Rapture's Rain

A novel by
Chris Pennington

DEDICATION

Beyond God's grace of enabling me to write this book, I dedicate it
to the following people:

My beautiful and loving wife
For her unwavering support. For how she holds our family
together and fills it with love. You are, quite simply, my everything.

My three wonderful children
Tyler: For his tender and loving nature – you are my inspiration.
Illy: For how she cares for others – you are my eternal valentine.
Stealth: For his strength and courage – you are my hero.

My mother
For her unconditional love and support that is beyond words. God
blessed me with the very best.

My brother
For always having my back and always giving me great advice.

Editorial and Creative Input
Lastly, I would like to thank Stephanie Brooks for her editorial
review and input as well as Donna Backshall for taking my story to
the next level by adding a beautiful creative polish.

PREFACE

Before reading *Rapture's Rain*, I would like you to know I am not a theologian, nor am I an expert on the Bible. Within these pages you will find many references to the Book of Revelation, and the Rapture, in particular. My goal in creating this book was not to try to explain this part of the Bible, but to create an entertaining work that, through God's grace, would hopefully touch you in a way that inspires your faith.

CHAPTER 1
HARMONY AMIDST THE CLOUDS

The tiny hand swept gracefully across the gentle waves of the white cotton fabric. One minute it was there, the next it was gone. Like a timid ballerina, the little girl danced and darted in and out of the sheets and pillowcases hanging from the clothesline.

Jason Stover chuckled watching his wife and daughter joyously pursuing one another amidst the array of bedding, pajamas, and other articles of clothing. He marveled at how adept they were at hiding from one another for fear of being tagged. With only the sounds of their merriment to confirm their presence, he mused at how cruel and desperate the world might be without their laughter.

It was mid-May in North Carolina, and the sleepy little community of Lake Royale was enjoying another beautiful spring Sunday. A lazy breeze floated across the lake, through the backyard of Jason's shady lakefront home, and into his study. The sweet scent of jasmine mingled with the laundered fabrics, filling his office with a profusion of seasonal freshness. Although their clothes dryer worked fine, his wife Kristina insisted upon line drying everything during the spring because, as she put it, "It

1

helped bring in the season and kept it closer to the heart." It was this spirit and her warmth that drew him to her nine years earlier. With flawless honey-toned skin and wavy brunette hair, she was beyond beautiful in his mind – she was ravishing.

Physically the Stovers were an attractive couple in their early thirties, with a love for the outdoors and a shared interest in spending as much time as possible enjoying the lake on which they lived. At six feet tall, Jason was lean and toned with sandy blond, shoulder-length hair that framed his green eyes. He could easily pass for the quintessential surfer dude.

Other than physicality, they were two different people from distinctly different backgrounds. She was a fun-loving extrovert from a large Latino family, while he was a self-proclaimed introvert from a small "white bread," as she called it, clan of half her family's size. Her family was loud, gregarious and always hugging. And if there was a karaoke machine within a hundred yards, they were guaranteed to be on it. On the other hand, Jason's family was soft-spoken, introspective, and could barely muster a handshake when showing affection. Jokingly, they would say her family was made up of clowns and jesters, while his were robots, but together it made for the best circus in town.

Along with their different backgrounds were their unique skills and talents. Kristina loved children and worked for social services in the foster care division. Though the pay was lousy and the hours were long, she never once thought to complain. Instead she'd often share her firm belief that every minute spent with a child in need or family in distress was a minute spent making a difference.

Jason, on the other hand, was a rare combination of academia and the creative arts. He was a high school science teacher with a Master's degree in Physics. In his spare time he loved to paint and write. If one thing was for certain, Jason Stover was a driven man who always had to be doing something. He was also a man of enormous pride who loved setting goals, then working himself to the point of exhaustion to accomplish them. In just the past year he had completed a full-length novel and had two gallery showings for his landscape paintings, all while taking on an additional teaching assignment at school.

Like her parents, their little girl Nikki inherited an overachiever's personality and was, without a doubt, the true definition of a precocious child. At five, she was drawing three-dimensional cartoon characters while her classmates were content with stick figures. At six, she was keeping a journal. Now, at seven, she had started to play the piano by ear. But what really set Nikki apart was how kind she was and how honestly she cared about virtually everyone and everything. If anyone was upset for any reason, Nikki was there to try and make things better. According to Jason, her heart was as big as all outdoors. He thought there was nothing she could ever possibly do to displease him.

One thing he knew for certain was that his little girl was truly a child of God. In his mind, he and Kristina had a solid Christian marriage. At every possible opportunity, they looked for ways to teach their daughter life lessons based on the scriptures or something their pastor had preached in previous sermons.

Before Nikki was born, their lives didn't actually include a lot of religion. They both said they believed in God and Jesus, but like so many others, that was the extent of it. In reality they were just checking the boxes. Go to church – check, pray before meals – check, give to an occasional charity – check. Neither had ever read a Bible verse, they didn't understand the concept of the Holy Spirit, and they didn't really understand the full meaning of why Jesus died for man's sins.

The year before Nikki was born, things began to change for the couple. Their love for one another was undeniable and they felt they were happy, but something seemed to be missing. They compared themselves to other married friends and were positive their marriage was as solid, or even stronger. And because they both loved their jobs, it couldn't be that either. Plus, they lived in a beautiful house on one of the most picturesque lakes in the state. From virtually every angle it was utopia – a misconception that was even fueled by friends and family.

Kristina's best friend, Erin, who lived two houses down the street, would often confess how she envied their marriage. Erin was a strikingly beautiful blond nurse just two days younger than Kristina. And like Kristina, everyone loved Erin.

Though beautiful inside and out, Erin had a unique perspective on their marital bliss. She had grown up a pageant girl, forced by her greedy parents to dress up, dance and twirl for money and prizes. By the time she was old enough to marry, her self-worth was based so heavily upon others' views of her, she had no idea how to demand simple things like respect and love from a friend, let alone a mate. She married an awful man, one who only wanted a trophy for his arm, and when he tired of her, he turned to heavy drinking, drugs and other women. The inevitable divorce left Erin in shambles, but in the daunting aftermath, and with Kristina and Jason's support, she had grown into the loving, giving and self-assured woman they were proud to call 'friend'. She often spoke of their strength as a couple, thankful to be a recipient of their unwavering faith and love.

Despite all outward signs that things were peachy in their lives, Kristina began to feel the need for change. She felt they were looking for happiness and fulfillment in the wrong places. She questioned why they were pinning so much on material things and relying only upon each other to make their family whole. So it came as no surprise to Jason when she began talking about finding a church to join. Because he loved her so much, he was happy to encourage her, even though deep down he would have admitted this wasn't a priority of his. After several months of looking they finally found Bay Bridge Fellowship. It was non-denominational, not too small and not too big. Plus the pastor was young, energetic, and possessed a sharp wit that made his sermons both engaging and approachable.

It wasn't long before Kristina approached Jason about joining one of the church's community groups.

"What's a community group?" he asked.

"It's just a small group of people from the congregation that get together once a week to discuss the sermon and talk about their personal needs and struggles. They also volunteer and do things as a group and they pray for each other."

Immediately Jason was silently opposed to the idea. They had just asked him to take on another class at school and his to-do list was growing exponentially every day. But more than anything it went against the grain of his personality. He wasn't comfortable expressing his feelings to anyone other than his wife.

"Kris, I'd like to, but honestly, I don't think I have the time." His voice was sincere and she did know how busy he was.

"I understand. Would it be okay though if I still joined one?" she asked.

"Of course, honey." Jason always encouraged his wife to pursue her interests, and because he knew this was important to her, he emphasized his approval with a big hug and kiss.

"I love you so much Jason Stover... and guess what?"

"What?"

"God does too," she said with a generous smile.

Over the next several months Kristina's involvement with Bay Bridge and her community group continued to grow. Jason's teaching responsibilities also grew, and he was painting and writing more than ever. He was a happy man, fully engaged in so many invigorating activities. Everything seemed to be working out well for them. So well, in fact, that on the anniversary of their first year at Bay Bridge, Kristina announced to him during the middle of a sermon that she was going to have his baby.

It was an incredible nine months of bliss for them. She was more radiant than ever and it seemed the house was always filled with family and friends. But it was Kristina's community group that really made an impact in their house. Once a week, without fail during her last trimester, someone from the group brought a covered dish so they wouldn't have to prepare dinner. Kristina loved these visits because they gave her husband an opportunity to get to know the members of the group. In fact, as she later explained, with a knowing smile, "Those visits were just part of my grand scheme to win him over to the group. Those, and of course, a lot of prayers."

After perhaps the fifth meal drop-off, Jason succumbed to his wife's tactics. "Honey, would you mind if I sat in on your group meeting next week?"

"Do what?" she exclaimed.

"Yeah, I think I might like to sit in and observe what you guys do for once."

"Are you sure you really want to?"

He nodded, "Why not? After all, they've been so supportive of us."

As soon as the words left his mouth, Kristina threw her arms around his neck and gave him a huge hug. "Thank you honey, thank you so, so much! I know you'll love it!"

That evening while he was working in his office he overheard his wife praying upstairs before going to bed. "Dear Lord, thank you for all of your blessings, thank you for the love of our family and for keeping us safe, and thank you so much for helping change my husband's mind about our community group. Amen." As she finished, Jason couldn't help but feel proud, knowing how happy he had made her.

The following week, everyone was in attendance in the group. There were four couples, along with an elderly widow, and a younger divorced man named Mike Branson. To Jason's surprise, the conversation was easy and enjoyable. As they transitioned from casual chit-chat to discussion about the past week's sermon, he found himself engaged in everything they were saying. When the group's leader, Ken Drolet, began explaining the chronological events leading up to Jesus' crucifixion, he found himself more than simply interested. He was spellbound.

From that moment on, Jason was at Kristina's side for every community group meeting. They even started doing things with members outside their normal gatherings. Jason especially liked hanging out with Mike, because they were about the same age and had similar creative interests. Mike was short and stocky with a seemingly permanent five o'clock shadow that accented his pudgy cheeks and constant megawatt smile.

Jason often joked that Mike was Santa Claus in the making, not only for his appearance but his perpetually positive attitude. He was also very intelligent, working as a technical lead for a business that implemented Internet security systems for large companies. Their talks outside of the community group always involved their jobs and they would always express, with a sense of pride, how important their careers were to them. It was always typical guy talk, but on one particular occasion over some beers, Mike opened up about his divorce.

"Jason," he said, with his eyes focused on his bottle, "I truly loved Karen. I guess I can't blame her for leaving, but she just didn't understand my commitment to the job. What I do is actually very important, and I take it seriously. These corporations depend on my expertise and if I don't do my job correctly, then millions of dollars and people's livelihoods, even their safety, are put in jeopardy. I know it sounds braggadocios, but it's the truth."

"What happened?" Jason asked, not wishing to pry, but hoping Mike would continue. He looked like he had the weight of the world on his shoulders.

After a thoughtful moment, Mike said with a sigh, "Karen disliked – no, hated – her job. I think she was actually jealous, resenting me for loving mine. Toward the end, we were at each other's throats all the time. She honestly thought I loved my job more than I loved her."

"A big regret of mine is that we never had kids, which I guess is best in the grand scheme of things. My parents, God rest their souls, believed wholeheartedly in the "be fruitful and multiply" tenet of the Catholic faith. Shoot, I was number six out of seven kids growing up! But being childless meant we could be granted an annulment by the Catholic Church."

Mike sighed, then continued, "I keep telling myself it wasn't meant to be, but I still feel like it should have turned out differently. I've spent my entire life working to make a difference, to do something important and make something of myself, but I never wanted to sacrifice having a family to do it."

Mike returned his focus to the beer in his hand, and the silence was heavy. The pain in Mike's voice had been evident, and it was obvious the loss had both bewildered and devastated him.

When Mike spoke again, it was to change the subject to a less weighty topic. "Want to order some wings to go with these beers?" Jason laughed, and the tension quickly dissipated.

Later that evening as Jason drove home, he felt saddened that Mike's marriage had been unable to withstand his love of career. Was it possible he could make the same mistakes? He reflected upon the strength of his relationship with his wife and a wave of contentment washed over him. Jason just knew that, unlike his friend, he certainly had his priorities in order.

CHAPTER 2
VANISHINGS

Jason couldn't believe how fast the years had flown by since Nikki was born. As he continued watching their game of tag under the clothesline, he felt a comforting warmth with the realization that his little girl was starting to look just like her mother. The one exception was a small, heart-shaped birthmark at the base of both his and Nikki's necks – the only physical attribute they shared. To Nikki's delight, Jason would often tell her that when he touched it he was touching hers too.

"Hey Nikki, have you been tagged yet?" he yelled out the window.

"Not yet!"

"Well, if you get tagged, you've gotta come on in for lunch okay?"

"Okay!"

"Hey, guess what?" he yelled back. "I'm touching our heart, so you've been tagged!"

"No fair! It's gotta be Mommy who tags me!" she giggled in mock protest.

At that very moment, the grandfather clock down the hall

started to chime, indicating it was noon. On the fourth chime, Jason turned to go into the kitchen when a weird sensation came over him. At first the hair on his arms stood up and a chill ran down his spine, making him shiver. Next his knees grew weak. He had a hard time balancing and his head began spinning like a top. Was he having a stroke or some sort of seizure? All of this happened within two chimes of the clock. He could barely think, given this sudden onslaught.

On the fifth chime, he tried turning back to the window so he could yell to Kristina for help. But as he turned, he was hit again. This time, he was temporarily blinded by three flashes of light that dropped him to his knees. It was as if he'd been zapped repeatedly by a Taser gun. He was numb from head to toe.

As he knelt motionless, the only thing registering with him was that there wasn't any actual pain. No other thoughts existed at that moment, except the sense that time was slowing down. As he remained motionless, he could hear the clock ringing out its chimes a half second slower with each ring.

On the twelfth and last chime his paralysis finally began to subside, and a couple seconds later he was pulling himself to his desk. When he finally righted himself, he leaned over his chair and let out a huge sigh. With his head still down he began contemplating what on earth had just happened. Whatever it was, he knew he had to tell Kristina.

He raised his head to look out the window, but everything was a blur. He wiped his eyes, realizing the physiological episode was still happening, or at least the side effects were. As he blearily gazed out onto the back lawn, everything was hazy and unclear. He wiped his eyes again, but still no clarity. Then it hit him. Instead of his eyes being unable to focus, he realized everything, including the trees, grass, clothesline, the lake, even the sky and clouds, all seemed to be vibrating. It was as if every atom of everything outdoors was dancing randomly back and forth and side to side at a million miles per second. It was both horrifying and sensational at the same time.

Shaking off the awe of the moment, Jason remembered he had to get to Kristina and Nikki. Everything but his eyesight seemed back to normal, and as long as he didn't look outside, he could move toward the back of the house without stumbling. As he walked through his office door, into the kitchen and out to his back porch, he kept his head down, focusing first on the carpet, then on the tile floor, and finally the wooden planks of his porch.

When he finally reached the screen door, he slowly opened it while still keeping his head focused on the steps leading out onto the lawn. At the base of the steps there was a flagstone path that wound its way through the middle of the yard, past the clothesline where Kristina and Nikki had been playing, and out to their boat house. If he stayed on the path, it would lead him directly to his family.

As he took his first step onto the path, he slowly and cautiously looked up. On his next step he raised his head completely. In order to reduce the effect of his visual abnormality, he tried squinting his eyes tightly. To his relief, the vibrating motions seemed to have stopped, but everything was still extremely fuzzy. The effects of the episode must be wearing off, he thought.

"Kristina, can you come here quickly?" he yelled. "I need you!" There was no response. He rubbed his eyes again. "Kristina, WHERE ARE YOU?" She had to hear him because where they had been playing was less than thirty yards away.

He looked directly toward the clothesline. Although everything was still a blur, he could make out the vague shapes of what he knew were his wife and daughter.

"There's something wrong. I need your help!" he pleaded.

A few seconds went by and no reply. Even odder was the fact that neither Kristina nor Nikki had come rushing to his aid. Here was a father and husband in obvious distress, and his family was ignoring his need for help. He took several more steps toward them and called out again. "Please come here quickly. I *really* need your help!" Their blurry figures remained motionless.

His distress continued to climb along with his frustration. "Why are you just standing there?" he shouted in both despair and anger.

Suddenly everything began to vibrate as it had before, but this time it seemed to be accelerating at an even faster rate. He looked at the figures of his wife and daughter and they appeared to be moving so fast he could actually see through them.

"For God's sake, Kristina, PLEEEASSSEE – HELLLLLLP – MEEEEEEEEE!" he screamed. His words lengthened like he was yelling into a black hole.

As if an atom bomb had exploded in front of him, a flash of blinding white light engulfed his world. No sound, no pain, no sensation at all, just an exquisite bright light, then – nothing. Jason's mind and body were depleted and he fell unconscious to the ground.

CHAPTER 3
THE AWAKENING

Noon turned to afternoon, afternoon to night, night to morning. It wasn't until around two o'clock the next afternoon when Jason's drained body began to stir. As he lay face down in the plush grass of his backyard, Jason slowly began to recover his senses. At first it was just a finger twitch, then a blink of an eye. With a labored groan, he reared his head off of the ground, but only for a second before it fell again. It was as if he were waking from a coma. Every muscle seemed to have wasted away over the past twenty-six hours. Again, he tried.

When he finally was able to reach a kneeling position, he had to stop. Standing seemed as challenging as climbing Mt. Everest, and he was only half way to the summit. As he rested momentarily, the previous day's events came rushing back to him in snippets of images, sounds, and finally his own thoughts. What happened, and how did he end up in the middle of his backyard?

As he continued to gather his strength, he struggled with piecing together the incredible events. Like a video set to fast-forward, he relived everything from the hairs on his arms rising to staring disbelievingly at the blurred images of his wife and daughter, then he drew a total blank. His memory stopped at the blurry translucent image of his family standing thirty yards away and his profound ache to reach them.

Where were Kristina and Nikki? As his strength began to return he staggered to his feet. He looked toward the clothesline where he had last seen them, seeing only the laundry waving gently in the breeze. He quickly surveyed the backyard, but there was no sign of either one.

"Kristina!" he yelled. "Kristina, Nikki, where are you?"

His voice was hoarse and dry from dehydration. He turned, looking in every possible direction. Adrenaline kicked in as he began to panic.

He called out desperately. "Kristina, where are you? Nikki, Daddy wants you to come here! Please, where are you?" he pleaded.

Confused about what to do, he began running back to the house, but started and stopped several times before finally deciding to circle the property. As he ran, he continued yelling for his wife and daughter. He ran into the house, stumbling over one of Nikki's stuffed animals left on the back porch steps. Within minutes he had scoured every room including the attic.

Suddenly it came to him – the boathouse! It was Nikki's favorite hide-and-seek spot. Given the right wind and wave conditions, it was often hard to hear anyone outside it, especially all the way up at the house. For a moment, he felt a sense of relief. At full speed, he ran back through the yard and down to the water's edge. As he approached, he noticed the boathouse door was slightly ajar and it was a wonderful sight to him. Practically every time they played hide and seek, Nikki left it cracked by mistake.

Flinging it open, he yelled, "Kristina, Nikki, are you in here?" Because it was a bright day, he was able to instantly see that the only thing inside was their empty boat. Jason's head dropped and he slowly began walking back up to his house. As he passed the clothesline, it finally came to him that they must actually be at someone else's house. That would certainly explain it. He almost felt stupid for not considering that possibility in the first place.

When he got back to his office, he retrieved his cell phone and tried calling Kristina. When he heard her ring tone singing from the next room, he hung up and hit the speed dial button for their community group leader.

"Hi, you've reached Ken Drolet, I'm away from my phone right now so if you would…"

Frustrated, he hung up before the message finished. He dialed the next number in his list, but again a voice message. Just as he started dialing his third number, he heard a faint whining sound in the distance. He stopped, listened harder, and finally he could make out that it was a police car passing through a nearby neighborhood.

On his next dial, another siren joined in from an opposite direction. A second later there came another and then another. He couldn't make out which was which, but several seconds later a fire truck and an ambulance joined the cacophony, followed by yet more sirens seemingly coming from all over town. Before long the air was filled with the deafening alarms of what must have been every emergency vehicle in all of Lake Royale.

A million negative images flashed before his eyes, all involving either Kristina or Nikki, or both. Were they somehow connected with whatever emergency was taking place? He prayed they were somewhere safe and thinking the same about him. He dialed his friend Mike.

"Hello," came a breathless voice on the other end.

"Mike, it's me, Jason."

"Jason," gasped his friend, "Where are you?"

"At home. What's going on? Have you heard from Kristina?"

"I…I…I don't know." He stammered. "Turn on the TV. It's all

over the news."

As he grabbed the remote, he asked Mike again, "Have you seen or heard from Kristina?"

"No, Jason, just please turn on the TV," he urged in a slightly more demanding, yet also somehow exasperated, tone.

"Okay, okay!" he replied.

At the top of the screen was a scrolling banner with the words, *Breaking News,* in bold letters. Underneath the banner stood a reporter interviewing a bathrobe-clad middle-aged woman, who looked both terrified and confused.

"Ma'am, where were you when you woke up?"

Sheepishly she replied, "I was in our hallway heading to the bathroom to take a shower when everything..." The woman's words trailed off, as she stifled a sob.

"Was it a similar experience to what others have been describing today? Did the same things happen to you as has happened to so many of us?"

Still on the line, Mike asked, "Jason, did you pass out too? Did you go blank just like everyone else?"

Jason heard him, but was too mesmerized by what he was watching to answer.

"Jason, did something happen to you too?" Mike asked.

"Mmm-hmm, something did happen to me," he mumbled while remaining transfixed on the TV.

Mike excitedly replied, "It happened to me! I went through all this crazy shit – chills, dizziness, double vision, and then BAM – these wild lightning flashes! The next thing I know, I'm waking up a day later – a *whole* day later!"

As Mike rattled on in one ear, Jason listened out of the other as the lady in the bathrobe continued describing virtually the same symptoms and sensations he'd had before everything went blank.

"That's what happened to me," said a man standing behind the lady being interviewed.

"Me too," chimed another.

Then a teenager, hanging on to a skateboard, leaned in from off screen, "Blew my mind, yo. Freaking insane!" he proudly exclaimed.

Suddenly the screen switched to a studio shot of the news anchor at his desk.

"We interrupt to bring you this latest update. We have received confirmation that the last twenty-four hours of, as yet, unexplained events and vanishings are not merely a regional occurrence. Reports from major cities across the world suggest this is a global phenomenon."

VANISHINGS? The word echoed in Jason's ears. What did he mean by "vanishings"? All he knew is that he had to find his family.

"Mike, I gotta go." Abruptly, he hung up and headed out the door, down to Erin's house. Certainly his wife would have headed to her best friend's house if there were an emergency. His heart hammered and his anxiety escalated with every step he took as he raced down the street.

In less than a minute he was on Erin's front porch. Without knocking, he opened the door and was startled to find Erin charging toward him. She flung her arms around his neck and sobbed uncontrollably.

"Erin, are you okay? Is Kristina here?"

"I don't understand! I don't understand it, Jason!" she choked. "What happened! What's going on? Why is this…" She seemed on the verge of hysteria.

"It's okay. Calm down. Just calm down."

"But, but, I'm afraid! What's happening?" she cried, "What's going on?"

"I promise you, it's going to be okay," he said, in what he

hoped sounded like a reassuring tone. "Just take a breath and try to relax."

She dropped her head into his chest and let her arms fall to her side. As Jason wrapped his arms around her, she slowly began to speak.

"I think I'm going insane," she sobbed, "I've been pulled through the ringer since yesterday afternoon. I...oh, you wouldn't believe me."

He took her face in his hands and gently lifted her head up to his. "Trust me, I guarantee I'll believe you." They stared at one another for a moment. Though neither one spoke a word, it became evident he truly understood everything she'd been through.

"Jason, something happen to you too, didn't it?"

"Yes," he replied softly.

"Was it like what they've been saying on TV and the radio?"

"Exactly the same."

"So you know what's going on?" she implored, as if she were a little girl asking her father to explain away a bad dream.

"I don't know much yet, but I'm sure everything's going to be all right." For the next minute, they held each other until finally he broke the silence. In the calmest tone he could muster, he asked, "Erin, have you seen or heard from Kristina or Nikki?" He held his breath in anticipation.

"No," she whimpered.

His heart sank. Dejected, he slowly backed away from her and collapsed into a chair in the hallway. He buried his head in his hands and in a muffled voice said, "Have you heard from anyone? From your family, maybe?"

"Only my loser uncle, Tony. He called right before you came in."

"Have you tried calling any of your other family members or friends?"

"No. Why?"

"You need to – *now.*" Then without another word, he opened the front door and strode purposefully out of her house.

"Wait! Where are you going?" she yelled after him.

Over his shoulder, he yelled, "Home! I need answers, Erin. I need to find my family!"

As Jason headed backed to his house, he became aware of the chaos emerging around him. Neighbors wandered through the street shouting the names of family members and friends. A young couple who lived on a nearby cul-de-sac stood on their lawn holding each other while someone appeared to be consoling them. He saw a car abandoned in the middle of the road, and fifty yards away there was a truck that had struck a tree, but no sign of the driver. Doors of homes sat wide open and the sounds of sobs and hysteria could be heard from within. Off in the distance, a fire licked the sky, pumping plumes of smoke into the horizon. Sirens and alarms blared from all corners of the city.

As he neared his house, a middle-aged man with a scraggly beard and clutching a half empty bottle of scotch ran up behind him, almost pushing him to the ground.

"Hey Jason, where you goin', buddy boy?" he slurred.

It was the neighborhood's most disliked resident, Larry Huffman. He cursed like a sailor and rarely had anything nice to say about anyone, especially not about his wife, who, by comparison was a virtual saint.

"Doris skipped out on me, Jay Boy! The bitch just up and left, didn't leave a message or nothin'. Can you believe that?" he said, while swaying back and forth.

Jason reached for Larry's shoulders to steady him. "Now I'm sure Doris didn't leave you, Larry. She's probably just visiting friends or is out shopping."

"Shopping!" Larry blurted. "That wench best not be shopping!"

"Maybe she's at a friend's house then?" Jason countered. "I'm sure that's it. Listen, I really have to go now."

As he turned to leave, Larry grabbed him by the arm. "Jason," he mumbled, "I don't want her to leave me." His glazed eyes filled with tears. "I'm no good without her."

Jason nodded in solemn acknowledgement, and looked carefully into Larry's eyes. "Listen to me. It's going to be okay. She's not going anywhere. I'm sure she'll be back soon, but I really have to go."

As he headed toward his house, Larry called after him, "Are you sure?"

"Yes!" Jason called back, without turning around.

When he finally got home, he ran to his answering machine. He had multiple messages! Surely one of them had to be from Kristina. As he pressed the play button his optimism quickly faded as the machine played one blank message, one indecipherable rambling from Mike, and a previous message Erin had left, pleading for him to call her.

It was all he could do to restrain himself from throwing the machine across the room. For a moment he just stood there staring at it with contempt. As he did, he began to wonder why no one from his community group had called. These were good Christian people who, in the past, had called just to alert them that a thunderstorm was approaching so they could make sure their boat was securely tied down. So why weren't they reaching out now during this obvious emergency?

The answer was simple and understandable. They were all taking care of their own families. That was what he was trying to do. Surely he would be hearing from them soon. He was positive of it.

In the meantime, he couldn't just wait. He had to do something. Although he was certain it was too soon to call in a missing persons report, he still did. He dialed the number and not to his surprise, the line was busy. He immediately tried again, and again a busy signal. After several more attempts yielding the same results, he started calling every family member, friend, and co-worker, hoping he could somehow begin to piece things together.

It was now going on twenty-eight hours and his desperation level was skyrocketing. In his panic, he couldn't help but imagine his options for finding his family were running out. When he picked up the phone again and began dialing, he received the automated message *"All circuits are currently busy, please try your call again later."*

"Oh, for God's sake!" he screamed.

With one hand, he grabbed the phone at the base and flung it across the room into the grandfather clock in the hallway, shattering its face and breaking the phone into a million pieces.

As he stood there, chest heaving, he pulled his cell phone from his pants pocket and dialed Erin. *"All circuits are currently…"*

He slammed the phone down and for a split second contemplated also hurling it across the room, before realizing it was likely his most valuable asset. But what could he do? Who could he turn to? He huffed and puffed while pacing the room, frantic to figure out his next move. After ten or fifteen minutes, he felt more helpless than ever. Rather than do nothing, he got in his car and headed out to find someone, anyone, who might lead him to his Kristina and Nikki.

As he drove through the countryside and through the city streets, the visual impact of what was happening in the world around him was overwhelming. The same situation existed outside his storybook neighborhood, magnified tenfold. Fires blazed, abandoned cars littered the streets and shoulders, and panic-stricken people rushed about while others wandered aimlessly in shock.

That evening and into the night, he drove to virtually every friend and family member he guessed his wife and daughter may have contacted. In total, he stopped at twenty-three houses, but in only nine did he find someone home. Each time it was the same story – no one had heard from or seen anything of his family. Each recounted the same progression of events he had experienced and with the same results. Either a loved one or someone they knew had gone missing.

On his way home he replayed each conversation in his head, hoping he had missed something that could help him in his search. As he did, he realized a rather odd similarity. No children. There were homes where one or more adults had vanished, but in every case where there were children, it was consistent that they had vanished without a trace. In these cases, the parents' anguish only served to drive Jason into even greater despair.

By the time he headed back home, he was an emotional and physical wreck. He hadn't eaten for, what, forty hours, and had been running on adrenaline since the moment he awoke on his back lawn. When he got home, it was three-thirty in the morning. He immediately went to check his phone and answering machine, only to remember how dramatically he had demolished it. He backed himself into the corner next to where the phone used to be, and as the last bit of energy left his body, he slid slowly down the wall, collapsing onto the floor. For the next twenty minutes, he sobbed uncontrollably until sleep mercifully took him.

CHAPTER 4
A CATASTROPHE REVEALED

At precisely 6:12 a.m. the next morning, a slow steady beam of light rolled across the Stovers' backyard, in through the kitchen, and down the hallway toward where Jason still lay asleep next to the grandfather clock. Like every other sunny morning on Lake Royale, the sun quickly flooded the Stover household, ensured by their unobstructed eastern exposure to the lake.

When the light reached his eyes, his senses stirred for a split second, but not enough to wake him. His ordeal had taken its toll. He had tossed and turned the entire evening, and was now completely out of it. It wasn't until seven o'clock, when the grandfather clock began to chime, that he rolled over to avoid the sunlight's increasing intensity.

On the third chime, the first memory of the previous day's events flashed through his groggy mind. Still half asleep, the horrific storyline began to play out. It was only a dream he thought. But with every chime of the clock a new and more vivid detail appeared, jarring him back into consciousness.

By the time the seventh chime rang, he was wide awake. As he slowly pulled himself to his feet, he saw the pieces of what used to be a phone scattered across the room. Like a sledgehammer to the gut, the full weight of his situation hit him. He doubled over and a fresh wave of despair engulfed him. He wasn't prepared yet to bear the burden of what had transpired, but he knew he had to gain his composure. His family needed him, and he needed them.

After grabbing a banana and a glass of water, he headed to the living room, where the TV was still playing from the afternoon before. Just as he expected, the news was continuing to override all other programming. The first channel to catch his eyes appeared to be broadcast from the depths of hell. The entire screen was filled with billowing smoke of unknown origin. As the camera pulled back, streaks of bright red and orange could be seen snaking their way through cracked earth, spewing a blizzard of ashes and soot. Jason absent-mindedly took a bite of his banana, transfixed on the hellish scene.

Suddenly, the camera shot changed to a reporter sitting in a news helicopter. As he struggled to be heard above the noise of the aircraft's blades, Jason could see a small town that lay in ruin below.

"What lies beneath us," yelled the reporter, "is just one of many small towns up and down the Washington and Oregon coastline that have been hit by a series of earthquakes since 1 a.m. this morning."

As the camera zoomed out the window and to the town below, Jason could see that the red and orange streaks were actually streams of lava flowing through huge crevasses, burning through the streets and into a once-peaceful countryside. He could also see broken power lines, overturned cars, and decimated buildings. The scene made Jason's heart ache, imagining the anguish the families of this town must feeling.

He flipped to one of the major network channels, hoping that their coverage might be more relevant to his own situation. This time the popular national news anchor, Russ Meyers, was interviewing someone in the studio. The caption at the bottom of the screen read, *"Mark Holloway: National Security Director."*

Intrigued, he leaned forward and turned up the sound. Mr. Holloway swiveled his chair around to a large monitor displaying a map of the continental United States, with each state marked in shades of either red or pink.

Mr. Holloway was a squared-off ex-marine, with a chiseled jaw and the expected high-and-tight haircut. He spoke plainly and clearly. Every syllable he pronounced was crisp and laden with authority.

"What we know at this time is that virtually every state in the country has experienced the same phenomenon. The red indicates states where the reported number of missing is in excess of 12 percent of the population. Due to the expansive scope of this event and the fact that these are initial figures, we expect these percentages to increase as more intelligence is gathered." As he continued, his expression grew grim. "Additionally," he paused a moment, "these statistics comprise a disproportionately high number of children in the infant to teenage bracket."

Jason couldn't believe what he was hearing. He turned up the volume again, just to make sure he wasn't missing anything.

"Director Holloway," the anchor continued, "what's the situation like globally?"

"We have been focused on homeland matters, but our sources report that, by all appearances, nations around the developed world are dealing with the exact same scenario."

"Do you mean to say they have all reported the same vanishings, as well as the same series of flash events and physical anomalies?"

"To my knowledge, that is correct, sir."

As Mr. Meyers was about to cut away, Holloway interjected,

"Let me also state that, given the magnitude of this phenomenon, we must acknowledge there are many law enforcement officials, emergency, and other security personnel from all over the country and around the world who are no longer with us. We find ourselves severely short-handed. As a result, we have already begun seeing a dramatic surge in vandalism and overall crime." He then turned gravely toward the camera before continuing. "I urge every individual to exercise extreme caution as they proceed into the days ahead. The continued safety of our citizens is our primary concern, and we require each individual's vigilance during these trying times. I assure you all resources and efforts are being utilized to maintain secure and safe conditions."

"Thank you, Director Holloway. Let's go now to our live feed from London, England, where we have one of the most renowned physicists of our time – University of Cambridge Dean of Physics and Nobel Prize winner, Sir Richard Teech."

Jason's eyes widened. Richard Teech was an icon in physics and a veritable hero in the scientific community. Anyone who had studied physics knew what a genius he was, especially in the field of theoretical physics. Jason somehow felt connected to him through his friend and fellow teaching associate, Silas McCain. To Jason's delight, Silas, who was a friend of Teech from his days in England, would recount his incredible tales of brilliance.

Just as Mr. Teech began to speak, his cell phone rang. Jason glanced down and saw it was Mike. He was torn between watching the one man who might have some answers and taking the call from his friend. Mike could possibly have information about his family. Simultaneously, he hit the record button and picked up his cell.

Before Jason could say anything, Mike blurted, "I've got some good news!"

Jason's heart skyrocketed with anticipation. "You've heard from

Kristina!" he exclaimed, as if pre-confirming what he prayed he was about to be told. There was a brief moment of silence.

"Uh – well, no," Mike sheepishly replied, knowing he'd mistakenly given his best friend a moment of false hope. "I'm sorry, Jason. I was just excited to let you know I've been in contact with a couple of our friends and some of my family."

Jason shut his eyes and swallowed back despair. He didn't care who Mike had found. If it wasn't his Kristina or Nikki, he wasn't interested. He glumly replied, "Mike, I'm going to have to call you back." As he hung up, he looked to the ceiling, and with outstretched arms he prayed, "Dear God, please help me. Please, Lord, help me find Kristina. Please help me find Nikki. Please dear God – PLEASE!"

After a few moments of silence, he lowered his arms and reached for the remote. When he clicked the resume button, the new image on screen was in sharp contrast to Director Holloway. It was hard to tell based on the camera shot, but Sir Richard Teech appeared to be a portly and amiable man in his early seventies. He wore large oval glasses and his mop of gray hair was disheveled, as was his tweed coat which appeared two sizes too big. He was, in fact, the stereotypical professor, which on a better day might have seemed amusing to Jason.

"Thank you for joining us, Sir Richard," The news anchor began.

With a slight nod of the head, Teech politely replied in a soft British accent. "The pleasure is all mine."

"Before we begin, I'd like to inform our viewers that we have approached Sir Richard because he is widely recognized as the world's leading authority on theoretical physics, which, for those who don't know, is a specialized field which uses abstractions of physics and mathematical models in order to rationalize, explain, and predict natural phenomena. Sir Richard, did I get that right?"

"Very well done," Teech replied with another quick nod.

"Given the nature of the phenomena, along with his lengthy credentials and reputation in the scientific community, we consider Sir Richard to be our most reliable source for speculating the origins of this global event."

As brilliant as he was, Teech was equally as modest. Such praise obviously embarrassed him, and he was quick to reply that, as favorably as he had been described, there were numerous other physicists who were equally as capable in theorizing the source of the vanishings as he.

Teech then cleared his throat as if about to deliver one of his lectures. "First, let me pre-qualify my comments by stating that at this stage there are virtually endless theories on what may have caused the global vanishing phenomenon. What we have to do is assess the absolutes and ascertain the commonalities between them. This will then provide us a logical path to follow. At this time, the only absolutes we possess are that the episodic events for everyone still present were identical in terms of effect and duration, and that there appear to be no residual physiological after-effects. Demographically speaking, the numbers of those missing is concurrent with the makeup of the global population. Additionally, all infants through children four years of age have vanished, along with a proportionally larger number of children five through twelve. The only other absolute we have to work with is an electromechanical occurrence that took place at precisely the moment of the blackouts, which we have determined to have occurred at the same time throughout the world."

Mr. Meyers interrupted, "Excuse me, Sir Richard, but what exactly do you mean by 'electromechanical occurrence'?"

Teech adjusted his glasses. "At exactly 1:07 p.m. Sunday, Greenwich time, every device operating via electricity stopped for .651 seconds."

Meyers interjected again, "You mentioned other absolutes, as if there were more."

"That is correct," Teech replied. "There was a substantial electromagnetic occurrence, as well."

"Electro – magnetic," the newsman said as if dissecting the word into two parts. "What do you mean by electromagnetic?"

"Yes...well, what was recorded was quite impressive indeed. Precisely one minute and twenty-three seconds prior to the electro*mechanical* occurrence, the earth's polarity increased by a factor of ten, creating an electro*magnetic* induction that continued to increase proportionately up to the blackout point."

"Sir Richard, would you mind translating that into layman's terms?"

"Certainly." He paused a moment as he looked for the best possible answer. "Basically, the earth experienced a significant and unprecedented increase of power we currently cannot explain. Typically, a solar storm accompanies any such power fluctuation, but none were recorded during this period. The power increase began at exactly the same moment everyone's physical anomalies began."

"When the hair rose on people's arms?" Meyers inquired.

"Precisely. The power then continued to increase, culminating in a huge surge at the moment everyone blacked out. Imagine the power surge you would experience in your home during a lightning storm. In this case, the home is planet earth and we, as individuals, were the electrical components in that home. The power spiked and our circuit breakers flipped."

"Correct me if I'm wrong, Sir Richard, but when that happens typically shouldn't there be some after effect or damage to those components? My computer got fried during our last electrical storm."

"They certainly can," Teech replied. "It's this particular result which has us most perplexed. As I stated earlier, thus far there have been no physical side effects reported that can be directly related to this aspect of the phenomenon." Teech stopped and cleared his throat again. "However, there is one after effect that may be of great significance." He paused once more. "Immediately after the surge dissipated, we have evidence of a global drop phenomenon."

As Teech continued, his demeanor became uneasy. He began rapidly tapping his fingers together as he lowered his head in an almost praying position.

"As the term implies, energy levels throughout the world dropped. Unfortunately, it was a dramatic drop. But on the upside, it was for a short period of time, which of course contributed to the .651-second electromechanical stoppage. Unfortunately, the drop effect extended to virtually every energy source we have, ranging from the food we eat to the coal and gas we burn."

Jason was glued to the TV. He had actually performed experiments involving energy drops. If this phenomenon had indeed taken place on a scale this large, he knew that there could be huge implications.

It was apparent that the news anchor had followed Teech's logic and shared the same concerns Jason did. In a hesitant tone he asked, "So, what exactly does that mean for us and the rest of the world?"

"Well, it's simply too early to tell, but I will offer this: approximately one to two percent of the world's energy has been depleted."

The reporter paused, taking this in. He then posed the only hopeful question possible, "How long will it take to regenerate?"

"That, sir, is another perplexing issue. It appears an energy drop of this type has never been documented." He hesitated a second. "We have begun investigating some theories regarding black matter, but it is not yet clear if these will prove pertinent to our current predicament. That said, we must recognize the firm possibility this energy loss may, in fact, be non-regenerative."

"Non-regenerative!" Meyers exclaimed, as if he forgot he was still on camera.

"Indeed," Teech answered impassively. "This means that although we get our power from the sun on a daily basis, it still isn't replenishing the grid. But a far more pressing concern…"

At that moment, the screen went black.

Jason quickly clicked to another channel to see if it was a system failure. A local reporter was interviewing a jewelry store owner who had just been robbed. He flipped back, and again, nothing but dead air. He jumped from station to station hoping that he would find another network carrying the same interview, but unfortunately all of them had also gone to black. What a crappy time for all these station outages, he thought. Teech had at least one more important bit of information to convey, and Jason had to find out what it was.

CHAPTER 5
WHERE ARE YOU, GOD?

Jason had always gotten the majority of his news from the Internet, so he headed to his office hoping his computer hadn't been barbecued during the energy surge. He was thankful when it turned on, but it was taking forever to finish booting up. This had to be related to Teech's explanation, he thought. As his home screen finished loading, he heard his back door open.

"KRISTINA!" he yelled, pushing his way back from the computer. "Oh my God, is that you?"

"It's just me," Mike announced, as he came bounding into Jason's office.

"What are you doing here?" Jason asked, unable to hide his disappointment.

"I tried calling you again, but my cell phone died and all the land lines are still out."

"I'm sorry, I was going to call you right back but I had to finish watching this interview..."

"About the end of days!" Mike blurted.

"What!" Jason exclaimed. "What end of days? I was watching Richard Teech, an expert physicist, who was explaining this whole mess."

"No, no, Jason, it's clear now. It's crystal clear," Mike replied.

"What, for God's sake, is 'crystal clear'?"

"The Rapture!" Mike exclaimed.

A moment of silence passed. Jason's brow furrowed, as he contemplated what his friend had just suggested. "Okay, you've *clearly* lost your mind!"

"No, it has to be!"

"No hard feelings, buddy, but there is a logical explanation for what's going on. I need to find it, and every minute counts."

"Every minute, now more than ever!" Mike exploded.

"Screw you and your fantasies, Mike! I need to get my hands on empirical data and concrete proof, and you're spouting biblical mythology." Exasperated, Jason abruptly turned and headed back to his office. "I've gotta get back to the computer."

"Wait a second," Mike pleaded. "I'm sorry, Jason. I'm not going about this the right way. Will you hear me out? Because I do have proof."

Jason slowly turned back around and mockingly replied. "You've got proof that God has taken all the good people to heaven?"

"Yes!" Mike exclaimed. Then he added, "Well, uh, maybe not the empirical proof you mentioned, but theoretical evidence."

Jason shook his head in frustration. "Theoretical evidence?" He could hear the sarcasm in his voice, but couldn't stop himself. "You can't have theoretical evidence. That's as ridiculous as saying we have a 'minor catastrophe' on our hands. It's either theoretical or it's… ah, forget it, Mike. I am truly sorry, but I've been watching the news and I haven't seen a single report that gave even a hint of what you're talking about."

"Why would they?" Mike countered. "News is supposed to be all facts and figures. Right now, they're just going with science and trying to help keep things from getting totally out of control. Any mention of the Rapture could possibly send things spiraling into total anarchy."

Jason looked at his friend impatiently and sighed. "So what's this so-called *evidence* you're talking about?"

"Remember in community group when Ken was describing the Rapture and all the things that happened and the different events that took place?"

Jason nodded. "I remember a few. And to be honest, the idea did actually cross my mind momentarily, but after listening to Teech, there's more data that yields a much more plausible cause."

"You're a science teacher, Jason. That's how you're trained to think. You've got to look at everything now and do it with faith."

"Faith – HA!" Jason glared at his friend. His whole body went rigid, and he clenched his fist in outrage. "What's faith got to do with figuring out why I've lost my family?"

Mike put his hand on Jason's shoulder and in an earnest voice said, "Jason, there's a reason why you and I are still here." He paused. "Neither you nor I had *true* faith."

"Oh, for God's sake, man!" Jason growled as he swiped Mike's hand off his shoulder. He turned and stepped to within inches of Mike's face and glowered at him. "I had faith. I had plenty of it!" he yelled. "I went to church. I volunteered and did tons of charity work. I was part of the same community group you were. I, I, I..." he stammered. In an instant, his rage was replaced with despair and an overwhelming sense of hopelessness. He fell to his knees and buried his head in his hands and began to weep. "I did *all* those things."

Mike bent down beside him. Softly, he said, "Jason, I know you did. We both did."

Mike remained patiently at his friend's side. Jason knelt with his head lowered, contemplating what his friend had just said.

Everything that had happened and every emotion he had felt over the past two days flooded his mind until he couldn't think any longer. He was exhausted in every possible sense and now he was shutting down. He just knelt there staring down at the floor. After several minutes, Jason wiped his eyes. He slowly shook his head.

"Why is this happening?" Jason implored.

Mike put his arm around him. "Can you get up?"

He nodded.

Together they picked themselves up, and with his arm still around him, Mike led him to the kitchen table.

"Sit here a minute and let me get you a drink." Mike returned in a few moments with two glasses of straight vodka.

Jason took a sip, while staring blankly at his glass. "Okay, I'm listening."

Mike looked at him cautiously. Jason could tell he was uncertain if he was truly receptive or merely placating him.

"Last night, I started recalling some of our group meetings when we talked about the Book of Revelation and how during the end of days people would just disappear. I tried reading the chapter, but to be honest, I had a hard time deciphering it so I did an Internet search for the high level stuff to see if it jived with what's going on." He paused and took a gulp, seemingly for courage to continue. "Jason, it all fits. Earthquakes – increased violence – economic collapse – threats of war – everything!"

Jason looked up from his glass. "All of those things have logical explanations. In fact, most of those things have been going on forever anyway."

"But not at the levels we're experiencing now."

"I'm sorry, Mike, but how exactly are you able to quantify any of this?"

"There's a site called *End Of Days, Fact Or Fiction*, and in it they list all the different events Revelation says we should expect, and compare those to what is happening now. It's even updated to today!"

Jason put down his drink and wearily rested his head in his hand. "Well, show me then," he said begrudgingly.

Mike excitedly ran out to retrieve Jason's laptop from his office. In seconds, he returned with it already opened. He pushed it in front of Jason.

"What's that web address, again?"

"It's all one word, with no hyphens: *endofdaysfactorfiction.net.*"

As Jason entered the address, he grumbled that no decent website would use a ".net" extension.

"Don't worry," Mike said, "most of what I found was the same on just about every Rapture-related website, both .com and .net sites. I thought this one was easiest to navigate and made the most sense."

"Okay, it's up. Where do I go from here?"

"Click the main nav bar tab that says 'Facts'."

He clicked the tab and began silently scanning the page. After about thirty seconds, he reached for the glass and sipped.

"Hmmm," he murmured. His eyes narrowed, as he clicked to the second page that displayed a list of biblical events from Revelation. Beside each event was a block of statistics supporting it. Next to earthquakes, it numerically described how dramatically their frequency had increased. The same was the case for the listings of global wars and violent crimes.

"So, what do you think?" urged Mike, obviously unable to contain his excitement.

Jason didn't respond, other than to hold up his hand in a 'give me a sec' gesture. In an almost inaudible tone, he began murmuring to himself.

"Statistically, all the data is well-presented. It's all referenced and attributed to what appears to be reliable sources."

As he spoke, he continued staring at the screen while clicking through the pages at an increasing rate. He was now oblivious to Mike's presence. His entire focus was directed toward processing the data in front of him and estimating its credibility. After about three minutes of near-silent scanning, he stopped, raised his hand to his chin and paused for a moment. "Hmm. So you read all of this?"

"Most of it. Well, just the stuff in the columns."

"All the statistics are pretty impressive, and they do represent a trending that correlates with the events from that chapter of the Bible."

Mike pointed eagerly to the screen. "Did you see how the number of global conflicts has dramatically increased and is at an all-time high? Remember how that was supposed to increase? And all these earthquakes! And the economic crisis, not just here but crippling most of Europe too?"

"I got all of that," Jason said evenly. "The only thing is that there's a lot more to the Book of Revelation than just this list of occurrences. What about the last page that mentions things like asteroids hitting the earth and the two prophets, Enoch and Elijah, coming back to prophesize in Jerusalem?"

Although Jason could feel himself warming to the whole concept, he still felt compelled to push back.

Mike must have sensed they were at a critical point, so he suggested, "Jason, just add all the information you read to the global vanishings, and it's all the evidence you need."

"Look, I admit this does add up to some degree, but if you step back, you have to be honest and admit there are lots of possibilities for coincidence."

"Are you kidding me?" Mike exclaimed in disbelief. "You can't just rationalize away the similarities between the Rapture and the most catastrophic event in the history of mankind as coincidence."

Jason looked at his friend and shrugged. "Mike, I don't know what to say. All I do know is that my wife and my daughter, the two most important things in my life, are missing and I'm helpless to find them. I'm dying inside. As much as I would like to indulge everything you're suggesting, I have one and only one focus right now, and that's to find my family."

"I understand," Mike apologized, "I just seem to be complicating things."

Jason looked at his friend, and immediately felt a pang of guilt. Not only had Mike lost his wife in a painful divorce, he had also lost both his parents to cancer. Who was Jason to whine to him about family, about loss? Here was a good man, his friend, sincerely trying to help and it seemed all he wanted to do was brush him away like a gnat.

"No, no!" Jason replied sympathetically. "I know you're really trying to help. It's just so much to consume. I think I just need to be by myself right now to sort through everything."

"Yeah, okay, that's probably best. Listen, I'll give you a buzz tomorrow okay?"

"Sure, that sounds good." Jason gave his friend a warm pat on the back.

Mike smiled gratefully, then turned and headed out of the kitchen. As he opened the back door, he yelled over his shoulder. "At least Elijah is already back!"

"What's that?" Jason yelled from the other room.

"Elijah. You know, the prophet that you mentioned from the last page of the site. There's a guy named Elijah who began a lecture series in Jerusalem this past week."

Jason heard the screen door shut.

"I'll talk to you tomorrow!" Mike shouted as he walked to his car.

The house was silent now and all that could be heard was the ticking of the kitchen clock and the low steady hum of the refrigerator. Jason sat slumped in his chair at the kitchen table. His mind was frazzled and he was an emotional wreck. Every second seemed like an eternity – an eternity filled with anguish, grief, and a sense of complete hopelessness.

Slowly, he pushed back from the table and turned to the cabinets directly behind him where he and Kristina kept all their medicines and emergency items. He opened the door and pulled out a large Tupperware box filled with a hodgepodge of drugs, bandages, ointments, scissors, and gauze. He reached in and pulled out a small box of over-the-counter sleep aids. This, he thought, was his answer. With this, he could escape.

He then pulled out two similar-sized prescription bottles. One was a powerful pain medicine, and the other a stronger prescription sleeping aid he had used several years ago to battle a case of insomnia. He turned back to the table and placed his selections between his laptop and glass of vodka. As he sat down, he lowered his head.

"I guess you really didn't think I believed in you," he said, as if speaking to someone standing in the same room. He raised his head and looked to the ceiling. His lower lip began to quiver. "Where are you, God? What did I do so terribly wrong?"

After a brief moment of silence, he poured out the contents of both prescription bottles in front of his computer, and then methodically punched out each of the individually sealed pills from the smaller box. As he stared at the blank screen, he picked up his drink with his right hand and with his left he grabbed half of the pile of medicine that lay in front of him. With one hand full of pills and the other holding his glass, a single tear rolled down his cheek.

"Forgive me, Lord," he whispered.

At that moment, the laptop crackled and popped, jolting Jason back into reality. The blank screen flickered several times, glowed warmly, and then displayed the last page of the Rapture website he had been reviewing with Mike. He blinked his eyes as his pupils adjusted to the now brightly lit screen. In the exact spot he had been staring was the section Mike had yelled to him about as he was leaving. The section header read:

Elijah Cohen Begins Lecture Series In Jerusalem

Underneath, was a blurb pointing out that Elijah was an important Old Testament prophet and how he, along with the prophet Enoch, would return and begin prophesizing during the time of the Rapture.

Jason's eyes remained fixed on the header. "Elijah Cohen," he muttered. His friend's theory still didn't hold water, he thought. Without Enoch, Mr. Cohen was just another coincidence. As he continued to stare at the heading, he slowly raised his fist of pills to his mouth. Holding them slightly above his lips he let the first one slip through his fingers. As the pill gently dropped onto his tongue, Jason shook his head and the pill fell to the table. He froze.

Slowly he lowered both hands to the table while his eyes remained glued on the name Elijah Cohen. Cohen. C – O – H – E – N! He rubbed his eyes, as he began rearranging the letters in his head. Then with a jerk he turned, grabbed a pen and pad from the countertop, and quickly scribbled out COHEN above the name ENOCH. His hand began to shake as he drew an individual line from each letter in the name Cohen to its matching letter in the name Enoch. Five letters in each name, and they all matched.

"Oh, my God!" he exclaimed. "Cohen IS ALSO Enoch."

CHAPTER 6
FIRE FROM THE SKY

On the other side of the world, the warm waters of the South China Sea gently rolled up on to the silvery sands of the Kanton Island. It had been another idyllic blue sky day in this serene tropical paradise, and now all fifty-four inhabitants of its sole village of Tebaronga were fast asleep, with the exception of twenty-one year-old Kim Hoach. She was getting married tomorrow, and although it was close to two in the morning, she was still too excited to fall asleep. Instead, she reclined in her bed gazing out the window at the beautiful canopy of stars sparkling down on her tiny little island. With only a half dozen lights in the whole village and the fact that they were out in the middle of the dark waters of a vast sea, it seemed as if every star in the universe was on display.

After scanning the sky intently for the perfect star, she finally stopped on one directly below Orion's Belt. Closing her eyes, she wished that she and her husband would have a beautiful baby boy and they would continue to live out their days in harmony on Kanton. While her eyes were still closed, a flaming fireball the size of a school bus ripped down through space, across the horizon where she had been looking and down into the South China Sea.

The explosion from the impact was deafening, causing her such a shock that she fell out of bed.

As she pulled herself up to the window, the noise of the blast subsided. Because her house was surrounded by thick vegetation, she was unable to see the beach, so all she could do was nervously stare out across the horizon looking for the source of the blast. For a few seconds, an eerie silence filled the air, and suddenly off in the distance, the sound of a train could be heard. Two seconds later, a massive black wall of water thundered through the trees obliterating her house, washing it and everything else on the island out to sea.

CHAPTER 7
THEORIES

As Mike was pulling into his driveway, his cell phone's ringtone began playing the Star Spangled Banner, indicating he had a text message. It was from Jason.

"Call me ASAP," was all the message said. Immediately, he hit the reply button. On the second ring, Jason picked up.

"Mike, I'm starting to think there's something to this!"

"What do you mean?"

"Mike – Elijah Cohen IS Enoch!" Jason shouted.

"What?"

"Just look at the letters that make up the word Cohen and rearrange them to form Enoch."

Several seconds passed.

"Whoa - You're right! Oh, my God, you're actually right! That means…"

"Both prophets are one!" Jason interjected. "We have to dig into this. Give me about forty-five minutes and I'll be over."

"Uh, okay," Mike replied. "Absolutely, I'll be waiting!" he said excitedly.

Jason hung up the phone and grabbed his laptop and car keys.

At that moment, he realized he was still clutching a handful of pills. As he headed to the garage, he stopped at the trash can next to the doorway. He opened the top, paused a second, and then let them spill out into the huge green container. Although he was still overwhelmed with grief, his feeling of hopelessness had been replaced with a sense that he might just be able to find some answers. And if he could get some answers, then maybe, just maybe, they might lead him to his family.

On the way to Mike's house he turned his radio to his favorite talk show, only to find the hiss of white noise. It was a small local station with low wattage. The poor signal surely had something to do with the power drop Teech had talked about. Even the larger and more powerful stations had considerable static. He was hoping he'd find at least one station discussing the End of Days theory, or more scientific explanations on the vanishings. Unfortunately, the static was driving him crazy, so he decided to use his drive time to contact friends and family who he hadn't tried to reach yet.

By the time he pulled up to Mike's house, the only people he had been able to reach were another teacher from his school, one of Kristina's uncles, and a cousin he hadn't spoken to in years. His phone also proved to be as aggravating as the radio, because every call dropped within about forty-five seconds. All he had time to do was say hello and get a fraction of an update on friends and family whom they had lost.

Walking up to Mike's house, he noticed sawdust shavings all over the front porch, along with a crumpled up box from a lock manufacturer. He rang the doorbell and within a few seconds Mike was on the other side unlocking what sounded like half a dozen locks. When he finally opened the door, Jason tilted his head and smirked.

"What gives with Fort Knox?"

Mike pointed proudly to a newly installed padlock and a

specially reinforced chain lock. "I put these in this morning."

"Why?"

"Aren't you following the reports? Crime's already way up. Because there are fewer security personnel to safeguard things, criminals are having a field day."

"I'm sure the increased power outages don't help things either," he added.

"Absolutely! Any good criminal is going to know that it takes power to run security cameras, and when they go out, then the cops are basically blind. But more importantly, it's a computer hacker's paradise. Outages wreak havoc on Internet security systems, leaving gaping holes that will allow them to waltz past the cryptographic protocol for certifying timestamps."

Jason rolled his eyes. "I know you're a tech wizard, but can you dial all that mumbo jumbo back a little?"

"Basically, it just means outages give Internet criminals an easier foot in the door to banks and other financial institutions. My company has been developing products for years to combat this very thing."

Jason panned the room as he walked in. Magazines and papers were strewn everywhere. And every table, chair, and countertop was covered with books and papers with techie sounding titles like *Network Collaborative Commerce Security* and *The Cyber-Attacker's Code Breaker*.

"Wow, if you had a bunch of stray cats wandering the house and a wall full of Post-it notes, I might mistake you for some sort of cyber serial killer."

"Will this do?' Mike grinned, as he opened the door to his office, revealing a long conference size table with five widescreen computer monitors lined up on it. On the other side of the room was a colossal whiteboard that reached from floor to ceiling. The entire thing was covered with a massive flow chart scrawled out with a dry erase marker, and there were Post-it notes peppered all over.

Jason shook his head as he looked around. "I think it's time for a little makeover."

For the next thirty minutes, they cleared the entire office of all techie literature and replaced it with Bibles and other related books to help them research the Rapture. Several hours later, Jason used the whiteboard to scribble out a long list of biblical events associated with the Book of Revelation. It was separated into two sections.

Section One was titled *Rapture* and included a small blurb that said *End-time event when Christians will be "caught up" into the air and meet Christ in the sky.* Beside it was a check mark along with a question mark.

Section Two, which was titled *Tribulation,* included a numbered list of items:

      1. Antichrist leads ten nations
      2. Enoch and Elijah prophesize
      3. Fiery hail
      4. Asteroid strikes
      5. Disease
      6. Volcanic activity
      7. Egypt rebels against Antichrist
      8. Enoch and Elijah killed

As Jason finished writing in the last item, he straightened up and arched backward to stretch his spine. "What's next?"

"It's pretty high level," Mike said from behind his computer screen, "but that seems to cover the major events for the first half of the Tribulation period."

"First half – really?" Jason asked.

"According to just about everything I've read, it's laid out like this. First comes the Rapture. Then there's a seven-year period of what's known as the Tribulation, which basically means the people left behind, like you and me, are tested. This period is broken into halves."

"So, if we're in the first half, then the events we just listed will take place over the next three-and-a-half years?"

"That's right. Then another three-and-a-half years follows, which includes about the same number of events. The second half also delivers the event most people are familiar with."

"666," said Jason uneasily.

"That's right. It's when people get marked with 666, which is the sign of the beast or the Antichrist."

"Mike, I don't ever remember discussing all of these other events in community group, do you?"

"No. But didn't you read Revelation? I thought you promised Kristina you were going to read the Bible cover to cover."

He put his head down. "I started to, but I just couldn't get into it like she did. I really didn't believe, not like she did anyway. I was interested in the Bible. It was fascinating, but the scientific, analytical side of me secretly rationalized away everything it said...at least the parts I did read." He slammed his hand against the whiteboard. "Why didn't I believe?"

Jason could feel himself slipping back into that bad place, and the panic must have been written all over his face.

"But don't you see?" Mike pleaded encouragingly. "If this is all true, then Kristina and Nikki are in a magnificent place just waiting for you. The answers you're looking for and how to get to them are right here. It may take some time, but you can do it. You can and *will* get to them!"

"Do you really believe that? Don't bullshit me, Mike. Do you honestly believe that?"

"I really do." He paused a moment. "The sad thing is that I was like you. I was only going through the motions. On the inside, I

47

didn't actually believe anything I was hearing either. Shoot, even the stuff I was telling others was a lie. Growing up in a big family, it's hard to get noticed, so I learned quickly that becoming a people-pleaser gave me an edge. I was just telling people what I thought they wanted to hear, to make myself look like a good Christian. And to be honest, I was just about to stop going to the community group and church altogether."

"So, what happened?"

"All this happened, you big doofus," Mike replied with a playful jab to his arm.

Jason smiled. Suddenly he was renewed with hope.

"You're right! If this is true…"

"And it IS true!" Mike interjected.

"Then I'll see them again. I'll find them and I'll be with them!" he exclaimed.

"That's my boy!" Mike shouted.

Jason stood, looking at the whiteboard, as his smile got bigger and bigger. Then his eyes welled up with tears. "Thank you, Mike."

"No. Thank you."

"Thank me? Why would you thank me?"

"Your lack of faith is what's kept my best friend around to help me actually make it through this."

Jason chuckled, then wiped his eyes. "Well then, if that's the case, I've got a lot of pressure on me to help you get your wings."

Mike smiled as he laid his hand back on his computer mouse. "Just remember, I'll need those wings in an extra-large, please."

Jason spun back to the whiteboard. "Hmmm, we've listed a lot of stuff. If we're in the first half of the Tribulation, then it really doesn't make much sense to look at the second half right now. Why don't we just look at what's supposed to happen in the first half and then visit the other half down the road?"

"I agree," said Mike. "There's nothing we can do to change

what's going to happen anyway. We just need to validate these events, so we can be aware of what's going on and be prepared for what we need to do."

Jason took his thumb and erased the question mark he had placed beside the word Rapture. "I think we're both in agreement that this one's confirmed."

"Absolutely!" said Mike.

Jason stood poised with his marker, waiting to place checks next to other items on the list. "So, going down the rest of these, what do we know or believe has happened?"

"Well, Enoch and Elijah prophesizing is a check." Mike said. "And I think number five – disease, soon will be. I forgot to tell you, but this morning I had one of my colleagues tap into the Center for Disease Control and…"

Jason shook his head. "You did what?"

"We, or rather he, hacked into their computer systems. We do it all the time. Not just the CDC, but a lot of other agencies and governmental departments. Remember, it's my job to prevent the bad guys from hacking into the good guys. Unfortunately, it means we have to know how to do it, too."

"So, I guess I'm an accomplice if you tell me what you found, huh?" Jason asked uneasily.

"Ehh, don't worry," Mike assured him, "we're so good we never get caught. Plus, with the power outage issues I told you about, it's actually been pretty easy."

"So, what exactly did you find?"

"Since the Rapture, an epidemic has broken out in Syria. It isn't a deadly disease, but something like boils and blisters. But it's spreading aggressively, and if it spans the globe, that'll definitely jive with what it says in the Bible."

Jason wrote a question mark next to *Disease*. "Okay, what else?"

"I think number six is a check."

Jason nodded and put a check next to the number six. "Yep, all the recent earthquakes and volcanic eruptions have to be associated. I heard on the news this morning that this is the most volcanic activity we've had in two thousand years. You didn't even have to hack into anybody's computer for that one."

"No, that's true." Mike paused a second and then took a deep breath. "But now that you mention it, we actually did do a little more investigative work."

"Oh, Lord!" Jason said in mock dismay. "Do I dare ask who or what you hacked?"

Mike looked around the room and scratched his chin. "This one's a little more sensitive."

He suspiciously eyed Mike. "What exactly do you mean by 'sensitive'?"

"Listen, don't get all squirrelly on me, but even though I'm a firm believer that we just experienced the Rapture, I had to know if it's being followed or researched by others."

"Well, of course it is. We're definitely not the only people who think this."

"I know that. What I meant to say is that I needed to find out if there were other organizations that may have bought into the idea and might have insider info the general public isn't privy to."

Jason took a quick step back. "Oh, no. Tell me you didn't!"

"Didn't what?"

"Tell me you didn't hack into the Vatican's system."

"No." Mike said.

"The Pope's computer?"

"Noooo, I said!"

Jason shrugged his shoulders. "Well, then who?"

Mike began scribbling something on a Post-it note.

"Would you stop that and tell me who you hacked into?"

Mike gave a quick glance up at him, as he pulled off the tiny slip of paper and shoved it into his pocket. "Okay, I'm telling you, but you can't freak out."

"I promise. I won't freak out."

CHAPTER 8
CONFIRMATIONS

Mike looked at Jason for a split second and then gazed out the window.

"I had one of my guys break into one of the government's most secure departments...the National Defense Department."

"Holy Crap! Are you insane?" Jason began pacing the room. "You've got to be completely out of your mind! Holy Crap!"

"I know, I know – holy crap," Mike said.

"Why on earth would you hack into the National Defense Department?"

"Because of this." Mike turned and reached into the top drawer of his desk and pulled out a scanned copy of a one-page document and handed it to him.

Jason's hands were trembling. Across the top of the page it read:

CLASSIFIED: PERSON OF INTEREST

"Holy Crap!"

"Enough already with the 'holy craps'," Mike said. "Do you want me just to tell you what it says?"

Jason handed the document back to him. "Yeah, I think you'd

better."

Mike laid the document in front of him on the conference table. He took a long drink from a ginger ale he'd been sipping earlier and then slowly placed both hands back on top of the document. He cleared his throat.

"This is huge. This document confirms *everything*."

Jason sat motionless, transfixed on his friend.

"Basically, what it says is that over the past three years the National Defense Department has been monitoring a certain politician from Turkey by the name of Mustaf Ebecan Younin. He's gained significant power and is currently lobbying for a ten-nation alliance with Egypt, Sudan, Libya, Iraq, Syria, Lebanon, Greece, Macedonia, and Albania.

"So, why's this so important?" Jason asked, clearly not getting it yet.

"Remember the website, *End Of Days Fact Or Fiction?*"

"Yeah, but I don't remember a Mustaf Younin."

"You're right. He wasn't actually named, but what was mentioned was a description of a politician who will rise up out of Turkey and begin to gain prominence. He'll take control of Turkey and form an alliance with Egypt, Sudan, Libya, Iraq, Syria, Lebanon, Greece, Macedonia, and Albania. It goes on to say that he'll also eventually rule over Syria and either Lebanon or Iraq. Jason, this person IS the Antichrist!"

"Whoa! What else did it say?"

"The rest of it is pretty cryptic, but from what I made of it they were outlining their recommendations for monitoring him. There were a bunch of codes and crazy sounding names like *Falcon Op 23*, *Tango Protocol*, and get this, there was even one called *Revelation Protocol*."

"WOW!"

"Don't you mean, 'holy crap'?" Mike replied, jokingly.

Engrossed with this new information, Jason looked down at the fingers on his left hand and began counting to himself. When he reached six, he looked over to his right hand and stopped.

"Mike, let me see that document."

Mike slid the paper across the table.

For the next few seconds, Jason sat scrolling across Younin's name with his index finger while counting to himself. "Whoa!" he said. "This is incredible!"

"What is?" Mike asked.

He spun the document around on the table so Mike could read it. "Take a look at Mustaf's whole name." With his index finger on the 'M' he pronounced his name and began scrolling across it counting each letter as he went. "Mustaf, one – two – three - four - five - six. Ebecan, one – two – three - four - five - six. Younin, one – two – three - four - five - six. Three names with six letters each!"

"Holy Crap!" said Mike. "666!"

Just then, the lights flickered. All the computers crackled and their monitors went black. The lights flickered two more times and then went out completely. A second later, they came back on and all the systems began rebooting.

Mike slammed his hand on the table. "Damn it! These outages are driving me nuts!"

"Look on the bright side," Jason said, "without these power failures you wouldn't have been able to hack into the NDD."

"That's true. And it's only going to get easier. Before long, we'll be able to hack into virtually any system in a few minutes." Just then, Mike reached into his pants pocket, retrieving the crumpled up Post-it note he had put there earlier.

"Listen, why don't you go into the living room and turn on the TV to see if there are any more updates? I need to back up the stuff we've been working on and save all the web addresses we think are most helpful. If I don't, we may start losing things the next time there's an outage."

"Sure," Jason said. "Maybe by now someone will be covering the situation from a religious slant."

CHAPTER 9
FIVE OUT OF EIGHT

Mike watched him as he left the room. When he heard the TV click on, he stuck the Post-it note onto the edge of the large computer monitor in front of him and pulled his keypad up close to his body and began typing feverishly. Every few seconds he would look to the door to make sure Jason wasn't coming down the hallway. After several minutes, he sat back and took a deep breath. Then with one hand he hit the send button and with the other he reached up and grabbed the note. Before putting it back into his pocket, he looked down at it one more time. Only two words had been written on the tiny piece of yellow paper – *Vatican* and *Pope*.

When Mike walked into the living room, he found Jason sitting on the edge of the couch watching the TV without any sound. His hands were tucked underneath his legs and he was leaning forward, staring intently at the screen. Mike followed his gaze and gasped.

The scene being displayed was one of mass destruction. Homes and office buildings had been turned to sticks and rubble. Those that weren't totally destroyed were missing windows, doors and roofs, and what remained was covered in mud and debris. Vehicles of every shape and size were scattered like broken toys. All that remained of the landscape was a fraction of what had been there before hell had rained down on this part of the world. There were no shrubs or bushes of any kind, and trees that did survive had only mangled trunks void of branches.

"What's wrong with the sound?" Mike asked.

"There hasn't been any since I started watching," Jason replied, without looking up. "They're having technical difficulties."

"I'll say," Mike quipped.

"The only thing I know is that something happened in the South China Sea."

"How do you know?"

"When I flipped to this station, there was a banner at the bottom of the screen that read *South China Sea Disaster Report*. Then right before you came in, it was replaced momentarily with another banner saying they were having technical difficulties."

Mike sat down beside Jason. "Are any other channels covering it?"

"Yeah, just about all of them are, but there's no sound on them either."

For the next few minutes they sat in silence and watched as a helicopter-mounted camera surveyed the surrounding area from above. As the shot zoomed out, it was apparent the waters of this massive beast had gone at least a quarter of a mile inland. As they came to the coast, the view revealed the horrific toll it had taken on those living there. Bodies floated through the still churning streets. They were lodged within the rubble of buildings or stuck between the wreckage of cars and trucks. Some had been dismembered, while others floated in pools of blood.

"Where are the survivors?" Mike asked.

"I don't think there are any."

Suddenly the scene switched from the aerial shot to a news

studio. There was a young professionally dressed Asian woman standing in front of a large computer-generated map of the Eastern Hemisphere. She appeared to be explaining the location of the event. When she waved her hand across the top of the screen, the map zoomed down to reveal just the South China Sea and its surrounding landmasses. As she moved her hand counterclockwise from the bottom of the screen upward, the bordering countries' names popped up along with numbers beside them.

Malaysia 189,877

Vietnam 233,646

China, 391,218

Taiwan, 95,138

Philippines 291, 385

Then, across the entire screen appeared the words, *Total Estimated Deaths*, followed by the number *1,201,264*.

Jason and Mike stared in disbelief.

A few seconds later, a thin, middle-aged balding man in a blue suit appeared in the upper right corner of the screen. With his right hand, he made a fist and stretched it upward, then slowly drew it diagonally down into the palm of his other hand, all the while appearing to narrate his motions.

Jason stepped forward and popped the side of the monitor. "This is nerve-racking without sound. Maybe we should go back online and try searching for whatever is going on."

Just then, the sound came on catching the lady as she was asking the man a question.

"So, the actual asteroid was only about sixty feet in diameter?"

"That is correct," the man said, "but it doesn't take a huge chunk of matter coming in from outer space at such high speeds to create disastrous effects. This particular asteroid was probably moving at around 800 miles per hour. When it hit the water, it was enough to cause a 1.7-megaton explosion, which in turn, of course, caused the tsunami.

Jason turned to Mike, "Tsunami! A friggin' tsunami now!"

"Shhhh." Mike held up his hand and then pointed his finger back at the screen. "Just listen."

The man had disappeared and the lady was back in front of the same computer-generated map. This time, however, there were red dots scattered all over it. Across the sea, they were spread out pretty evenly, but along the coastlines there were large clusters. In some places they were so closely grouped they formed massive blobs of red. At the top of the screen, the words *Shipping Toll* appeared.

"In addition to the massive loss of life and huge coastal destruction is the incredible loss in shipping." She pointed to one of the red dots. "Each dot on our map represents a vessel that has been lost, due to the effects of the tsunami. The majority of the loss, of course, occurred along the coast. It's much too early to give reliable estimates, but some experts are telling us as much as a third of the entire world's shipping fleet may have been destroyed."

Mike reached around the corner of the TV monitor and clicked the off button.

"Hey! What are you doing?" Jason demanded.

"Follow me." Mike turned and headed down the hallway.

As they entered his office, Mike grabbed a Bible off the conference table and tossed it to Jason. "Start scanning the Book of Revelation for the words "meteor," "asteroid," or anything like that coming from out of the sky. I'm going to do the same on the computer."

Jason started flipping pages. "What else should I be looking for?"

"Any references to trade, shipping, or anything like that."

After several minutes, Jason sighed. "Man, I'm not finding anything. Mind if I use one of your computers?"

"Sure, but I think I just found what we're looking for."

Jason walked around the back of Mike's chair and leaned over his shoulder. Mike was again viewing the *End of Days Fact Or Fiction* website, and he pointed to the screen. "It says here that an asteroid will strike one of the earth's oceans, killing a third of the surrounding life and devastating a third of the ships sailing the seas."

Jason picked up his marker and walked over to the whiteboard. "That's almost verbatim with what the reporter mentioned when she said the tsunami was estimated to have destroyed a third of the world's shipping fleets. But what about that part about killing a third of the surrounding life?"

"I'm not sure about that part," Mike said, "but I'd bet my 401k that when the final numbers come in, they'll match up."

Jason nodded his head. "With more than a million deaths and a third of the world's shipping fleet destroyed, I'm going to check this one off as a definite."

After a quick flick of his marker he stepped back and surveyed their list of biblical events. "Antichrist leads ten nations – check! Enoch and Elijah prophesize – check! Volcanic activity – that's a check! Disease – we checked that one, but we'll have to wait and see, since your report said it is just starting to spread. And finally, asteroid strikes – that's a big check. Now all that leaves us with is fiery hail, Egypt rebels against Antichrist, and Enoch and Elijah killed. That's five out of eight. I don't know about you, but I'm definitely on board with the Rapture theory."

"We've got company then." Mike said peering over the edge of his computer monitor. "You, me, and more than three billion people. I just did a search on the word "Rapture" and that's how many times it's been searched in the last two days!"

CHAPTER 10
CHRISTMAS GUEST

For the next seven months, Lake Royale slowly became a beige and desolate community. The rich colors of fall were all but forgotten, amidst the sorrow and suffering of the vanishings. As the winter months progressed, temperatures continued to stay warm, while the normally placid emerald green waters turned choppy and muddy. What used to be a flourishing ecosystem surrounded with beautiful foliage and bountiful wildlife was now turning brown and barren. Just a few dozen sparrows perched in the leafless trees of the surrounding woods, and the cheerful chirping of the orioles and robins was gone. Only the occasional caw of a black crow could be heard, echoing across the dying lake.

Winter used to be a festive time in the city, especially around Christmas. But since the vanishings, it was as if the town's very soul had been sucked from it. Instead of hanging holly wreaths on their doors, people installed deadbolts and security latches. And instead of outlining their windows with colorful Christmas lights, they had either boarded them up or installed crossbars over them. Crime continued to rise as power throughout the world continued to slowly diminish. Gangs started to form, and it became increasingly dangerous even to leave the house.

Everything had become more difficult. Food supplies were dwindling, and prices on products and services were escalating. Schools were closed because there were no children to attend them. Hospitals were always full. Manufacturing plants were all running at half capacity. Every business and industry had been adversely affected, as a result of not having enough people to perform the labor or not enough power to meet the demands. But of all the after-effects from the previous months, the worst was the overwhelming grief that had swept across the globe. Almost everyone had either lost someone or knew someone who had vanished. The security, love, and bond of family and friends had been vaporized. All that was left was a heavy blanket of sadness covering every city, town, and village throughout the world.

Even though Jason continually had to fight off his own feelings of despair, he knew he was luckier than most. He had his friends to bolster him. He and Mike were connected at the hip, as they remained engrossed in their belief in the Rapture theory.

His relationship with Erin had also grown stronger. If he wasn't with Mike, he would most likely be with her, sharing the one major thing they had in common – the lake. It was a substantial source of solace for them both, and they would spend hours walking along its shores together or just hanging out on her deck admiring the view.

On Christmas day, Jason invited Mike and Erin to his house for a traditional turkey dinner.

"Do you mind if I bring someone along?" Mike asked.

"Of course not, I'm pretty sure nobody's going to be asking for seconds, so there should be enough. Who's your mystery guest?"

"It's a surprise," Mike said coyly.

"Oooh la la," Jason said. "Could it be that curvy red head from across your street?"

"Even more heavenly!" Mike said.

At precisely seven o'clock, Erin showed up on Jason's doorstep. As soon as he opened the door, she threw her arms around his neck and planted a big kiss on his cheek.

"Merry Christmas!" she exclaimed, as she handed him a small, tightly wrapped box with a tiny white bow.

"Ah, you shouldn't have," Jason replied. "But thank you so much".

She looked around. "Is Mike here yet?"

"He just texted me. He'll be here in about five minutes."

"Good!" she said. "You can go ahead and open it before he gets here!"

"Well alrighty! I'm always ready to open a present."

Meticulously, he slowly unwrapped the box. Erin smiled and bounced up and down on her tiptoes in anticipation. Finally, she couldn't restrain her excitement any longer.

"Oh, just rip that puppy to pieces!" she finally blurted out.

Jason jerked his head up and looked at her feigning surprise. Then together they began laughing as he now tore into the little package. After all the wrapping paper was gone, it revealed a small mahogany box the size of a credit card, about a half inch deep. He looked at it and smiled, then looked up at Erin.

"You're too much, you know that."

"Open it, silly!" she persisted.

Inside was a tiny blue velvet bag. He pulled it out. "You got me the cutest silk baggy…how sweet."

She tilted her head and grabbed his arm. "Are you going to open this, or do I have to give it to my dentist?"

"Oh, alright!" he said. Then he reached in with two fingers and pulled out a silver heart-shaped medallion the size of a fifty-cent piece.

"That's beautiful – absolutely beautiful," he said.

"Read the inscription!"

He narrowed his eyes slightly and read:

Love, Erin

She motioned for him to flip it over. "That's the backside. See what the other side says."

He turned it over and read:

To New Beginnings

She put her hands together as if about to pray. "Do you like it?"

"It's wonderful. I do. I love it – I really do! Thank you so much." He placed it back into its bag and then neatly laid it into the box. "I know just where to put it," he said. Then he hugged her tightly, raising her off the floor as he leaned back. "I'm so lucky to have you in my life."

Erin took a half step back and gazed into his eyes. Her hands were trembling. She looked off to the side and then down to the floor.

"Jason, I – I don't know if you know this," she began, "but for the longest time…" Then she stopped.

"What is it?" he asked. A few seconds passed. He lightly placed his hand under her chin and gently pulled her head up to where her eyes met his. "What is it?" he said softly.

Just then, two car doors slammed shut out in the driveway.

"Gobble gobble, your best friend is here to hobbnobble," Mike yelled as he stepped onto the front porch.

Jason looked at Erin with a crooked smile. "Hobbnobble? What the heck is hobbnobble?"

Both laughed and turned toward the door, just as Mike was entering. Behind him was a tall bald man who appeared to be in his late fifties. His shoulders were broad and his build suggested he was once an athlete. He had a large, slightly crooked nose that suggested he'd probably been in a fight or two back in his day. In contrast were his eyes - they were big and brown and conveyed sincerity.

Mike immediately gave Erin a full hug and then leaned over and took Jason's hand while giving him a typical men's chest bump. "Merry Christmas, one and all!" he bellowed, followed by a hearty "Ho, Ho, Ho!"

"Well, Merry Christmas to you too, St. Nick," Erin giggled.

"I think Santa's already been hittin' the eggnog," Jason added.

They all laughed, and then Mike turned to the man who had entered with him and said, "Erin and Jason, I'd like you to meet Father Timothy Lanier."

"Please, call me Tim," he said.

Erin reached out to shake his hand. "Welcome, Father Tim." She paused a second and then sheepishly said. "Oh, I'm sorry. I was raised Catholic, so it's a habit. Do you mind if I stick with Father Tim?"

"Of course not," he chuckled. "You can call me anything you want. My college buddies had several other names for me, but I'm afraid they were a little saltier."

Erin laughed. At that moment she knew she liked him.

"Father, welcome to my home," Jason said. "I'm not much of a cook, so I'm afraid this might not be a great first impression."

"Just allowing me to be a part of your group on such a special evening is the best impression you could ever make."

"Well then, since you're brave enough to test my culinary creations, why don't we all head into the dining room and start our little feast? Erin, will you show Father Tim where the dining room is?"

As Erin escorted their guest down the hallway, Jason grabbed Mike by the arm. "So, this is what you meant by *more heavenly*?" The two burst into laughter.

After they all sat down, Jason looked to Father Tim. "Father, I don't mean to put you on the spot, but would you mind saying the blessing?"

"Certainly, it would be an honor." He paused thoughtfully, then began, "Bless us, oh Lord, and these bountiful gifts of food and friendship. This is such a significant time for your people. As we rejoice and celebrate the birth of your son, our Lord and Savior Jesus Christ, we also rejoice in the new beginning, which you have so graciously granted us. May you be with each of us in the days ahead, and may you comfort us in the trials and tribulations of this time. Through Christ, our Lord. Amen."

"Thank you, Father," Jason said. "Everyone, don't be shy. Go ahead and dig in."

His friends began reaching for dishes and passing them around. Immediately the room was filled with the clatter of silverware and polite small talk that quickly progressed to more jovial banter about how Jason had spent two days prepping for the evening. The atmosphere was festive with a warmth that had not been present in his home since before the vanishings. And even though Jason was enjoying how his evening had started, he was dying to move past the idle chitchat and to start quizzing Father Tim. He was still seeking answers, and he was anxious to find out what someone from the clergy knew or thought about the vanishings and how everything related to the Rapture.

When there was a lull in the conversation, Jason made his move. "So, Father, I'm curious to hear what the Catholic Church thinks about everything that's been happening over the past seven months."

All eyes turned to the pastor.

"Well, as you may know, Catholics don't generally use the term Rapture, nor do we believe in a Rapture that will take place some time before the Second Coming, as do many Evangelicals. However, the evidence certainly does support a divine occurrence. I don't have a hard and fast answer for what the line is from the church because so many of our leaders have vanished. But what I will say is that, Rapture or not, most of us left behind believe one undisputable thing."

He stopped and looked around the table. "It was our lack of faith – our not truly believing that caused us to be left behind."

Jason nodded. "I'm sure Mike has mentioned to you that he and I have been researching all of the events that have been occurring. Are they related?"

"Most of them certainly appear to be. But again, I can't say whether or not they are Rapture related or not. By the way, no one has asked yet, but the reason I'm here is because Mike actually sought me out as part of this research you've been doing."

"I'm so sorry," Mike said. "I totally forgot to tell you guys how I know Tim. As you know, I was raised Catholic, and my parents were very active at St. Francis of Assisi. Father Tim was there for my family both times when my father, and then my mother, passed away. It was because we had grown so close through that painful time that Karen and I asked him to preside over our marriage. Sadly he was also there during our divorce and to guide us through the annulment. It was a shot in the dark when I called him, and to be honest, I never thought he'd be left behind. He has been such a source of strength for me over the years."

The room grew quiet and a sudden look of sadness crossed Tim's face. He sighed.

"Well, let's just say even those in the clergy sometimes have faith issues." Then he clapped his hands together and said with a smile, "But that's all behind us now. Our faith is rock solid and the Lord, through His grace, is offering us the chance to still enter His kingdom."

"Amen to that!" said Mike.

"So, Father," Erin said, "what exactly do we have to do?"

"It's simple, yet hard. The simple part is that we have to live like those who were taken. And like them, we have to have faith."

"What's the hard part?" she asked.

"The hard part is simply enduring the unknown, fighting all the crime and just surviving. And we have to constantly be on guard against Satan and protect ourselves against the deceptions he'll try to employ. He'll come in many shapes and forms. Our very souls are his prize and he'll use our own weaknesses to obtain them." He paused, looking at each one of them individually. "Now, listen to me carefully." His voice grew stern. "The one major weapon we have against him is our faith. It's our shield against him. Those without it will be more susceptible to his presence."

Just then, Erin noticed something that seemed to move behind the Father. But all that was there was a mirror directly behind him that reflected out the room's bay window into Jason's driveway. As he continued to talk about being prepared for the Tribulation, Erin's attention remained on the mirror. Suddenly she was jerked back into the conversation when Jason asked her to pass the cranberry sauce.

"Oh, sure," she said.

As she passed him the plate, he mouthed to her, "Are you okay?"

With a quick nod, she whispered, "Yeah," then turned back to Father Tim.

As the conversation continued, Mike engaged the clergyman with more questions about the different views of the Rapture from various religious denominations. As the Father spoke, he turned his attention away from Erin, giving her the opportunity to look back to the mirror. But all she could see was the vague outline of Mike's car against the backdrop of light reflecting off the lake in the distance. She continued to stare at the mirror, wishing she could turn around and look directly out the window.

After a moment she decided she had just been seeing things and began to turn back to the conversation. Just as she did, something caught her eye. Out in the driveway, a black object appeared from out of nowhere and appeared to be hovering just above the car's roof. Then, as quickly as it had appeared, it was gone. She blinked and tried telling herself it was just something floating out on the lake.

In a flash, it reappeared. She made a quick glance at Jason, but he was engrossed in what Father Tim was saying. When she turned back, there was nothing. But something was different. This time the car door was open. Her palms were sweating and she started feeling sick.

"Excuse me," she said, "I need to get some ice. Does anyone want some?"

"No, thanks," they all replied.

When she reached the kitchen, she grabbed a dishcloth from beside the sink and soaked it in cold water. Then she bent over and held it to her face while letting the water fall into the sink. The sensation of the water on her skin and the cool darkness of the cloth gave her immediate relief. After a minute, her hands had stopped shaking and she was feeling like herself again.

She stood up and slowly pulled the cloth back from her face. With her other hand she wiped her eyes and gazed out the window over the sink and into the dark foliage of an overgrown bush that stood about three feet from the house. As her pupils adjusted to the light, she began to see its shape more clearly. Slowly, the branches became more defined. In an instant, they began taking on another shape.

On the other side of the window, hidden in the dark details of its branches, was the figure of a man. She dropped the dishcloth, and her body froze. She couldn't move or even scream. As if in a trance, Erin's eyes were transfixed by the ominous figure before her. The silhouette was that of a large man wearing a long black

69

coat with a black hood revealing nothing of his face, except a large protruding chin. Startlingly, from within the dining room came the sound of breaking glass followed by chairs scraping across the floor.

CHAPTER 11
PROTECTORS

"What the hell?" yelled Mike.

"Wait, don't go!" Jason screamed.

A second later, Father Tim was bursting through the back door and sprinting toward Mike's car. A figure darted from behind the car and ran in the opposite direction. Jason grabbed a baseball bat from his office and ran out the back door just in time to see Father Tim tackling the fleeing trespasser at the far end of the yard. In a split second, he had him pinned to the ground.

When Jason got to the scene he was out of breath. "What, what the heck, Father?" he panted.

Father Tim didn't appear to be winded at all. The man he had subdued, however, was wheezing uncontrollably. He was about six feet tall, two hundred pounds, and appeared to be in his mid-thirties. He wore jeans and a black hoodie. And although he didn't look menacing, there was an undeniable look of desperation in his eyes.

As the Father stood up, he pulled his captive with him. It was obvious by the hold he had on him there was no way he could break free.

"Jason, would you mind calling the police?" Tim's tone was almost comical in how calmly and politely he asked.

Jason looked at him and couldn't help but crack a smile. "Why sure."

Mike came running up. "I've already called the police. What happened? Who is this guy?"

Jason grabbed Mike's arm. "Where's Erin?"

"She's in the house. Don't worry, she's all right. A little shaken, but she's okay."

In minutes a police car screeched through the driveway into the middle of the backyard. Seconds later, two more followed. The entire lawn quickly filled with flashing blue lights and policemen.

As the police took the suspect into their custody, Jason excused himself to check on Erin. Tim and Mike remained to help the police with their report of the incident.

Jason found her sitting in his living room with her arms tightly crossed against her chest. She was staring blankly at the wall.

"Erin, are you okay?"

She turned to him and sighed. "I'm okay now," she said, as her lower lip began to quiver.

He quickly sat down and put his arm around her. "It's okay. Everything's alright now."

"Did you get him?" she whispered timidly.

"Yes. He's outside right now being questioned by the police."

Mike entered the room. "The police need all of us outside to verify this is the guy who was trespassing."

Jason helped her up, and they all headed to the back of the house.

"Mike, wasn't that incredible how Tim took that guy down?"

"Oh yeah! But to be honest, I'm not too surprised."

"Why not?"

"Well, I was saving this fascinating tidbit for later on in the evening, but since we had our little interruption, it kinda put it on hold. It just so happens that our good Father was a decorated Navy Seal before he turned in his camo gear for a cloak."

Jason looked at Mike and shook his head with a grateful smile. "Man, oh man. The Lord truly does work in mysterious ways."

When they reached the backyard, only one police car remained, along with the arresting officer and Father Tim.

"Erin and Jason, this is Officer Jonathan McNabb," Tim said. "He just needs to ask you guys a couple of questions."

"Howdy, folks. I'm sorry you've had this little disturbance this evening, but I'm glad it turned out okay. Mr. Tim made things pretty easy for us. As a matter of protocol, I just need each of you to look at the man one last time and tell me if he's the fella who was trespassing." He turned to Erin. "All except you, ma'am. Since you were inside, you wouldn't have been able to see him."

"But, sir, I did see him. I saw him when I went to get ice."

"You did?" Jason asked.

"Yeah, I was looking out the kitchen sink window and he was standing directly in front of me, in that big bush outside your house."

"Hmm. Well, okay then." the officer said, while making a note on his report. Then he walked over to the back of the car and opened the door so they could see the suspect sitting in the back seat. "Folks, would you confirm for me that this is the person who was trespassing on your property this evening."

"Yes," they all said in unison, with the exception of Erin who stood there shaking her head.

"No. That's not the man. The man I saw looked different."

"How so?" asked the policeman.

"The man I saw was all in black like this man, but his face was different. I couldn't see his eyes because of his hood, but their chins are different. The other man had a much bigger chin. It was kind of creepy, actually. It was big and pointed." She paused. "And it had a huge zigzagged scar across it. It was like a Halloween mask type of chin."

"Do you think it *could* have been a mask?" asked the officer.

"No. I'm sure it was real."

The men looked at one another.

Then the officer said, "Well, there may have been an accomplice." He looked at Erin. "But if there was, you can rest assured that other guy is long gone. After he saw what Tim did to his boy, he's not going to be coming back to this house, that's for sure."

They all laughed, but Erin just stood looking back at the house shivering. It had grown cold since all the commotion had started, and Jason saw that she was not handling the sudden drop in temperature well.

"Hey, Mike, would you mind taking Erin back to the house? I need to finish up with officer McNabb. And Father Tim, would you mind staying?"

When Erin and Mike were out of hearing distance, he turned to the policeman. "Do you think there was somebody with this guy?"

The officer looked back toward Erin and Mike, then walked over to the police car and shut the door where the suspect was. "Mr. Stover, I could tell your friend Erin was pretty upset. If I had disputed what she said, it would've upset her more and you'd be spending the rest of the night calming her down. But between you and me – well, I'm pretty sure it was just the guy in this car."

"What makes you think that?"

"Two things. First, I've been on the force for more than twenty-eight years and I've been trained how to interrogate suspects in situations like this. There wasn't anything this guy said that would indicate he had an accomplice. And second, our guys surveyed the entire outside of your house and unless someone can levitate, there's no way she could have seen anybody directly outside that particular window."

Jason nodded. "That's right." He turned to the Father. "That window is almost fifteen feet off the ground."

"What if he climbed the branches, or used a ladder?"

"It's just an overgrown bush," the officer said. "It's only stems and twigs that couldn't even support the weight of a cat. There also was no trace of a ladder being used anywhere around the house. And if an intruder were trying to enter your house, this is the last place he would have tried."

"Are you positive?" Father Tim questioned.

"You can never guarantee something like this. But I'd almost stake my badge on it. I'm afraid your friend was just seeing things."

"So what did you find out about the guy in the back seat?" Jason asked.

"It looks like he was here to steal your car. It'll be in my report, but he said he was laid off. He worked at a manufacturing plant that just cut its workers down to a skeleton crew. He said he needed the cash to support his family. He's probably not a bad guy, just a very desperate one."

Jason reached out and shook his hand. "Thanks again for everything, Officer McNabb. You guys were great."

Father Tim placed his hand on his shoulder. "Please, thank the rest of your guys, too. You've got a great team."

As the police car pulled out of the driveway, Jason and Father Tim headed back to the house.

"Father, what do you think about tonight? Was this guy by himself?"

He shook his head. "I'm not sure. All I know is that we're entering a time when we'll be seeing all sorts of things that make us question everything. Personally, I think Erin witnessed one of those tonight."

When they reached the house, Mike met them at the back door.

"Tim, are you ready to head out? Jason probably needs to unwind a little."

"Yep, I'm good to go." He turned to Jason. "Would you tell Erin goodnight for us? I'm sure she's probably still a little shaken."

"Sure," he said. "Thank you both for coming tonight. I didn't plan that bit of entertainment, but I hope you at least enjoyed the first half of the evening."

Father Tim walked up to Jason and gave him a huge bear hug. "Everything was perfect. We'll just have to remember to bring our workout gear next time, in case we have to get physical."

They headed to the car and Jason waved goodbye. "Mike, I'll call you tomorrow, buddy" he yelled after them.

When he went back into the house, he found Erin lying on the living room sofa with a blanket neatly tucked around her. He knelt down beside her.

"How ya doin', young lady?" he whispered.

"Umm, okay," she said softly.

"Do you want anything? Tea, coffee – cocoa, maybe?"

"No, I'm fine."

"Are you sure you're okay?"

She sat up and looked at him. Her usually radiant complexion was pale and she looked exhausted.

"I'm scared, Jason. I can't shake the image of that, that man. I didn't say anything to you guys earlier, but there was something so strange about him."

"In what way?" he asked.

"There was this sense of evil. I don't know how to explain it, but when I was staring at him all these horrible feelings came over me. It was like I was feeling depressed, lonely, and angry all at the same time. It felt like he was there *for me*. And there's something else I didn't tell you guys. I didn't want you to think I was crazy or just imagining things." She paused then took a deep breath. "I was standing there looking at him. Honestly, I don't know how long it was. It could've been five seconds or five minutes. Time just kind of stood still, but when all the commotion began it made me blink. When I did, he was gone. In that split second, he just vanished into thin air."

He put his hand on her knee. "Erin, I want you to know I will believe whatever you tell me. These are terrible times. All kinds of crazy things are going through our heads. I'm not saying you imagined anything but..."

"No! I *didn't* imagine it," she pleaded

"Okay, I believe you. All I'm saying is..." he stopped. "All I'm saying is that I believe you. I really do." He knew that she was committed to her feelings and that it would be useless trying to convince her otherwise.

Almost in a whimper, she said, "Will you walk me home?"

He hugged her. "Sure, I'll walk you home. Why don't you keep the blanket around you and I'll grab a jacket?"

The walk to Erin's house seemed to reinvigorate her. She even started joking about how silly everyone probably thought she was. Jason had always loved her sense of humor and he couldn't help thinking how cute she looked all bundled up in his blanket. She was by far the most attractive lady in the community and her vulnerability only magnified her beauty.

When they reached her front porch she turned to Jason and playfully bumped up against him. "Thanks ya big lug for walkin' a gal home.

"Pleasure's all mine, little missy."

She shuffled nervously back and forth. She tried looking him in the eye but then looked down.

"Erin, what's up? You okay?"

"I don't want to seem forward, but would you mind sleeping...I mean staying here tonight?"

His eyebrows rose slightly.

"The only reason I ask is that I don't feel safe," she continued. "I was actually going to ask if I could sleep on your couch, but I knew I'd be too scared there."

He smiled. "Of course, and before you say anything else, I totally understand."

"Thank you so much!" she said.

Erin's house was a small bungalow, but it was beautiful. When Jason walked in, all the lights were off with the exception of several cinnamon scented candles burning in the living room. Their scent and the flickering candlelight gave the house a warm and inviting feel.

"Would you like anything?" she said. "I have some red wine opened, if you'd like some."

"I'm fine. I'm actually pretty exhausted to tell you the truth."

"Let me know if you change your mind. I'm going to go put my pajamas on, but I'll be back in just a minute. You'll find blankets in the corner cabinet, as well as a goose down pillow. Make yourself at home."

Jason took off his jacket and shoes then retrieved the items from the cabinet. Several minutes later, she returned wearing just a long T-shirt made of thin white cotton.

"We're you able to find everything?" she said.

"I did. I just need to put it all together and I'm good to go."

"Oh, let me do that, please," she said, as she took the blanket from his hand. As she spread it out and began tucking in the corners, the backlight from the room's candles revealed the silhouette of her beautifully toned body. As he watched, he thought how much of an idiot her ex-husband was to have messed up their marriage like he did. She was a beautiful woman, both inside and out.

78

After tucking in the last corner, she stood up and made a quick turn. As she did, she tripped over one of Jason's shoes and began falling backwards. He reached out to grab her but lost his footing too, and together they fell onto the couch. As they lay there laughing, the scent of her perfume suddenly replaced that of the candles, and he found himself gazing into her eyes. His heartbeat quickened, and he felt a lump in his throat. Slowly, she leaned in and kissed him tenderly on the cheek. "Thank you," she whispered in his ear.

For a moment, the two lay side-by-side, motionless, until finally Jason broke the silence. "Umm. Well, uh, you're welcome," he stammered.

Quickly, he jumped to his feet and began straightening the coffee table that had moved during their tumble.

"Are you sure you want such a klutz guarding you?" he joked.

She stood up and pretended to dust herself off. "There's no one else I'd rather have." She smiled and then headed down the hallway with the scent of her perfume lingering behind. Jason watched until she got to her room. She turned and leaned against the doorframe. "If you need anything – anything at all, I'm right down here." She smiled again and disappeared inside.

He stood staring into the hall. After a few seconds, he sighed and lay down on the couch. As he pulled the covers up around him, he reached into his pants pocket and pulled out the box she had given him earlier. He opened its lid and pulled the heart-shaped medallion from the silk bag. He flipped it over and reread the inscription, then looked back down the hallway. What a truly special gift it was. He rubbed the back of his neck where his birthmark was, and then closed his eyes and remembered the small of his daughter's neck and the heart-shaped birthmark that was in the exact same place as his. Yes, this was truly a special gift.

CHAPTER 12
THE RAIN

The next morning, Jason awakened at the break of dawn to the smell of bacon frying and fresh coffee brewing in the kitchen. He wiped his eyes and slowly sat up. Erin came into the living room carrying a large plate of waffles, bacon, and scrambled eggs. He couldn't believe how someone could be so energetic at this time of day. But more baffling was how someone could wake up looking just as beautiful as they had the night before.

"Good, you're up!" she said. "I thought you might be extra hungry, since we didn't get to finish our dinner last night, so I whipped up a little extra."

He stretched his arms behind him while leaning back trying to shake off the effects of his night on the sofa. "You read my mind. I'm famished!"

"Good! I love a hearty eater. I'll be back in a minute with some coffee." When she returned, he had already spread out the meal onto the table next to the sofa.

"Mind if I see what's on the news?" he asked.

"No, I'm kinda curious to see what they have to say about a Christmas Tribulation," she said with a smile.

Just as he was reaching for the remote, all of the power in the house went out. "Ah, man! Not another outage," he moaned.

"Well at least I was able to get our breakfast done," she said. "Would you mind hitting that switch directly behind you?"

He flipped the switch and instantly the gas logs in the fireplace lit up the room with a soft warm glow. Together with the pastels of the early morning sun, the room was a picturesque image of serenity and peace – a far cry from the drab and gloomy feel Jason's house had taken on over the past months. As they ate, their conversation was easy and relaxed. It evolved from the events of the previous evening to a wide range of topics including their hopes and fears for their futures.

It was approaching eleven o'clock by the time they realized they'd been chatting it up for almost the entire morning. Jason loved talking to Erin and expressing himself to her comforted him in a way that he had been longing for. "Can you believe what time it is?" he said. "I haven't talked like this since…" he paused.

"Since Kristina was here?" she said softly.

"Yeah, since Kristina."

"Hey, wanna take some Christmas day video this afternoon?" she said snapping things back to a lively mood.

"Well, sure. What did you have in mind?"

Erin bounced up and down in her chair. "It's been a tradition of mine for the past few years to email a video to all my family and friends wishing them a merry Christmas. This year I thought I'd go down by the lakeshore and do it from there. You could be my videographer!"

"That sounds like fun – I'm in!"

"Awesome! Why don't I go freshen up and get changed?"

"Do I have time to run back to the house and get a quick shower? I need to give Mike a call, too."

"Sure. How about you meet me back here at 11:45? We'll take

the video and then grab some lunch."

"Sounds like a plan." He grabbed his jacket and headed out the door. It was a beautiful day. The weather continued to be unseasonably warm, and there wasn't a cloud in the sky. And the fact that he had an afternoon planned with one of his best friends lifted his spirits even more. When he reached his house, he found his cell phone and called Mike.

"Merry Christmas!" he shouted the moment his friend picked up.

"Right back at ya, buddy!" Mike said in his usual jovial manner. "So were you able to get a good night's sleep after all the ruckus?"

"Actually, it was one of the best I've had in a long time, even if it was on a sofa."

"On a sofa? Why'd you sleep on your sofa?"

"It wasn't my sofa. It was Erin's."

"Oh, really now? Do tell," Mike coaxed.

"Man, get your mind out of the gutter," he chuckled. "You saw how upset she was. I just stayed on her couch because she was so scared."

"Well, I'll give you that one, but you gotta be blind if you can't see how much that girl's in to you."

"What? She's my friend. Actually, besides you, she's my best friend."

"Friend or not, she's all about Jason Stover. You can tell by the way she looks at you. Shoot, even her tone of voice is different when she's talking to you," Mike laughed. "It's all ooohhh and ahhh and Jason this and Jason that!"

"Oh, whatever! Listen, I just wanted to give you a call and let you know I'll be over later tonight, probably right after dinner if that's okay."

"Sounds good. See you later."

Jason quickly showered, changed, and headed back to Erin's.

He loved that she only lived a few houses away, but on a warm, clear blue sky like today, he almost wished it was longer.

When he arrived, the front door was still open. He stuck his head inside. "Yoooohoo! Is Miss Claus ready for her close-up?"

"Come on in. I'm in the kitchen," she yelled back.

When he entered the kitchen, Erin was standing in the middle of the room with her hands on her hips and head tilted down in a come-hither look straight out of Cosmopolitan. She was wearing a fluffy Santa hat, a red mini skirt revealing her long slender legs and a low cut red V-neck cashmere sweater that accentuated every curve of her body.

"Wow!"

"What do ya think?" she purred.

"I think you look absolutely stunning." He blushed.

With a quick peck on the cheek she said, "You're so sweet." Then she grabbed him by the hand. "Come on. The light down on the lake is perfect, and besides, it's almost noon and I'm hungry again."

On their way out the door she grabbed her video camera, and like kids just out of elementary school, they ran all the way down to the lakeshore behind her house. When they stopped, Erin handed Jason her camera, then stretched out her arms and began spinning around.

"Finally a pretty day!"

Jason powered on the camera and began circling her as she continued to spin. "Can you believe it?" Jason said while filming her. "This place has been so depressing and glum, but today it's like a whole new world." He stopped. "Listen! Do you hear that?"

"Hear what?" she said.

"The Lake Loons – I haven't heard them in months. They're calling for each other. Man, how I've missed that sound."

Erin leaned her head back. With her arms still outstretched, she took a long deep breath. "And smell the air. It's so fresh and clean."

He smiled and sighed. "Who knows, Erin? Maybe this is a sign that things are about to change."

He lifted the camera back to his face and clicked the record button. Just as he was about to focus in on her, she reached up and placed her hand on top of it. Slowly she pulled it down. She was now standing less than a foot from him. For several seconds the two stood motionless, her crystal blue eyes confirming what Mike had said earlier.

As Jason stood there mesmerized by her beauty, she leaned in and tenderly placed her lips to his. Then gently, she placed her hand to his cheek and began passionately kissing him. His mind began swimming, as the warmth of her lips filled him with desires he hadn't felt for so long. His heart and body raged against one another, as thoughts of Kristina suddenly filled his mind. He let loose of the camera. As it fell to the ground, he grabbed her by the shoulders.

"I can't do this. It isn't right." He turned away and looked off across the lake. "I loved Kristina. I still love her – I always will." He turned back to her. "I'm so sorry."

Erin was looking down, unable to meet his eyes. "No, don't be sorry," she said in a strained voice. "I'm the one who should be apologizing. I've been feeling so lost and lonely, and you've been so wonderful through all this..." Her voice trailed off and a tear ran down her cheek.

"Erin, please don't feel bad. This is a crazy time and it's got all of us out of sorts." He tried to sound matter of fact, but he knew she could hear the anxiety in his voice.

"I know but I should've known better. I saw, I mean I see, how you still love Kristina. I loved her too. I really did, and now I feel like I've betrayed her and messed up our friendship."

Carefully he put his hand under her chin and raised her head so her eyes met his. "You didn't betray anyone, and you certainly didn't mess up our friendship. There's absolutely no reason to apologize."

She pulled off her Santa Clause hat and let it fall to the ground. "Why couldn't I have found a guy like you before I met the jerk I got married to? Ugh, never mind that. My mind was so messed up back then, I wouldn't have known a good man even if he rode up on a white stallion with a glass slipper in his hand."

Jason tilted his head, glad for the opening, "Maybe, if we finish this video, I'll post it online and your Prince Charming can find you over the Internet."

She smiled. "You're just too sweet."

He gave her a big hug and asked, "Do you still want to do the video?"

"Sure. I think I'm…" She stopped mid-sentence. Then with two quick steps, she backed away from him while stretching out her arms in front of her. She looked down at them blankly, as if she didn't recognize them as her own.

"What's wrong?" Jason asked.

"Do you feel it?" Her tone was monotone, but with a sense of dread.

"Feel what?" Jason asked earnestly, anxiety building in his chest.

"The tingling!" she said. "The tingling!" She looked at him with wide eyes pleading him to understand.

At that moment, the hair stood up on Jason's arms and a chill ran down his spine. He suddenly remembered the feeling and knew why Erin was panicking. It was the same sensation they had experienced during the vanishings.

He grabbed her arms. "It's going to be okay." He stared into her eyes. "Just focus on me, okay? Everything's going to be all right."

As they huddled together, the entire sky began to change. Large threatening clouds seemed to blow in from nowhere. It was as if a thunderstorm had instantly appeared. But unlike normal solid gray storm clouds, these were a mix of various shades of blue.

Erin's head rolled to the side. "Ohhhhh," she moaned, collapsing to the ground.

"Erin!" he yelled.

He tried pulling her up, but couldn't. She was dead weight and he was suddenly so very weak.

The next thing he knew his balance was gone and he fell to the ground next to her, unable to move. He tried yelling to her, but his lips wouldn't move. Nothing would. As he lay there, all he could do was stare at her across the grass, apprehensively awaiting the next series of events. Suddenly, there was a loud clap of thunder, followed by a bright flash of light that filled the entire sky. For several seconds, the sky was illuminated with the most brilliant white. It only lasted a few more seconds before it began to fade. As it did, Jason drifted into unconsciousness. The last thing he remembered was the rain on the horizon.

The next conscious sensation Jason had was when his body jerked, awakening him from a coma-like sleep he'd been subjected to. He wanted to sit up, to see what was going on, but his body felt like a sack of bricks. Like the aftermath of the vanishings, he was as weak as a newborn calf. All he could do was to lie there until his strength returned.

"Erin," he croaked. "Erin, can you hear me?"

She was in the exact same position as when she had collapsed. Her hair was tossed across her face hiding her eyes.

"Erin, can you hear me?" he repeated. Then he closed his eyes and fell back into sleep.

What seemed like only a moment later, he was awakened by a small and weak voice.

"Jason, are you okay?"

He opened his eyes to find Erin feebly stretching her arm out to him. Slowly, he moved his arm across the ground and grabbed her hand.

"Can you get up?"

"I don't think so," she whimpered.

He let go of her hand and pushed himself up onto his side. Then with all his might, he pushed himself into a kneeling position. His head dropped and he let out a big sigh.

"Erin, just lie still," he said in a long, forced breath. "Wait until your strength starts coming back."

For the next few minutes, she continued to lie in the same spot while he remained kneeling beside her until his strength returned. As if preparing to lift a heavy object, he began rapidly breathing in and out. After a few seconds he lunged upward and on to his feet, staggered a half step closer to Erin, and then leaned over her.

"Are you feeling any stronger?"

"I think so," she replied.

"Do you think you can get up?"

"If you'll help me."

Jason bent down on one knee and with one hand pulled her arm over his shoulder, then with the other pulled her up by the waist until they were both standing.

"Don't move," he instructed her. "Wait until you get your balance and you feel strong enough to stand on your own. It should come back pretty quickly now."

After a few more seconds, she nodded. "You're right. I think I'm good now."

Jason moved his arm around her waist, giving her support in case she lost her balance.

"I'm okay now," she said.

As the effects of their ordeal continued to wear off, they stood side by side, staring out across the lake silently wondering what had happened to them. The sun was shining brightly and there was a gentle breeze with no clouds. If they didn't know any better, they would have thought they had just passed out for a few seconds. The only difference was the dozen columns of black smoke rising into the sky over the lake's tree line.

Erin turned to him. Her face was ashen and distressed. "How long do you think we were out?"

He reached into his pocket and pulled out his cell phone and checked the date.

"Another whole day."

"We were out for a full day?"

"Just like last time," he said.

"Can we go back to the house?" she pleaded.

"Sure." He took her by the hand and they began slowly walking back to the house.

"Wait," she said, "don't forget the camera."

Jason ran back and scooped it up along with her Santa hat.

When they got back to the house, it was eerily quiet. No hum from the refrigerator or ticking of the clock. Jason flipped the ceiling light switch, but nothing.

"Crap!" he said, as he ran into the living room. "Erin, where's the TV remote? Wait, never mind, I found it." He clicked the power button, but nothing. "For crying out loud!"

Erin ran in after him. "Is all the power off again?"

"I'm afraid so."

For a minute they stood in the middle of the living room, not sure what to do next. Suddenly the silence was broken, as the TV crackled on and all of the appliances and electronics surged on in a simultaneous hum. Seconds later, off in the distance a siren began to wail, followed by another and then another. Within minutes, every alarm and siren in the city seemed to be blasting away.

"Nooooo!" She cried. "Not again! I can't do this. I can't – I just can't."

"Relax." He put his arms around her and pulled her head into his chest while covering her ears with his hands. "Just relax!"

She pulled away. "No – YOU relax! I'm telling you, I can NOT handle this! All these people vanishing, the power outages, the crime, the evil, this whole Tribulation stuff, passing out, all these sirens." She fell to her knees. "God knows what's happened now!" Then, she buried her head into her hands and began to sob.

Jason knelt down beside her and wrapped his arm around her. "Erin, look at me."

Slowly, she dropped her hands away from her face.

"Everything will settle down again, just as it did before. Trust me."

She looked at him sorrowfully, then started shaking her head. "You're stronger than me. I don't think I can make it through all of this."

"Sure you can. You've got me. You've got Mike, and now you've got Father Tim. Together, we'll make it." He stroked her hair. "Listen, why don't you go lie down in your room and I'll bring you something to help soothe your nerves."

"Okay," she nodded, but still seemed unconvinced.

As she headed down the hallway, he rushed out the front door and sprinted to his house. The sirens and alarms were deafening. Just like the events of the vanishings, there were people running everywhere, panicking and screaming. There were wrecks up and down the street. Clouds of smoke filled the sky. Jason couldn't help but think that this may be the end. All he could think about was whether or not he was prepared. Was he saved? Was he forgiven for not believing as he should?

When he reached his house, he ran to his kitchen cabinet and pulled out his pill box from when he was on the verge of ending his life. He grabbed the small box of his prescription sleeping aid and headed back to Erin's house. The moment he hit the sidewalk, the sky above him exploded, propelling him up and onto the pavement. Sparks and smoky streamers rained down on him, as he lay there covering his face. Then, BA BAMMM! Another explosion a block away. BAMMM, BAMMM, two more explosions off in the distance. In an instant, the sound of bombs bursting could be heard echoing throughout the city.

As he attempted to gather himself, the sound of warfare continued to rage. Then, as suddenly as it had begun, everything went quiet. Not even the wailing of the sirens or blaring alarms was present. Only the rustling of the leaves as the wind swept through the tree branches.

Slowly, he looked up preparing himself to see the wreckage from the bomb that had landed so near to him. He looked in front of him, but there was nothing. He looked to his left and right, but still nothing. He looked all around, baffled, but couldn't find any evidence of destruction. Then he remembered Erin. In a panic, he jumped to his feet and ran to her house.

When he arrived, he flung open the front door and ran straight into her bedroom. She was sitting up in the middle of her bed. She had pulled her blanket up to her mouth and was clutching it tightly while rocking back and forth, staring blankly at the wall. He sat on the edge of the bed next to her.

"Erin," he said, as gently as he could manage through gasping breaths, "are you okay?"

She stopped for a moment and blankly looked more through him than at him, then turned back to the wall and began rocking again. He reached into his pocket, pulled out the box of prescription pills and quickly popped one out of its wrapper. He gingerly pulled the blanket away from her mouth. With the other hand, he gently placed the pill against her lips.

"Here, honey, take this," he softly coaxed. "It'll help you relax and sleep."

"Okay," she mumbled between white lips.

He grabbed a half empty diet coke bottle from her bedside table and held it out in front of her. "Here, this will help make it go down." After she swallowed the pill, he fluffed her pillow. "Now just lie back and close your eyes."

For the next twenty minutes, Jason remained by her side, gently stroking her hair until the effects of the sleeping pill kicked in. As she began to drift off, a rifle shot rang out from across the lake.

CHAPTER 13
THE HUNT

A large oafish man covered in camouflage from head to toe was kneeling behind a huge fallen maple tree, aiming his 30.06 rifle into a dense thicket of trees and scrubs. Another camouflaged man, this one rail thin and wearing a filthy red hat, was sitting directly behind him.

"Didja hit it?" whispered the man with the hat.

"I think I wounded the bastard. Come on, let's get trackin'."

Both men leapt to their feet and began running through the woods.

"Hellllll yeahhh!" yelled the one with the hat. "I'm gonna eat me some deer meat tonight!"

"Shut the hell up, ya idiot. If I didn't hit him, he might could still be hanging around and yer ruckus'll scare him away."

After about thirty yards, they stopped next to an opening among a small grove of maple trees. Both men bent over panting. The man with the gun got down on one knee. With his index finger, he swiped a large rock protruding from the ground.

"That's blood, Bubba." He held it up to his friend, revealing a smear of deep crimson.

"Well, I'll be danged. You did hit 'im!"

The gunman stood up. Still panting, he looked around in every direction. "We gotta keep lookin'."

"Aww man! Cain't you go look and let me wait here?"

The large man turned. "Listen, ya little shit. You're the one who's starvin' and who ain't been prepared for all this crap. If you wanna eat, you gotta hunt. You ain't got a gun, but yer scrawny ass sure as hell can dog after this bitch." He grabbed the skinny man by the arm and whipped him out in front of him. "Now go on now, hunt Fido, hunt!"

"Come on, Gene, quit it. I was just kiddin'."

"Well, come on then. Let's get movin'. Sun's going down and we only got about an hour left to find 'im."

For the next forty minutes the two arguing men searched the woods to find their wounded prey.

"Gene, I'm about beat, bo. I wanna eat tonight, but I'm tapped out."

The bigger man looked at him, while wiping his forehead with his sleeve, then looked over to a nearby ridge about fifty yards above them. "Come on, let's get ourselves up on that ridge and take a look-see from there. We'll be able to see just about everything up that high."

"Then can we go home?" Bubba whined.

"Yeah, I reckon."

When they reached the top of the ridge, the view around them was clear. The only problem was that it was now dusk and visibility was negligible beyond seventy yards. It had been a steep climb. As the men caught their breath they panned the forest below them looking for a glimpse of the wounded deer.

"This is gonna suck if we can't find him," grumbled the smaller man.

"Shush," the man whispered, pointing his gun down the hill to a little crevice jutting out from the side of a small ravine about fifty yards away. "See inside that crevice?" he said.

The smaller man squinted his eyes. "I don't see nothin'. Wait, yeah I do see it. It's moving some." He paused. "But Gene, that ain't no deer. It's too white."

"I know! I think it's one of them albinos," the bigger man said as he pulled his rifle up to his cheek. "I ain't ever seen no albino deer."

"Wait!" The smaller man grabbed the rifle, pushing it down. "How do ya know it's a deer?"

"Man, don't ever touch my gun," the man growled as he took aim again. "You wanna eat or not? By God, I'm gonna bag me a trophy buck and some eats all in one shot."

Just as he promised, the man pulled the trigger. The sound of the blast startled the other man, causing him to lose his footing, stumble to the ground and roll down the hill several yards. When he came to a stop, he was engulfed in a cloud of dust. He wiped his eyes and swatted away the dust. As he turned in the direction of the crevice, all he could see was a pale figure of something rolling down the hillside.

"You got 'im Gene! You got 'im!"

At that moment, a small weak moan floated up the hill from where the man's prey lay below. Whatever had been shot wasn't an animal at all. A bolt of panic ran through Bubba as he held his breath, hoping desperately that what he had just heard was his imagination. He waited, but nothing came.

"Gene! Oh God, Gene! That won't no deer!" he bellowed as he frantically clamored up the hill. When he reached the top of the ridge, he looked around but his friend was nowhere to be found. "Gene!" he cried out. "Where are you?" He turned in circles looking in every possible direction. "Gene, where'd you go, you ugly son of a bitch?"

Bubba then looked straight down at the ground, at the spot where the larger man had been standing when he took the shot. It was hard to tell because of how the colors blended in, but scattered over a ten-yard radius were thousands of small pieces of camouflage material. He bent down and scooped up a handful of the pieces. Their edges were jagged and charred. His heart began pounding as he continued to survey the scene. Then he recognized a familiar object at the base of a small bush – a riflescope. He scanned past it. Another ten feet away was the rifle itself, along with a singed hunting boot that was still smoldering.

"Oh, my God! What just happened?" he thought. His hands started shaking and he couldn't catch his breath. Nothing made any sense. He couldn't piece anything together. All he knew was that he had to get out of there pronto. He snatched up the rifle and started running down the hill, away from the camo pieces, away from whatever or whoever Gene shot, just away.

By the time he reached the lakeshore, some five minutes later, he was gasping for air. He leaned on the rifle for a minute while he caught his breath. Then with every bit of energy he could muster, he flung it as far out in the lake as possible.

CHAPTER 14
BANDING TOGETHER

The next morning, a tiny ray of sunlight slipped around the corner of Erin's bedroom drapes and across her face. It inched its way languidly over her eyes, awakening her unhurriedly from a deep and dreamless sleep. From down the hall she heard the murmur of men's voices. She sat up in bed and stretched.

"Jason, is that you?" she called.

A moment later Jason poked his head around the door with his eyes squeezed shut.

"Are you decent?" he inquired, in a playful voice.

She chuckled, "Yes, I'm decent. You can come in."

He opened his eyes, smiled, then walked over and sat down on the bed next to her. "How do you feel?"

"Great, actually. I haven't slept like that since college. How long was I out?"

He looked at his watch. "Oh, about ten hours."

"Wow. What'd you give me?"

"Just a regular sleeping pill. I think it, along with all the adrenaline you expended yesterday, is why you were out for so long."

She rubbed her eyes. "Did anything happen while I was out?"

He hesitated a second. "No, not really. The power is still out, so we haven't been able to get any news updates or anything like that. But Mike and I were still able to find out some stuff. He's actually in the kitchen right now."

She wrapped her comforter around her and they headed down the hall.

"Gooooood morning, Missy!" Mike said, as they entered the kitchen.

She yawned, then smiled. "Hi, Mike. How are you?"

"I'm pretty good considering our recent turn of events. Would you like some coffee?" he asked, while handing her a cup.

"Oh, you're such a darling. That is exactly what I need." She grabbed the cup with both hands and started to take a grateful sip, then stopped. "Wait, how'd you make it? Jason just told me we haven't had any power."

"We used his generator, of course." Mike turned to Jason and winked. "Mine was too big to haul over here on Jason's motorcycle just to brew a few cups of joe."

"Whatever," Jason said with a smirk.

"So, catch me up. What have you two geniuses uncovered?" she asked.

"Well, for one, I was serious about Jason's motorcycle."

"What do you mean?"

Mike looked pointedly at Jason. "You're the physics teacher. You can explain this better than I can."

Jason turned to Erin. "Remember the explanation I told you that famous physicist, Richard Teech, gave for why the energy started to drop after the vanishings? And how its overall level throughout the world has been decreasing since then?"

"Yeah," she nodded.

"And of course you remember what happened yesterday."

She nodded again.

"It appears that a similar energy drop, like what occurred during the vanishings, happened again yesterday, but this time on a much more dramatic scale."

She put down her cup, no longer smiling. "What's that mean?"

Jason looked at Mike, then back to her. He knew how emotional she was and didn't want to upset her, but there was no way to skirt it.

"I've been running tests for the past month to monitor our energy levels." He took a deep breath. "It appears that our energy is continuing to drop."

She gasped, as she fell back into a chair.

He held out his hand. "But don't be alarmed. The good news is that it has been very gradual. It's enough to continue to screw things up, but not enough to do us in. At the rate it's going, the Tribulation period will be over long before it's down to a catastrophic level." He took another long pause. "However, the energy spike yesterday wreaked such havoc on everything that even cars aren't working."

"What do you mean cars aren't working?" she asked in disbelief. "Mine's been running okay."

Jason shook his head. "Not since yesterday. The energy spike was so severe it knocked out the car batteries and other electrical components. I'm lucky that I was able to reconfigure my motorcycle and to create enough of a battery supply to get it cranked."

Erin put her hand to her mouth, her eyes widening with every new piece of information being thrown at her. She began thinking she should have stayed in bed.

"And remember hearing all the bombs going off yesterday?" he said. "Those weren't bombs at all. They were transformers blowing up. They were exploding all over the city. Evidently the energy spike was so massive it blew all of them."

"So when do you think we'll have power back?" she asked tentatively.

"I'm not sure. I don't think it will be anytime soon."

"Okay, so what do we do now?"

"Mike and I have talked and we think it would be best if we all move into one house. It's simply not safe for us to live alone anymore. We have to prepare for crime to skyrocket, and besides, it will be easier going forward if we pool our resources."

Erin nodded in solemn agreement. "Okay, so whose house?"

"We decided on Mike's because his house is much bigger and is overall much safer. He's also got a communications room that, if we're lucky, we might be able to get operative again."

"Is that okay with you?" Mike asked Erin.

"Yeah, I guess."

Jason put his hand on her shoulder. "Don't worry, it's going to be okay."

Mike clapped his hands together in an effort to look enthusiastic. "Okay, now that that's settled, we need to get a move on before it gets dark."

"Right," Jason replied. "Erin, Mike and I need to see if we can get my generator over to his house, so he and I need to head out for an hour or so. This'll give you time to pack some things and get ready. Think you'll be okay until we get back?"

"Sure. How much should I bring?"

"Just enough for a couple of days. We'll come back for more later."

He gave her a hug and quick peck on the forehead. "Don't worry. We'll be back in no time." He and Mike headed out the door.

Erin sat silently in the kitchen contemplating everything she had just heard. Her mind went back to her childhood, where everything had to be just so, as her parents pushed her through all those dance lessons, modeling schools and pageants. She had survived her parents treating her like an object, just a doll to dress and make up, and show off for money and prizes. She had moved past that, survived an abusive marriage and a bitter divorce, and after everything had been able to create a comfortable living not just for herself, but more importantly *within* herself. Surely she could survive several days, or even weeks, of inconvenience. No power? Living in someone else's house? It was actually kind of liberating to consider letting all the complexity go, embracing the simplicity thrust upon them.

As Jason and Mike walked back to his house, Jason looked at his friend and asked, "Do you think she understands that she may not be able to come back here again?"

Back inside, a strange sense of peace was coming over Erin as she went to pack. After about fifteen minutes, she had filled just a small duffle bag and a toiletry case. It was certainly the lightest she had ever packed in her life, but she was enjoying the idea of roughing it a bit. She grinned to herself as she changed into a no fuss outfit: jeans and sweatshirt.

After freshening up, she grabbed her comforter and headed to the back porch for a final look at the lake. She loved the panoramic view from that part of her house and wanted to spend as much time as she could enjoying it before heading to Mike's house.

The weather was a carbon copy of the day before, except a tad cooler. She bundled up in her comforter and sat back in her favorite Adirondack chair and took a slow deep breath. She loved how pure the air off the lake was. It always seemed to invigorate her. She looked out over the water and thought about how she was going to miss the view. She'd often told people that her home was her favorite place in the world and that she would never move. She loved it so much, she easily gave in to all her ex-husband's demands during their divorce in order to buy him out. Financially, it had put her deep into debt, but she didn't care. You can't put a price on peace, she'd told herself.

As she scanned the lakeshore, she spied a Kingfisher perched atop a small elm tree. Its beautiful blue and orange plumage was a wonderful spot of color against the gray tree branch it was using as its lookout for prey. After several seconds, he spotted his next meal and swooped down just past the shoreline and into the water to retrieve a tiny minnow. As she followed him flying out over the water, something caught her eye.

About a hundred yards out was something bobbing up and down. The reflection on the water made it difficult to make out, but she could tell that it was around five feet long. She leaned forward and squinted. At first, it looked like a log, but as it continued to drift closer a horrific transformation occurred. What at first looked like branches now appeared to be more like outstretched arms and legs. Not wanting to believe what it could be, she hesitantly stood up and went to the edge of the porch to get a better look. Still unable to make it out, she ran inside and retrieved a pair of binoculars that she used for bird watching. When she returned moments later, the wind had changed turning the mysterious object back toward the middle of the lake. As she rotated the knobs on the binoculars, the object slowly came into focus. Whatever it was had floated away from her making it more difficult to discern what it was.

For the next few minutes she remained fixed on the object, patiently waiting for it to turn back around. The combination of the bobbing and the angle kept it a mystery until suddenly the wind changed course. Slowly, it turned lengthwise, and she could tell exactly what it was. She gasped. Floating less than two hundred yards away was the pale figure of a young girl with dark hair. Her dress was billowing out from her body and her arms were stretched

101

straight out from her sides. Just then she felt the pressure of something on her shoulder, startling her so much that she dropped her binocular.

"Oh! I'm so sorry," Jason said. "I didn't mean to scare you."

Erin put her hand to her heart. "Phewww," she exclaimed. "You startled me."

"I'm sorry. I actually said your name as I was coming up."

"No, it's quite all right." She bent down and picked up the binoculars and thrust them at him. "Here, take these and look at that object bobbing up and down straight out that way. You'll see why I didn't hear you."

He readjusted the focus until the object appeared clearly. "Is that – a body?"

"I think so," she said anxiously. "It looks like a girl or young woman from what I can tell."

"Yeah, it sure does," he said in amazement. "I can't make out details too well, but it looks like she's been in the water for a long time. Her skin looks incredibly pale. Actually, it looks just plain white. Maybe it's a mannequin."

"A mannequin?" Erin said.

"Yeah, that would explain why it's so white."

"But wouldn't a body that's been out in the water for a long time also turn white?"

"Actually, it should be blue. I'm not a forensic expert, but I recall from that reality police show that people turn blue, not white, when they've been in the water for a while."

Erin shook her head and sat down. "From here, it just looks so real."

Jason put the binoculars down. "They do make those things pretty life-like. I'd go out in my boat and pull it in, but like all the cars, boats or anything motorized aren't working." He picked up the binoculars and looked back out at the lake. "And unfortunately, the wind's picked up and is moving it farther away." He pulled the binoculars away from his face and turned to Erin and smiled. "I think all we have here is a case of a missing department store mannequin."

"Yeah, I guess you're right," she said. "I can't tell you how close I was to freaking out again."

"Well you're about to freak out for real when you see what we've got set up at Mike's house. We were able to get my generator back to his house. And when we combine it with the mega monster one he has, we're going to be set for energy for a while. He's working right now on getting his computer system up. We've already got the TV working, but unfortunately no stations are broadcasting."

"That sounds fantastic."

"Plus, he's already got supper going."

Erin clapped her hands. "Oh good! I'm starving. I'm all ready to go if you are."

"I'm ready too, but there's one thing I forgot. We need to clean out your cupboard and refrigerator, and take everything edible with us."

"Sure, but you do realize it's only going to be a small box, right?"

"That's fine. We just need everything we can get a hold of." After a few minutes they had packed up a small box of canned items and staple goods and secured it, along with Erin's duffle bag and toiletry case, to a makeshift trailer he had rigged up to the back of his motorcycle. He threw his leg over the seat of his motorcycle, then pulled his helmet from the handlebars and gave it to Erin.

"If you'll put this on, we can be on our way."

"Where's yours?"

"That is mine, but I don't have an extra one."

"But, what if we crash?" she said while pulling the helmet down over her head and jumping on behind him.

"First, my head's way too hard to crack," he said with a smile. "And second, we'll only be going about ten miles an hour. I've got precious cargo onboard and I can't afford to jeopardize it."

"Ahhh, you're so worried about my canned goods, how sweet." They both laughed as Jason cranked the engine. As they slowly drove out of her driveway, Erin turned back. "Bye-bye beautiful house, beautiful lake. I'll miss you!"

When they reached the street, Jason stopped and turned off the motorcycle. He had waited until the very last minute to unload what he was about to tell her, because he didn't want to give her enough time to worry and chance her choosing not to come. He swiveled around on the seat so he was directly facing her.

"Listen, there's something I've got to prepare you for."

"Okay," she said hesitantly. "What is it?"

"You've got to be solid on this, okay? Getting to Mike's house is going to be a little more difficult than us just slowly driving over there."

She pulled off the helmet, and gave him a wary look. "Now, you're scaring me."

"I'm sorry. I really don't mean to scare you, honestly, but we do need to be on our toes."

"Jason, just tell me. What's so spooky about driving to Mike's?"

"Nothing's the same, Erin. It's a war zone beyond this driveway. A lot more has happened than just what we discussed back at the house, and none of it is pretty. I didn't want to alarm you into staying, because it's not safe and if I'd told you earlier, I don't know if you'd have come. Some of the stuff you'll see is so bad…" Erin covered his mouth with her hand.

"You don't have to tell me. I'm going to see for myself anyway." She pursed her lips together and nodded. Then quickly she pulled her helmet back on. "Let's just do this."

Jason managed a slight smile. "Okay then."

With a quick kick, he jump-started the motorcycle and they were on their way.

CHAPTER 15
EVIDENCE

As they drove out of their neighborhood, Erin wrapped her arms round Jason's waist. At once it was obvious what he'd been trying to tell her. The only other vehicles on the road were those that had crashed when their drivers had passed out at the wheel. But unlike the vanishings, when people were taken from their vehicles, the occupants' dead bodies remained with the wreckage. Erin's stomach churned, as it appeared many of the drivers and passengers had not survived. Every other car or truck seemed to have corpses within the vehicle, or out in the road, or off to the side, where they had been thrown.

As they continued, they drove through a section of town where houses and office buildings had burned to the ground. Some buildings were still aflame, and others were smoldering. And many of the remaining buildings had broken windows and graffiti sprayed across them. The only people on the streets were police and soldiers. Some had their weapons drawn and appeared to be searching for someone or something. Occasionally the sounds of gunshots could be heard off in the distance. She squeezed Jason harder, wishing they could move faster than a snail's pace.

Jason turned his head to her. "So far, so good. We're only about ten minutes away. Are you doing okay?"

She nodded. "But can you please go any faster?"

"If I do, I'm afraid we'll lose everything we're pulling in the trailer."

Just as they were approaching an intersection, Jason noticed a man helping another man climb out a jewelry store window on the corner. At their feet was a box overflowing with necklaces, bracelets, and other shiny trinkets. As they drew within a few yards, the man being helped out the window noticed them.

"Hey, where'd you get the ride, buddy?" the man said in a raspy voice.

Jason continued as if he had not heard him. As they passed the two men, one of them began jogging after them.

"We said, where'd you get your bike?"

Erin leaned over Jason's shoulder. "Please, can you speed up?" she begged.

He knew that he could easily accelerate and lose the man if he wanted. He just didn't want to lose the supplies he was carrying at the same time.

"We'll be out of distance in just a few seconds," he replied.

Suddenly, Erin screamed, "GO! GO!"

Jason turned around to find both men sprinting after them.

"We need those wheels man!"

With a quick flick of his throttle, they easily accelerated about fifty yards out in front of their pursuers. After a few seconds they had managed to outdistance themselves, while still keeping their cargo in tow. But just as they began to slow down, Jason noticed another more menacing group of men at the end of the block. It was a much larger group of around six or seven and they were all standing in the middle of the street. He couldn't tell for sure, but it appeared that most of them were carrying baseball bats. He had seen firsthand how desperate men had become and knew that what lay ahead of them meant nothing but trouble. Fortunately, Erin had her head turned against his back and wasn't able to see the oncoming threat.

He ran his options through his head. Turn around and go back, or keep going and try to maneuver past them. There would be a split second window of opportunity, but he knew it would be easy to lose them if the bike could manage to break past them. If any of the men grabbed them or knocked them off balance, it would cause them to wreck and then they'd be done for. Suddenly, his strategy came to him.

He continued his slow steady speed of ten miles per hour, but as they came to within a hundred yards he began to steer toward the right side of the street. As he had hoped, the gang mirrored his action by moving in the same direction. When he was sixty yards away, he accelerated again while steering even farther to the right. They took the bait and all of the men continued to move with him leaving the entire left side of the street open.

As they approached within thirty yards he yelled over his shoulder, "Hang On!"

"Why?" Erin yelled back.

"Just do it – now!"

A second later, he gunned the accelerator, rocketing them to within ten yards of the men, their bats raised and ready to swing as they anticipated him trying to plow through them. At the last moment he veered hard to the left, causing their makeshift trailer to whip around from behind and snap off at the hitch, flipping it across the street and slamming into the gang like a bowling ball knocking them all off their feet. In an instant, the street was wide open and they were zipping down the road at a brisk fifty miles an hour.

Several minutes later, they pulled into Mike's driveway. The moment Jason put the kickstand down, Erin was off the bike and tugging at her helmet with clear irritation.

"Hold on – easy now," he said while calmly unfastening her chin strap.

The moment he had finished, she yanked off the helmet and threw it to the ground.

"What's going on? Has the whole world gone insane?" she screamed. "And what's with you? What kind of James Bond crap was that? We could've been killed!"

Just then, Mike came running from around the house. "What's happening? I heard screaming."

"I'm afraid we ran into the less than civil part of what our world's become," Jason said.

"You think?" Erin mocked. Then she turned and raced to the house.

"Wow! What just went down?" Mike asked. "And what happened to the trailer?"

Jason shook his head in frustration. "I'll tell you later." He turned to the back of his motorcycle and then smiled as he reached down to untangle Erin's duffle bag, which somehow had gotten its shoulder strap caught just above where the hitch had broken off. It was badly scraped, but there were no rips or tears.

"I'm not sure how this survived, but not losing this bag may have saved us some stress this evening. Come on, let's get the bike in the garage and ourselves back in the house before today gets any worse."

After taking care of the motorcycle, they walked into the house where they found Erin sitting in the living room with her head hung down. When she heard them enter she looked up.

"I'm sorry Jason," she muttered. "I didn't mean to get so upset. It wasn't at you. Honestly, it was just the shock of what could've happened."

"I know, I know," he said sympathetically. "Anybody would have been upset."

"Do you forgive me?" she asked.

He gave her a hug. "Of course I do. Do you see now why we need to all be here?"

She nodded, then buried her head in his chest.

"Do you think all of this has something to do with the Rapture and the first vanishings?"

"I'm not sure, but what I do know is that I've seen at least one miracle today."

She lifted her heard. "What?"

"I don't know how it managed to survive, but somehow your duffle bag stayed with us during our trip here." He pointed to the corner of the room where he had laid her bag.

"Oh my gosh! How in the world?" She looked back at him, then rushed over to it. She pulled the zipper and quickly started feeling through its contents until suddenly, "There it is!" she said as she pulled out her video camera. "And not a scratch on it!"

"Not a scratch on what?" Mike said as he entered the room.

Jason pointed to Erin. "Her video camera didn't get smashed into a million pieces during our ride here."

"That reminds me," Mike said, "you owe me one tall tale about you and missy's great adventure this afternoon. But right now, it's time to eat."

"Goody!" Erin said. "I'm starving."

"You don't have to tell me twice," said Jason. "I'll see you guys in the dining room."

"Actually, I've got us in the conference room tonight. I thought I'd introduce Erin to our headquarters while we eat."

"That's a great idea," Jason replied.

"Mind if I bring my camera?" she asked as they headed down the hall.

"Sure, I think we may have a monitor you can use to play video." He and Jason broke out laughing.

"What's so funny?" Erin said.

Mike opened the door to the conference room.

"Amazing!" Erin gushed as she looked across the conference room table. She counted, "One – two – three – four - five. You have five monitors. Seriously, who has five monitors?"

"Actually, six," Mike said proudly pointing to a huge five-foot screen on the wall at the opposite end of the room.

"Holy cow!" she said.

"I told you he was a techie," Jason chuckled.

Spread out between the monitors and keyboards were bowls and plates of mashed potatoes, corn, fruit, biscuits, and a small ham.

"You neglected to mention he is also a master chef."

Mike grinned. "I hope you like how I've integrated the technical components of this evening's meal along with the culinary elements. It's my latest masterpiece of traditional Southern fare, with a tech infusion."

Erin giggled and Jason rolled his eyes, "Oh, brother."

After they sat down, Jason said a prayer, then proceeded to tell Mike about the afternoon's motorcycle ride.

As they were talking, Erin grabbed her video camera and pointed it at them. "Lousy battery," she said, while repeatedly pressing the power button.

Jason turned to her. "It's not going to work. Remember, the power drop and how it's affecting everything?"

"Oh…yeah," she said disappointedly.

"No need to worry," said Mike. "Wait here." He sprang to his feet and headed out of the room.

A minute later she and Jason heard what sounded like a car engine turning over from outside. Suddenly, the entire room lit up and all of the monitors popped on. Instantly, the house was abuzz with electricity.

Erin looked around the room with her mouth open in amazement. "Wow!"

Just then Mike walked back in, looking rather pleased with himself. "Pretty cool, huh? It was about time anyway, so I went ahead and cranked up our generators."

Jason turned to Erin. "The way we've got things planned is that we'll go through the day without using the generators. Since they run on gas, we've gotta conserve as much as possible, especially since it's not as efficient as it used to be."

"But don't worry," Mike said, "I switched out the fuel in my propane tank with gas and also built a second tank as a reserve. We should be good for a while."

"Then what?" Erin asked.

"We continue to prepare for every obstacle we may encounter during the Tribulation period." Mike said.

"Are you guys still holding to the Rapture and Tribulation theory?"

"Of course!" Jason said. "Are you still doubting what's going on?"

"Well, no. I was just asking."

Jason cocked his head and looked at her. "Are you sure?"

"Yes, very."

Jason could tell she wasn't entirely on board. If she truly believed, she wouldn't have asked the question in the first place. But it had already been a long day and he wasn't prepared to go any further with the subject, especially on their first night together. He figured he'd have plenty of time for that later.

Just then, Mike broke off their conversation by handing Erin her video camera. "Try it now. I hooked it up to the big monitor while you two chatterboxes were talking Tribulation."

"Ohhhh, thank you!"

Mike turned off the lights. "Alrighty, the screen's all yours. I'm ready to be entertained," he jokingly demanded.

"I don't really have anything on here that's entertaining. I was just going to take videos of you guys on our first night."

"Actually, you do have something," Jason said. "Remember the Christmas video we were doing. Can we look at that?"

"Well, I guess." She clicked a few buttons, and a second later a picture of a young lady on a jet ski floating out on the lake appeared. "Oh, that's my friend Bethany. Her jet ski conked out on her and she was... Ohhh, I'm sorry guys. Let me fast forward."

"Hey, wait. She's kinda cute," Mike said. "Is she taken?"

"She's taken all right! She's taken in the Rapture kind of taken."

"No problem, I'll just have to call on her later."

Erin and Jason burst out laughing.

Jason smiled at his friend. "That's my boy – always the supreme optimist."

"Here we go," she said. The scene suddenly switched to Erin in her sexy Santa outfit spinning in circles down by the lakeshore.

Mike shot Jason a quick glance with a raised eyebrow.

"Where's the sound?" Erin asked, tilting the camera from side to side.

"Can I see it?" Jason asked, as Erin gladly surrendered the camera.

For the next few minutes Jason and Erin fumbled with the controls while the video continued to play.

Suddenly Mike blurted, "Go back! Reverse it and go back a few seconds. I think this is when the blackouts occurred."

Jason held the reverse button down a moment, then hit play. The scene was a jerky flash frame of images: Erin – the water – the ground – Erin's shoes – Jason's leg – the ground – the sky – then suddenly a still image of Erin's backyard from ground level.

"That's when I must have dropped the camera," Jason said.

"Wait, here it comes." Mike said.

At that moment, the lower half of Erin's body appeared to stagger into frame, then suddenly collapse off screen.

"That's when I passed out."

A split second later, a blur of Jason's back moved into frame then fell off camera in the same direction.

"And that's when I passed out trying to help you up."

The only things remaining on screen were the billowy blue clouds over the Lake Royale horizon and part of Jason's leg from where he lay just outside the camera frame.

Ten to fifteen seconds passed, the screen flickered, and then a blast of white light filled the entire screen.

"I guess the camera got zapped too," Mike said. He got up to turn on the lights.

"No, wait!" Jason pointed him back to the screen.

Slowly, the landscape reappeared as if coming out of a cloudbank. But something was different. Instead of the blue clouds, like before, the sky was now completely gray.

"How about that?" Mike said. "The entire sky changed colors."

Another ten or fifteen seconds went by.

"This should be when it starts to rain." Jason said while remaining fixated on the screen.

"Rain?" said Mike.

"It's the last thing I remembered – look, off in the distance. See those streaks of light. I told you. It was starting to rain."

Mike squinted. "Oh yeah."

At first, just a few appeared. Within seconds, the entire horizon was filled with flashes of light streaking to earth. But it was suddenly apparent this wasn't a typical rain storm. Unlike raindrops falling to earth, these left a shimmering silver trail that seemed to electrify the sky. As the storm grew nearer, the trails of light grew bigger.

"Is this a meteor shower?" Mike asked, almost in disbelief.

"I can't tell," Jason replied. "I don't see any impacts."

As the strange storm rapidly approached, the camera started to flicker and the image began to break up and become pixelated. It was like looking at a giant puzzle with pieces randomly disappearing and then reappearing. After a few more seconds, it was almost impossible to tell but it appeared that a couple of streaks of light fell within forty or fifty yards of the camera.

The three of them sat on the edge of their seats squinting their eyes trying to discern what was happening, when suddenly Mike leapt out of his chair.

"Did you see THAT?"

"I saw it!" Erin yelled.

At that moment, the screen went black.

CHAPTER 16
THE ANALYSIS

For the next thirty minutes Erin, Jason, and Mike replayed the last five seconds of the video over and over trying to figure out what it was they had seen.

"Run it back again," Mike said. "And this time go frame by frame."

"My camera won't do that," Erin said.

"Here, let me do something," he said grabbing the camera. He went to his computer, plugged it in and a minute later the video was back on screen.

"What'd you do?" she asked.

"I copied it over to my hard drive and am going to run it back using some software that allows you to see it frame by frame."

Mike pressed a couple keys on his laptop and the video began advancing one frame at a time. As the frames progressed, the pixelated images began to appear. The entire screen became one giant mosaic with dozens of missing pieces randomly disappearing and reappearing.

"Here it comes," Jason said anxiously.

They all leaned forward in their seats as the frame displayed the first image of what they had so eagerly awaited. In the upper right corner of the screen was the curved edge of an unknown object that was about to descend within twenty to thirty yards of the camera. As the frame advanced, the full length of the object was revealed amidst several large pixelated sections of the video. Whatever it was must have been moving at an incredible speed, because the image was such a blur. The only thing distinguishable about it was that it was bullet-shaped and approximately four to six feet in length. The leading edge appeared to just be touching the ground while the end tapered off to the top edge of the screen.

The next series of frames showed the object exploding into a ball of white light that progressively filled the screen, then fading quickly. It was the last three frames that the three were most desperate to see. As the first of these frames displayed, it showed the white light converge back to its origin and into the oval bullet shape it had descended as.

In the next frame the light faded to a hazy cloud. It was difficult to make out, but in the center was a blurry silhouette of what appeared to be a person. As the last frame advanced, Erin gasped. She leapt out of her chair, holding her hand over her mouth.

"Oh, my God!" exclaimed Jason.

The white cloud had completely faded, and standing in place of the silhouette was a young girl with long brown hair that fell straight down covering her face. Her skin was ghostly white. The next frame went blank and the camera clicked off. They all sat in silence staring at the screen. For several more minutes, they played the last three frames over and over.

"Maybe it's a latent image from a previous video you recorded," Mike said.

Erin shook her head. "It couldn't be. That video card was brand new. That's the first time it had been used."

"Besides," Jason added, "that girl is crystal clear. A latent image

117

wouldn't be that clear."

"What about where the thing came down?" Mike asked. "Was there a hole in the ground or was it burnt or anything like that?"

"Nothing," Jason replied. "Whatever it was, it came down within yards of us. And where it landed was right where we walked back to the house. I'd have noticed something like that. Man, this is too freaky."

"Erin, are you okay?" Mike said.

She was staring down at the floor, her brow furrowed as if she were trying to solve a problem.

"Yeah, I'm okay. I just can't get the other image out of my head now."

"What other image?" asked Jason.

"The image of that girl or mannequin or whatever it was floating in the lake."

"What?" exclaimed Mike.

Erin turned to him. "You mean Jason didn't tell you we saw something that looked like a girl floating out in the lake this morning?"

He glanced over at Jason with a puzzled look.

"We did actually see something," Jason said. "It was floating about a hundred yards offshore. It was hard to make out, but it did look like a girl. The only thing is that the skin didn't look real. It was so pale, it looked more like a mannequin."

"That's just it," she said, "it *was* pale white. It looked like the image of the girl we just saw in the video."

Mike began pacing the room. "Can you guys believe all of this? I don't know what you saw in the lake, but what we just saw on that video is just freakin' incredible."

"What do you think it was?" Erin asked.

Mike stopped pacing and stood there contemplating her question.

"What about aliens? It could've been an alien, couldn't it?" said Erin.

No one responded as the idea sunk in. The room was silent. Only the hum of the generators could be heard as they struggled with their thoughts of what it could have been. A couple of minutes passed, then finally Jason broke the silence.

"An angel," he said nodding his head. "It was an angel."

Mike turned to Jason, then Erin. "An alien or an angel, huh?" He looked back at Jason. "You're the scientist. Can you logically explain how it's an angel?"

Jason looked at him. "Hold on a minute! You're the first person who should be agreeing with me on that. You're the one who came preaching the whole Rapture theory. There are angels all throughout Revelation. This could be the first sign of them — right?" Jason was almost pleading with Mike to agree with him. He was fully committed to the idea and desperately wanted to see it lived out. He knew that if it was, then he'd see his family again and that was all that mattered. "Isn't this just more evidence that we're in the Tribulation period?" he pleaded.

Mike looked down and scratched his forehead. "Well, it kinda is and kinda isn't."

"I don't understand."

"You're right about angels in the Tribulation period," Mike said, "but there's nothing about them coming to earth at this stage. They come near the end."

"Then this may be the end," Jason said hopefully. If it were the end of the Tribulation, he was that much nearer to being reunited with his family.

Mike shook his head. "I'm sorry, buddy, but it's been less than a year and the Tribulation lasts seven years."

"But Mike, you know it's hard sometimes to take the Bible literally. Maybe the seven years is more like seven months or seven seasons."

Mike sat down at one of the monitors and began typing.

"What are you doing?" Jason asked.

"I'm going straight to the source."

Jason and Erin looked at each other. "Are you contacting Father Tim?" Erin asked.

"No," he said. "Higher – much higher."

"Come on, Mike. What's going on?"

He continued typing. "Remember way back when I lowered the boom on you about tapping into the National Defense Department?"

Erin jumped out of her chair. "You did what?"

Jason held his hand out motioning her to sit back down. "Wait, Erin, just relax. It's alright," he said. Then he turned to Mike. "Okay, what's up now?"

He quit typing and sat scanning the monitor. "Well, you mentioned something back then that prompted me to act."

"I don't remember saying anything that..." Suddenly he stopped. "Oh no! I do remember now. You hacked into the Pope's computer, didn't you?"

Mike didn't respond for a moment, then turned to him. "No, the Pontiff is no longer with us, so it didn't make much sense to do that." Then he turned back to his computer screen. "But I did tap into the Vatican's system."

Erin threw her hands up in disbelief. "How can you get away with that?"

Jason looked over his shoulder at her. "Trust me. Our friend here is a cyber-master with some wicked skills." He turned back to Mike and shrugged his shoulders. "I guess it really doesn't matter though at this stage of the game who is hacking whom."

"Hmmm," he said, as he leaned closer to the monitor.

"What is it?" Jason asked.

"This is a conversation thread I've been following for the past several months. As you can imagine, there are hardly any religious figures left, especially in the Vatican. However, there are a handful of Vatican priests, some bishops and even a few cardinals who didn't get taken during the vanishings – excuse me, I mean the Rapture – and these guys have been conversing via their internal instant messaging system. They've been talking about the Tribulation and pretty much been confirming all our original thoughts about it. I've been reading it every day, except I've missed the last couple of days because of all the weirdness going on."

Suddenly he stopped and sat back in his chair. "Wow!" he said while still staring intently into the monitor. He leaned back to his computer screen. "This one priest is telling a cardinal he's gotten reports from parishes around Italy that angels have been witnessed.

"Can you tell what time he's sending the emails?"

"Sure. The time stamp indicates it's around twenty-eight hours ago."

"That would pretty much jive with what we saw on the tape," Jason said.

"Wait! Here's another one from a priest a few hours later saying he's gotten several similar reports from farther out. One from Spain, two from Ireland, and another from Poland."

"I told you guys!" Jason crowed.

"Hold on a second," Mike said. "The cardinal is telling them not to encourage anyone to believe these are angels. Here's exactly what he says:

'Please be advised that in times of crisis God's children will be more susceptible to experiencing unsubstantiated "miracles". During previous world crises, we've experienced reports similar in nature. Rely upon your faith and the teachings of the Roman Catholic Church as you investigate these reports, and above all, be prudent as you shepherd your congregations and others of faith.'

"Okay, so all he's saying is to be cautious," Jason said. "But the fact still remains there have been sightings that could actually be angels. And if there are angels among us, maybe we should seek them out."

"So how exactly would we do that?"

He looked down as he thought through his response. "We need to be more mobile. We can't just stay holed up in here, only venturing out when we need food or supplies. We have to make an effort to reconnect with other people."

"So when you say mobile, do you mean our cell phones?"

"No. I mean mobile like getting our cars working again. I don't think we can get both going though. Yours is a lot bigger and would be an energy hog, and besides, I'll need the battery from your car to rig up mine."

"That's fine with me. What about Erin's car?"

Jason looked at her. "No offense, but it's so old that it wouldn't be able to handle the system I'd be setting up."

"Well, my divorce sapped me financially. It was either keep my house or buy a new car. And you guys know how I love that house."

He smiled, then turned to Mike. "If you're ready to get started we could go ahead and take your battery out now, then get up early tomorrow and head to my house."

"Sounds like a plan," Mike said. "We'll probably want to get over there before the sun comes up though. We don't want another adventure like you guys had today."

Jason put his hand on his shoulder and the two headed out to the garage while Erin cleaned up.

CHAPTER 17
FIRST CONTACT

The next morning at five o'clock, Mike and Jason woke up and prepared for the short trip to Jason's house. After eating a bagel and orange, Mike placed his car's battery inside his backpack and with Jason's help strapped it on. Five minutes later, they were heading to Jason's house under the cover of darkness and without any lights on.

It was an eerie ride. The predawn silence was unnerving. With no power, there were no streetlights or interior lights from homes or office buildings. The only lights were from small fires that peppered the landscape as the homeless tried keeping warm. Within fifteen minutes, they had arrived at his house.

"Ah, man," Jason said as he got off the motorcycle.

"What's wrong?" Mike asked.

"Someone's broken in. See the back door? It's been kicked in."

As Jason began walking to the house, Mike threw his arm in front of him. "Wait." With his other hand he reached around and pulled off his backpack letting it fall to the ground. "We'll need these." He reached in and pulled out a small lighter and a large black and silver handgun. He looked up at Jason. "We've gotta be very careful."

Jason gave a reluctant nod, then took the lighter and slowly walked up to the back of his house, while Mike followed closely behind. As he gently pushed the broken door out of his way he flicked on the lighter. The small flame created a dim glow, casting long shadows across the room. A quick scan of the kitchen revealed that whoever had broken in clearly was desperate for food. The refrigerator doors were standing open and all of the cabinet draws had been pulled out. Everything edible was gone, while all the utensils and other items had been left intact.

Side by side, the two hesitantly walked through the kitchen and into the dining room making sure not to let the weight of their bodies cause the floorboards to creak. If there was anyone still inside, they wanted to make sure they had the element of surprise on their side.

As they slowly moved from room to room, it became evident the intruder's motives were driven purely by hunger. After they finished inspecting Jason's office, they stepped out into the hallway when suddenly Mike grabbed him by the arm and pointed back to the kitchen.

"Did you hear that?" he mouthed.

Jason shook his head.

"Listen," he whispered.

Just then a dish crashed to the floor. Jason looked at him, his eyes wide with anticipation. "What the..!" he mouthed.

Mike motioned Jason to move behind him. As they switched places, he carefully aimed his gun toward the kitchen. When they were inches away from the doorway he turned his head slightly and out of the side of his mouth whispered, "On three, okay?"

Jason nodded.

Mike mouthed, "One - two - three."

In a flash, they both rushed in. Mike wielded his gun in every direction, as Jason raised his lighter above his head trying to illuminate the room in order to locate their intruder. For several seconds they frantically scanned the area, but nothing was there. The refrigerator doors and cabinet drawers were still in their same positions, and there wasn't any sign of someone who had come in or out. The only thing different was the smashed dish that lay in pieces in front of the refrigerator.

Mike shrugged his shoulder and dropped his gun to his side. "The plate was probably just loosely placed on a shelf and our bumbling around tipped it over."

Jason sighed, "I guess so."

Just then something moved on top of the refrigerator. Mike whipped around. As he did, he stepped on the broken plate, causing him to slip and fall. Jason jumped back into the corner waving his lighter back and forth trying to find the source of the noise. As Mike pulled his gun up, a large black cat leapt from the top of the refrigerator onto the kitchen table and across his outstretched weapon. As it flew by, its tail hit him in the face.

"Damn it!" he yelled. "Damn it to hell!

Jason let out a huge sigh as he watched the furry fiend scurry out the back door.

He reached down to help Mike off the floor. "Man, my house is giving me the creeps. Let's get a move on and get out of here."

"Absolutely," Mike chuckled. "I'm going to have a heart attack if we don't."

As they walked out of the house, Jason looked at his watch. "We've gotta hurry. It's going to take us about forty-five minutes to rig my car, and we've only got about an hour before sunrise."

For the next half hour, Mike held a candle over the engine while Jason frantically worked to install Mike's battery into his car.

"Okay, I think I've got it rigged," he said as he stepped back and wiped the sweat from his forehead. "Let's crank her up."

Jason slid into the front seat and inserted the key into the ignition. When he turned it, nothing happened. He waited a moment and tried once more – again, nothing. He got out and walked back to the front of the car.

"Hey, Mike, can you hold the light down into the middle of the engine for me? I think I may know what the problem is." With a wrench in one hand and a screwdriver in the other, he dropped to the ground and crawled under the car. After several minutes he crawled back out shaking his head. "Man, I really zoned out on this one. I forgot to bring a second length of copper wire. If I'd remembered to bring it, we'd be out of here in ten seconds."

"We may as well head home and come back this evening," Mike said. "It looks like the sun's about to come up. We'll be an easy target for every thug wanting the motorcycle if we wait any longer."

Jason turned and looked across his back lawn and over his boathouse where the sun always rose during the winter months. In the short amount of time it had taken him to discover the problem, the sky had changed from dark blue to a pinkish hue and the tip of the sun was starting to peep between the tree branches on the opposite side of the lake.

"Wait! I just remembered something. I've got an entire spool of wiring next to my boat."

"Awesome! Let's go get it," Mike said.

"It might actually be better if you stay here," Jason said as he sprinted off toward the boathouse. "You'll need to protect the bike in case anybody's been watching us and decides to try and take it."

When he got to the boathouse he noticed the door was slightly ajar. What if the person who had broken into his house was inside? He hesitated for a second and then thought, "So what? If someone is there, I'll just turn and bolt back toward Mike."

Just to play it safe, he peeked through a tiny crack along the doorframe. Although he couldn't really make out much, he could see the large doors where he pulled the boat in and out were open.

Ever so slowly, he opened the door. As he did, the first rays of the morning sun came over the horizon and through the rear of the boathouse, temporarily blinding him. As he stood in the doorway letting his eyes adjust, he slowly began to make out the silhouettes of the boat and the docking slip that surrounded it. He breathed a sigh of relief. No intruders.

With his hand still in front of his face he carefully began side-stepping his way around the front of the boat and toward the tiny shelf in the back left corner where he had stored his box of wire. When he reached the shelf, he pulled down the box and opened it. Just as he had remembered, inside was a small roll of the copper wire about the size of a spool of thread. As he put it in his pocket, something from the opposite side of the boathouse moved. He turned with a jerk.

Standing at the back edge of the boat slip was the silhouette of a young girl with long hair. He couldn't tell if it was the backdrop of the sun against her or what, but her entire body was aglow with a soft halo framing it. She didn't speak or move, except to raise her hands slightly above her waist with her palms facing up. For a minute he stood motionless, not able to breathe.

Slowly, she raised her hands to her chin as if about to pray. Jason's heart skipped a beat and his hands began to tremble uncontrollably. Could this be what he thought? Was he dreaming? Was this an angel? Breaking the ghastly silence, Mike came bounding through the door.

"Everything okay down here?"

Jason took a much needed breath as he turned to his friend.

"What's taking so long?" Mike asked impatiently.

Jason didn't say anything, but instead turned and pointed to the other side of the boat. He gasped. Nothing was there. The girl had vanished.

"What's wrong?" Mike asked as he looked to the vacant space.

"Right there, in that spot was something," he exclaimed. "I, I," he stuttered, "I think it was an angel."

Mike searched his face, unsure he was hearing Jason correctly. "An angel?" He looked back to where he was still pointing. It was simply the back of the boathouse, with a bunch of boxes stuffed in a dark corner. "Are you serious?"

Jason nodded gravely, obviously still shaken.

Mike cautiously inched his way to the front of the boat, then stopped and leaned to the right as he inspected the back of the boathouse. He looked back at him and shrugged his shoulders. Jason motioned him to continue all the way to the back.

Mike turned and took two more steps, then suddenly stopped. His mouth fell open. He glanced at Jason then pointed to the back corner of the boathouse where all the boxes were stacked against the wall.

"Something's behind those boxes," he whispered. His heart began beating rapidly. Slowly he pulled his gun from his pocket and aimed it in the direction of the boxes. "Come out from behind there!" he yelled. There was no response. "I said come out. We know you're there!" Still no response. He swallowed. His gun hand was shaking so much that he had to use his other hand to steady it. "Come on now," he said as he continued to move his way closer. "We know you're there!"

When he came to within three feet of the boxes he stopped, then with his right foot he reached out and kicked the stack, sending them flying across the boat and out into the water. Behind where the boxes had been was the shadowy figure of a girl lying curled up on the floor. Mike took a small step toward her. As he did, she cowered back into the corner clutching the end of her dress and whimpering. He stopped and turned to Jason.

"What do I do?"

"Just wait a second," he replied. "She's gotta be scared to death," and then added, "I know I am."

For several seconds, no one moved. The only sounds were those of the girl's faint sobbing mingled with the water as it gently lapped against the hull of the boat.

As Mike continued to point his gun into the corner, Jason worked his way over to his side. With his left hand he gently pushed Mike's gun down while side stepping around him.

"Let me try," he said.

Jason turned and slowly dropped to one knee. Like a trapped animal the girl had pushed herself as far back into the corner as possible. Her head was tucked into her chest and her hair fell down over her face. She was curled up into a tight little ball and was shivering. Other than her hair the only discernible feature was part of one hand, which was clutching part of her dress near her chin.

In a soft, gentle voice Jason said, "Don't be afraid. We aren't going to hurt you." He turned his head to Mike. "Maybe you should go outside."

Mike nodded and quietly left as Jason continued to try and persuade her he meant no harm.

"Please don't be afraid. Are you okay? Can we help you?"

A few minutes passed and still the girl did not move. The left side of the boathouse began to fill with light as the sun came pouring through the open doors in the back. But in the far right corner where the girl lay it was still dark. As his eyes began to adjust, he was able to make out that her hair was either black or dark brown and that her dress was white with mud stains across the bottom.

Just as he was about to speak again, she reached her hand up and pulled her hair back just enough to see him. Jason tilted his head and slowly lifted his hands as if to pray.

"Please, won't you let me help you?"

Slowly, she lifted both hands up to her face and started to part her hair. As she pulled her hair away from her face he suddenly lost his breath by the sight of how her eyes pierced the darkness like two glowing orbs. They were ice blue, a searing blue he had never seen before. But beyond that, what made them so remarkable was that they seemed electrified. The blue actually shimmered and the outer edges radiated like microscopic neon circles. They were breathtakingly beautiful, but alarmingly unreal at the same time.

Jason wasn't sure if he was looking into the eyes of an angel or an alien. What he did know was that this girl was extremely vulnerable and scared. He knew beyond a doubt she would not harm him. After a few moments, he realized his staring was starting to make her uneasy. She looked back down and her lower lip began to quiver.

"I'm sorry. Oh gosh, please don't cry." With his palm up, he slowly reached out to her. When he got within a foot of her hand he stopped. "I'm here to help you."

She raised her head again and stared down at his hand. Her lip stopped quivering. She hesitantly moved her hand to within a few inches of his, then stopped.

Jason smiled. "It's okay."

The edges of her mouth turned slightly up as she reached out to take his hand. As her index finger touched his palm, a tiny spark snapped his skin, sending a prickly sensation up his arm. A tiny surge of energy washed over his body when she wrapped her fingers around his palm. For a few seconds, he felt light and strangely energized. As the sensation subsided, he took his other hand and placed it on top of hers. "My name is Jason."

As carefully as he could and without rushing her, he helped the girl to her feet. Once she was standing he asked, "Will you follow me?"

She leaned her head to the side and looked at him bewildered.

"Can you follow me outside?" he said slowly and deliberately.

With her left hand, she pointed to her left ear and then to her mouth, while shaking her head.

"Oh, you can't hear or speak." Jason muttered to himself. He wasn't sure what to say next, then realized it didn't matter anyway. He simply had to communicate now through gestures and would have to be patient. After a few seconds, he nodded and motioned with his hand for her to follow him. With his other hand, he led her around the boat and back to boathouse entrance. When they reached the doorway he turned and nodded to her reassuringly and then slowly led her out.

As they walked across the tiny bridge and onto the yard, Mike came running up to meet them. When he got within ten yards he stopped cold.

"It's okay," Jason said. "Don't be alarmed. She's harmless."

When he turned back to the girl, the sun's light revealed all the features he had not been able to ascertain in the boathouse. Her hair was dark brown and her skin was as white as alabaster with a light blue hue. She appeared to be between eleven and twelve, but her skin was indescribably even more youthful and absolutely flawless. Still the most remarkable feature was her eyes. Even in the light of day, they were mesmerizing.

He turned back to Mike. He hadn't moved and was gaping at her in the same hypnotic way that he knew he had been.

"Mike, don't gawk. It'll scare her."

Mike looked to the ground, then off to the side, then quickly back to Jason. He didn't want to alarm her, but wasn't sure how to react either. All he knew was that if he looked back at her he wouldn't be able to look away. He promptly decided Jason's comment about angels appearing on earth wasn't so far-fetched after all.

CHAPTER 18
THE GAUNTLET

After Mike composed himself, he looked at the girl and sheepishly tried introducing himself. "Hello. I'm Mike."

The girl tilted her head then looked away.

"I'm afraid she can't hear you," Jason said. "And she can't speak either."

He started to apologize, then realizing its futility, he stopped. "Are you able to communicate to her at all?"

"She seems to understand my gestures."

"Okay, well – uh, that's good," Mike stammered, still feeling uncomfortable about what to say. Changing the subject, he turned to Jason. "Are you ready to get out of here?"

"Yeah. I've got the wire, so it'll just take a couple of minutes to finish configuring the battery setup."

He continued to hold the girl's hand as they walked to the car. The entire time she kept looking down at the ground while clutching her dress below her chin and pulling it up close to her mouth. Occasionally, she would steal a quick glance at them, but then go back to looking down.

"She really is timid, isn't she?"

Jason nodded. Then he turned and gave her what he hoped was his best reassuring smile.

When they reached the car, he opened the trunk, pulled out a blanket and wrapped it around her. Then he motioned to her that he was going to go under the car. As he dropped to the ground he gave her the okay sign. She nodded as he disappeared under the engine. After just a few minutes, he crawled out and ran around and jumped in the front seat. This time when he turned the ignition the engine roared to life.

"All right!" he yelled. "We're in business." He looked up at Mike. "Would you mind taking the motorcycle so I can take the car with the girl? She'll definitely feel much safer in it."

"I'm good with that," Mike responded. "I'll follow to make sure your system doesn't crap out. Also, I was thinking we should bypass the way you guys went last time. The sun's already up, so we're a lot more vulnerable now. There has to be a safer route."

"Yeah, I think you're right. What'd you have in mind?"

"It's a little longer, but what if we go through the city park? It'll add another ten minutes, but it should be a lot safer."

Jason thought about it for a second then jumped out of the car and walked the girl around to the passenger side. As he helped her inside, he looked at Mike and nodded. "It's worth a shot. Let's give it a try."

As they pulled out of the driveway, he turned to see how the girl was doing. She was no longer clutching her dress and appeared to be a little more at ease. He started to ask her a question, but stopped. As much as he wanted to try and speak to her, he knew that it wouldn't result in much. Right now, he had to concentrate on driving. From his previous experience he knew the trip from his house to Mike's was a gauntlet of danger, no matter which route they took. Having a working motorized vehicle made them a target for any desperate man wanting to gain an edge.

After several minutes, they passed over a short bridge that led up to the main entrance of the city park. It was a large and scenic tract of rolling hills with a small pond, bike trails, a carousel, and a four-mile running loop. There was also a small tree-lined road that ran from the entrance straight through to the opposite side. They had hoped to take it, but unfortunately it was closed off with several big metal pylons. Typically, the park would have been filled with joggers, picnickers, and other people enjoying all of its amenities, but now it was desolate.

In order to get to Mike's house, they would have to circle the park by taking the road that ran around its perimeter. As Jason was turning the car around, he looked back and saw that Mike had stopped about a hundred yards behind him. He finished his u-turn and sped back. As they pulled up alongside of him, he rolled down the window.

"What happened?"

"I don't know," Mike groaned, as he unsuccessfully tried to crank the engine. "I was moving along okay and then it just slowly died on me."

Jason got out, walked over and began inspecting the motorcycle. After a few minutes, he stepped away from it while scratching his head.

"The engine seems fine," he said.

"Do you think it could have something to do with how you rigged it up?" asked Mike.

"Nope, that looks okay." Then he looked at Mike. "Oh, I bet I know what it is." He leaned across the handlebars and looked at the gauges, then thumped the gas tank with his finger, producing a hollow ting sound. "She's bone dry. That's the problem."

"You've gotta be kidding! All that work for nothing," Mike said. "I guess we'll just have to abandon it now."

"No way," Jason said as he opened the trunk of his car and

pulled out a small, six-foot hose. We'll just siphon some gas from the car to the bike."

Mike looked at his friend and grinned. "I'm so proud to be your friend."

"Well, I think you suck!" Jason replied as he tossed the hose to him.

Mike cocked his head and shot him a sideways smile. "I'm grading that pun a solid D-minus." He inserted one end of the hose into the car and began sucking on it until gas came running out the other end.

After a couple of minutes of transferring gas between the car and motorcycle, Mike clapped his hands together. "That should do it." Then he pulled the hose from out of the two vehicles and tossed it in the trunk.

Just then Jason motioned with his head back toward the park. "Take a look."

Coming down the running loop from the left side of the park were two men in hoodies. One was on a bike and appeared to have something long and narrow strapped across the handlebars. Another was pulling along a snarling dog by a leash.

"We need to get a move on." Jason said as he jumped back in his car. "Let's take a right and loop around the park from that direction."

Mike hopped on the motorcycle and with a quick kick-start was ready to go.

"I'm right behind you!" he yelled, as they headed back toward the park.

As they approached the entrance the man with the dog suddenly dropped the leash. "Go get 'em, boy!" he commanded.

When Jason saw the dog running toward them he punched the accelerator and zoomed around the corner with Mike following about twenty yards behind. The dog reached the turning point just as Mike veered his bike to the right. When he came within three feet, it lunged out to bite his leg. At the same moment he lifted his leg causing the dog to leap, nose first, into the red-hot muffler. Even above the roar of the engine, he could hear the dog yelp with pain. After about fifty yards, he looked back over his shoulder to see the dog standing in the middle of the road pawing at his nose.

For a second, Mike felt a sense of relief until he then noticed the man on the bike was racing through the park in the direction they were heading. He wasn't sure why he would be heading that way or why he was peddling so fast, but he knew it couldn't be good. As they drew closer to the back entrance to the park, his suspicions were realized.

At the edge of the gate lay the man's bike, but its rider was nowhere in sight. Even though he couldn't see him, he knew he had to be somewhere close. He motioned to Jason to speed up, but his friend was focused on making sure the girl was okay.

Just then he turned to see the man squatting in a sniper's position from behind a nearby bench. He had a rifle propped on top of it and was aiming directly at Jason's car. It was obvious he was waiting until he got within range to pull the trigger. If he waited until Jason made the turn, it would be an easy shot of less than thirty yards.

Mike waved frantically, hoping his friend would see him in the rearview mirror or better yet draw attention to himself and divert the shooter's focus. Unfortunately Jason was still oblivious to what was going on. As he began to make his turn, a shot rang out.

Jason's driver-side window shattered.

Almost instantaneously, the shooter's park bench exploded into millions of pieces. Tiny burning ashes fell across the park's back gate.

"NOOOO!" Mike yelled, as he watched Jason's car jump the curb and swerve toward an embankment.

At the last second, the car veered back onto the road.

Mike caught his breath. "Oh dear God, please let him be okay."

Just then Jason's arm appeared out the broken window and he gave a thumbs up.

"Thank you, Lord! Thank you, thank you!" Mike exclaimed.

Several minutes later they arrived at Mike's house. As Jason was getting out of the car, Mike ran over to him and almost knocked him down as he threw his arms around him.

"Man, I thought you were gone. I thought you'd been hit for sure."

"Hit?" Jason said. "Hit by what?"

Mike looked at him quizzically. "You mean you don't know what happened?"

"All I know is my window blew out, but I don't know why." He paused a second. "Wait. Do you mean somebody was shooting at me?"

"Remember, the guy on the bike back at the park?"

"Yeah."

"Well, while we were circling around the park, he cut through and was waiting on the other side with a rifle."

"No way! He actually tried to kill me!"

Mike nodded. "I assume he wanted the car."

Jason shook his head. "Just so he could take my friggin' car."

"So you didn't see what happened to him?"

"No."

"You won't believe this," Mikes eyes grew large, "but he exploded!

"WHAT?"

"He exploded into a million pieces. He just blew up!"

"How?"

"I have no idea, but I'm telling you, the exact moment your window blew he just vaporized. It was incredible. All that was left was a black snow falling across the back of the park."

"How could I have missed that?" Jason looked back at the car. Suddenly he realized the girl was still inside. "I've gotta check to see how she's doing. She's been curled up in the corner ever since the window blew out."

As he ran around to the other side of the car he could see she was still curled up against the door. Obviously she was still shocked by the window being blasted apart. He didn't want to startle her, so he slowly lifted the handle and opened the door just a few inches.

"Are you okay?" he said through the small opening in the door.

There was no response or movement. He pulled it open a few more inches. As he did, her head dropped forward and the full weight of her body fell against the door, pushing it open. As the door swung by, her body toppled into his arms.

"Mike, come quickly!" he yelled as he cradled her limp body.

"What's wrong?" he asked as he came running up.

"I don't know." He gently pulled her away from the car and out onto the grass. "She just fell out when I opened the door."

"Check her pulse."

Jason brushed her hair away from her face. Her eyes were shut. He placed his fingers on her neck.

"I can't find a pulse!"

Mike bent down on the other side of her. "Let's check her pupils."

As Jason continued feeling for a pulse, Mike pulled up her left eyelid.

"What the..." he exclaimed.

Jason looked over at Mike then down into the girl's eye. The magnificent glow had vanished. There was no electric shimmering brilliance as before. And the ice blue coloring was now just an average everyday brown.

"What happened to her eyes?" Mike asked.

"I don't know," he muttered as he pulled his hand away from her neck.

Mike pointed to his hand. "Are you bleeding?"

He looked down. His pinky was dripping with blood. He quickly reached back under her hair and around to the base of her head. Almost instantly his expression indicated that he had found the source. Slowly, he turned her to the side revealing blood-soaked hair.

His head dropped to his chest as he rolled her back. "The whole back half of her skull has been crushed," he said solemnly.

"Or shot," Mike countered.

"Shot?" He paused, then nodded. "Shot. Yeah, that's gotta be it."

"The sniper's bullet that shattered your window and missed you struck her instead."

Jason slapped the ground with his blood-soaked hand. "This is just senseless! Killing for a friggin' car, for a friggin' car!" He hung his head down and stared at the ground.

The two men remained kneeling next to her lifeless body; neither one saying anything as they silently mourned the tragedy of the innocence girl's death. After a minute, Mike put his hand on Jason's shoulder.

"Stay here." He disappeared into the garage and reappeared with two shovels. He walked over to Jason and held out his hand to help him up. As he got to his feet he handed him one of the shovels. "Come on. We need to put her to rest."

"Shouldn't we call the police first?"

Mike just looked at him with raised eyebrows.

"Never mind," he corrected himself. "I don't know how we'd explain it anyway."

CHAPTER 19
BUILDING A FORTRESS

Mike's home was located just outside the city in an upscale but rural suburb. Every lot was large and fairly secluded. His sat on the back half of an acre lot with a long driveway running from the road through a hundred yards of densely covered natural area. It was a sprawling ranch with a detached garage situated on the right side of the house. A quaint, ivy-covered walkway that led up to the kitchen back door connected them. A large privacy fence wrapped around the sides and back of the house, huge cypress trees lined the side fences, and an easement full of tall pines bordered the back.

Other than the two gas tanks next to the left side of the garage, the only other features of his Spartan backyard were a cobble-stoned patio with a gas grill and a large oak tree in the back left corner. Growing up in a large family ensured Mike would be an outgoing and gregarious person, but this also meant he cherished his privacy. This type of lot gave him exactly what he needed. This relative seclusion, and the fact that it had perimeter security cameras and an actual working communication system, was why they had decided they should all stay there.

Jason looked around the backyard contemplating a burial site for the girl. "It's your yard, Mike. Where do you think we should bury her?"

He pointed to the far end of the yard. "Let's carry her to the oak tree."

"Okay. But, what about Erin? She's inside. If she looks out and sees us burying a body, she'll freak out for sure."

Just then Jason noticed a large man dressed in dark sweats and a baseball cap lugging a huge backpack and jogging down the driveway.

"Holy crap!" Jason exclaimed. "Hide her!"

"Quick, grab her arms. I've got her feet," Mike said while dragging her to the opposite side of the car. After three or four yards, he gently laid down her arms.

"Hold on a minute." he said peering down the driveway. "There's no need to worry," he sighed. "It's just Father Tim."

Jason turned and watched the clergyman as he increased his speed from a jog to an all-out sprint. When he reached the edge of the car he flung his backpack to the ground and collapsed beside it as if he'd been shot.

"Whoooo Weeee," he exhaled loudly as he lay on the ground panting. "Not bad for an old Navy seal, huh?"

"You ran the entire way here?" Mike asked.

"Sure did."

"All seven miles?"

"Yep," he said as he stood up. "Well, except for the one time when I had to tie my shoe." He bent over to catch his breath some more, then leaned forward and stretched from side to side. "I started out from my house this morning about the same time you guys were heading out to rig up the car."

Mike turned to Jason. "I forgot to tell you that I invited the good Padre to join us here at the house."

"To live?"

"Yeah, I thought we could use a man of his spiritual stature to help guide us in our journey." He grabbed Father Tim's left bicep with both hands. "Not to mention we need these guns."

"I am so good with that!" Jason exclaimed happily, as he walked over and patted him on the back. "Welcome aboard, Father."

Just then, Mike caught Jason's attention and with his eyes led him to the other side of the car where the girl still lay. "Tim, your timing couldn't be better. We're actually in dire need of some spiritual leadership."

"Really?"

"I'm afraid so. I'll go into the details later, but right now we need to take care of something before Erin finds out."

Father Tim looked sideways at him. "What exactly have you boys been up to?"

Mike led him around the back of the car where the girl was laying.

"Oh, my Lord!" he exclaimed, placing his hand to his heart. "Is she – dead?"

"I'm afraid so."

"Please tell me one thing. Was it an accident?"

"Well, kinda and kinda not," Mike wavered. "But it wasn't our fault. I promise!"

Jason interrupted, nodding toward the girl's body. "I don't mean to be rude, but could you possibly tell him the whole story while you... you know."

"Bury her," Father Tim said, relieving him from having to finish his sentence.

Mike turned to the Father. "He's right. We need to do it now before Erin sees us and comes out of the house."

"Sure," he said.

Mike looked at Jason. "If you'll go in and keep Erin busy we'll take the girl and lay her to rest behind the big oak like we'd planned. That should give us enough cover and it's a fitting spot, don't you think?"

They all nodded. Then Jason turned and headed into the house while Mike and Father Tim went about the task of figuring out how to inconspicuously get the girl's body to the back of the yard.

As Jason entered the house, Erin was coming out of the kitchen. "I thought I heard you guys," she said as she gave him a hug. "Everything go okay?"

"Easy peezy. Actually it was a piece of cake."

"Was there somebody else with you?" she said craning her neck over his shoulder toward the front door.

"Oh, yeah. Father Tim is here."

"Really?" she shouted. "I just love that man. Let me go say hi."

"Wait!" he exclaimed, jumping in front of her. "Mike and he are talking about some pretty serious stuff. I don't think they should be interrupted right now."

"What type of serious stuff?"

"Oh, well, um…security issues," he stated, nodding gravely. "They're talking about ways to keep the house and property safe."

"That's not so serious."

"Well, maybe not serious in that sense, but they need some uninterrupted time to figure out a couple of things we need to do around the house. Besides, they'll be in shortly."

She shrugged her shoulders. "Well, okay. I'll wait. Oh, I made some coffee. You want some?"

"Absolutely." What a perfect way, he thought, to keep her mind off going outside. "Would you mind bringing it to me here in the living room? I need to plop down in the recliner and chill out for a bit."

"Sure." She disappeared into the kitchen. A minute later she was back carrying an oversized cup of hot coffee. "Here you go. The fellas must be installing something in the back. They're digging up a storm behind that big oak tree way back there. They even drove your car out there to unload it."

Jason almost spilled his coffee. He had completely forgotten the kitchen had a clear view to the oak tree.

"Yeah, it must be part of the increased security system they were talking about."

For the next hour, Erin was captivated by Jason's easy conversation. Keeping her distracted was hardly a chore, and Jason almost felt guilty for getting such an easy job compared to what the boys were dealing with outside.

Just then they heard the sound of boots being scraped of what was likely mud outside the back door. Erin jumped out of her chair. "They must be finished," she said excitedly, then ran through the kitchen and flung open the door.

"Hey stranger!" she yelled past Mike out to Father Tim.

"Well, hello to you, Missy." He gave her a big bear hug. "How in the world have you been?"

"Pretty good, actually. I'm even better now. Jason just told me you're moving in and joining our motley crew."

"If you guys will have me."

"Of course! Come on in," she smiled. "Did you bring your things with you?"

He pulled his backpack up to his chest and patted it. "Everything I need is right here."

"You're such a guy," she laughed. "That would be considered a cosmetic case for a girl like me."

She turned to Mike. "Can I help him get situated?"

"Why, sure. He'll be in the bedroom at the far end of the house."

"Come on, Father," she said prancing down the hall like a grade school girl preparing for her first slumber party.

Mike and Jason went into the living room where Mike

immediately flopped down on the couch. "Man, I'm absolutely beat."

"So did you explain everything to Father Tim?" Jason asked. No response. "Did you tell him about how we found the girl and how the shooter exploded and..." He leaned down toward his friend. Mike's eyes were shut and he was snoring like a buzz saw.

Fifteen minutes later Erin came bounding into the room followed by Father Tim.

"Is he asleep?" she whispered.

Jason chuckled. "You couldn't tell by that hideous chainsaw he's got running through his nose?"

"So Erin saw us installing some of the new security system out back," Father Tim said.

Jason lifted his eyebrows realizing he was able to play along with the story he had concocted for Erin.

"What security system?" Mike said jerking up out of his catnap.

"How was your mini-siesta, Señor?" Erin joked.

"It was good. What security system are you guys talking about?"

"Wow, you really were out of it," Jason said. He turned his back to the others and gave him a concealed wink. "Erin saw you guys installing part of the new security system out back."

"Oh, yeah, right. Man, I really was out of it." He scratched his head while yawning. "Yeah, we got it up okay." He looked at Father Tim and then Jason. "Guys, that's something we really need to work on even more."

"What do you mean?" Jason asked.

"Our security system – we need to beef it up."

Erin tilted her head. "Weren't you guys already discussing this?"

Jason quickly diffused her inquiry. "Yeah, we did, but we kinda got side-tracked. Let's finish talking about it now, and of course you need to hear all of it too, Erin."

"Thanks. Just consider me one of the boys," she smiled.

Mike continued, "Father Tim and I were talking, and in addition to the perimeter and house security, we need something for the gas tanks."

"We also need to protect our vehicles," Father Tim added. "Our most important assets are transportation, fuel, food, shelter, and of course each other. If any one of those is compromised, we're in trouble."

"Spoken like a true Navy seal," Mike said. "And I agree about the car and motorcycle. We need to protect them as much as we can."

He nodded. "Guys, we're actually set up pretty well here. We've got ample supplies, mobility, and a darn good team. Jason's our physicist, Mike's our communications and information officer, and Erin's nursing skills make her one heck of a medic. All we need is a long-term survival strategy."

Mike looked at Jason. "What's with that big grin you've got going there?"

"I'm just so incredibly thankful you invited this man to join us."

"You aren't going to get all emotional and start crying are you?" he joked.

Father Tim slapped him on the shoulder. "Thank you, Jason. You certainly make me feel welcomed." Then he turned to Mike and Erin. "If you guys aren't too tired, would now be a good time to convene in the conference room and discuss our strategy?"

Resoundingly, they all agreed. Father Tim clapped his hands together. "Well, then. Let's get crackin'!" The guys all headed down the hall to the conference room, while Erin stepped toward the kitchen. "Guys, would you like some coffee to keep us going?"

"That'd be fantastic," Jason said.

"Absolutely," Mike chimed in.

"Great, I'll just be a minute."

As the three men entered the office, Father Tim stopped and

turned in a slow circle. He let out a grateful sigh. "Man, I love this room."

"Why's that?" asked Jason.

"It reminds me of our briefing rooms when I was in the service." Then he chuckled. "But this is actually a lot more sophisticated than what we had back then."

Just then Erin let out a high-pitched scream from the kitchen. "Guys, guys get in here! Quick, get in here!"

In a flash, all three men were sprinting back to the kitchen. "What's wrong?" said Mike.

She was pointing out the kitchen window toward the gas tanks. "There was somebody out there, out next to the gas tank."

Father Tim threw open the back door and they all rushed out onto the patio looking in every direction.

"There he goes!" Jason pointed to the back right corner of the yard where the intruder was climbing over the fence.

Mike started to run after him, but Father Tim grabbed him by the arm. "It's no use. He's long gone."

Jason reached down and picked up a four-foot length of hose. "Looks like he left something behind."

"Yeah, and there are a couple more things he forgot," Mike said pointing toward two empty plastic milk jugs next to the edge of the gas tanks. "Looks like he was going to try and siphon off some of our fuel supply without permission."

"That's exactly what he was trying," Father Tim said. "Erin's scream scared the pants off of him." He turned to the three of them. "So much for a secured perimeter. Now that he knows there's a fuel supply here, he'll be back. And who knows how many others know about it? Guys, this is a serious situation. I can guarantee there'll be more attempts like this."

Erin was still staring blankly at where the man had climbed over the fence.

"I'm sorry," Father Tim said, "I don't mean to alarm you."

Suddenly she snapped out of it. She shook her head and turned to go back inside. "Alarmed? Hell! I'm just mad now."

The men smiled at one another.

"Come on, boys," she said as she stepped into the house, "we need to strategize."

CHAPTER 20
STRATEGIES AND CALCULATIONS

As the four walked back into the kitchen, Jason stopped at the pantry closet. "Before we get started, do you guys mind if I grab a snack?"

"I was going to ask the same thing," Mike said.

"Me too," Erin said. "What about you, Father Tim. Are you hungry?"

"I had about five protein bars before the run over. Usually that keeps me going for an entire morning, but for some reason I'm hungry again."

Jason grabbed a bag of pretzels and they headed down the hallway. When they reached the conference room, Mike sat down in front of one of the computer monitors while Erin and Father Tim sat next to each other on the opposite side of the table. Jason walked over to the large whiteboard on the wall and grabbed the marker from its tray and held it up in preparation for writing down their key talking points.

"So what are the main things to discuss?"

"I think it comes down to the basics," Mike said. "Security, communication, and of course, food and fuel."

Jason turned to the board and wrote out each item in big block letters. When he was finished, he swung around toward Father Tim. "I think we all agree you're the best to lead us on Security. Would you mind laying out a plan?"

"Wow. I'm flattered," he smiled. "It's definitely a different ministry than I've been involved with in recent years, but I'll give it a shot." He scratched his chin, then stared intently at the whiteboard as if he were invisibly writing out his action items. In an instant, his demeanor changed from a humble clergyman to an authoritative military commander.

"Tactically, we have to secure from the perimeter inward. Mike, the cameras you installed at each corner of the property are good, but they're only useful at night when the generators are on."

Mike frowned. "You know, you're right. Man, I thought I knew what I was doing."

"Don't be bummed. We'll definitely use them, but we have to adjust. At night, we'll watch the monitors in shifts. And for the daytime, I suggest we simply plant punji sticks around key areas of the house, the gas tanks, and garage.

"What's a punji stick?" Erin asked.

"It's a set of booby-trapped stakes that are placed upright in the ground and camouflaged. In our case, we'll use nails sticking up through boards. When an intruder steps on one, it'll stop him dead in his tracks."

"Sounds good to me," Jason said. "Is that it for Security?"

"There'll definitely be more, but that's it for now."

Jason pointed his marker at Erin. "Okay, Miss Communications Director, what do you have for us?"

"Oh, you want me to lead?"

"Sure." Mike said. "You're the chattiest of all of us, so why not?"

"I think that's you, but I'll give it a shot anyway." She paused a second as she contemplated her response. "I think it's actually pretty straight forward. Whenever we're apart we just have to have a way of staying connected in case of emergencies. Our cell phones are sporadic at best, and we have to assume it's only going to get worse."

Jason looked at the others and nodded, "Unfortunately, she's right."

"In that case," she continued, "we need another device that isn't an energy hog and is more reliable."

"Like what, though?" Jason said skeptically.

Mike's eyes lit up. "Like a blast from the past is what." He ran over to a small metal filing cabinet in the corner and began rummaging through it. After a few seconds he turned around and held up a small black square object in the palm of his hand.

"How about these?"

Jason squinted. "Is that a pager?"

"Sure is."

"Aren't they kind of obsolete?" Erin asked.

"Oh, no," Mike said turning back to the cabinet. "Pagers are what hospitals and other emergency and communication-critical organizations use to stay in contact." After a few more seconds of digging he pulled out a shoebox.

"Jackpot!" He pulled off the lid and dumped five pagers and six chargers onto the table. "These, ladies and gentlemen, are military grade pagers used by elite special ops. They've also been standard issue for the president and his staff for the past five years. They were developed specifically for situations like we're in now. They use hardly any energy, they're almost indestructible, and they work virtually anywhere."

"How'd you get them?" asked Jason.

They were given to my department when we helped them install a major upgrade to their Internet security system.

Jason gave him a suspicious look. "Exactly what organization gave them to you?"

Mike broke out laughing. "Why, the Department of Defense, of course."

"What's so funny?" Father Tim asked.

"You're going to have to give Father Tim confession right now," Erin jokingly demanded. "Father, Mike's a cyber-criminal. He hacks into places like the Department of Defense all the time, and then they give him awards and prizes."

"All for the good of fighting evil and getting us safely through the Tribulation," Mike added with a cheeky grin.

Father Tim slowly shook his head, "Well, I do believe the good Lord will forgive you." Then he smiled. "But just to play it safe, you'd better say ten Hail Marys before going to sleep tonight."

"Ohhh, you got off easy mister," Erin laughed.

Jason waved his hand directing their attention back to him. "Okay, it looks like we're set for communication, so that leaves Fuel and Food, which probably falls to me." He walked away from the whiteboard and sat down at the end of the table.

"We all know that since the vanishings, the earth's been gradually losing energy. The power outages and the lack of energy efficiency in our fuel, most importantly food, show this. At that time I had estimated that if we procured enough food on a regular basis and maintained an adequate level of intake we could easily survive the seven-year Tribulation period."

"But what worries me now is that since the second blackout phenomenon, we don't know how rapidly energy is being lost on a daily basis. So there's no way to effectively plan our intake. There's also the problem of how much we can eat. When we get full, we can't eat anymore. We can't keep stuffing ourselves, in order to make up for the lack of energy the food provides."

"So, do you have a plan?" Mike asked.

"Yeah, I just have to run another food and fuel efficiency test and compare it against the tests I ran prior to the second blackouts."

"Is it complicated?" Erin asked.

"No, not at all. For food, it's basically just burning the food and measuring the heat output. It's even easier for gas. Just burn some fuel and see how long it takes before it goes out. I've got all my previous figures, so it'll be easy to make the comparison, which will then allow me to do all the calculations. It'll only take me about forty-five minutes."

"That sounds good to me," she said. "Guys, if you want to crank up the generators, I'll go and make us something to eat while Jason does the test."

"Great," Mike said. "I'm hungry again."

Father Tim slapped him on the back. "While those two are doing their thing, do you mind helping me start to pull together the materials for our punji stake strategy?"

"Let's go," Mike said. "We'll meet you guys back here in about forty-five minutes."

They went off in their respective directions. Before Jason headed to the patio to do his tests, he went to his room and grabbed the journal he had been using to record and calculate his findings. He also grabbed a small cardboard box that contained the equipment he had been using to conduct his experiments.

Included in the box were a small food scale, a beaker, a cork, two tin cans, a box of matches, a paper clip, and a thermometer. In addition, there was a bag of potato chips, a small baby jar filled with gasoline, and a sewing thimble. When he got outside he went over to a round glass patio table and poured out the contents of the box.

With precise and steady movements he quickly assembled the device he would use to burn and measure his food subject. In this case, he would use one of the potato chips from the same bag he had taken his measurements from before. Just as he was about to begin, he stopped and silently prayed that the results would be in their favor. A few minutes later, he was all but finished. The only thing left was to record his data and do his calculations. He reached over and scribbled his measurements into his journal, then sat down and began performing the calculations in his head. "This can't be right," he said aloud.

"Sure it can," said Mike, as he came up and slapped him on the back.

Jason jumped around. "Man, please don't do that."

"What's wrong, buddy?" Mike asked.

"Oh, nothing. I think I messed up my test and need to redo it."

"Can I help?"

"No, it's just a matter of going through it again. It'll only take a few minutes, then I've got to test the gas, which shouldn't be too long either."

"Okay," Mike said, "I think Erin's almost finished though."

"You guys start without me. I'll be in soon."

"All right."

As Mike walked into the house, Jason rushed back to his testing equipment and began the process again. A couple minutes later he was recording the output. "This just can't be!" He looked to the house and then to the bag of chips. One more time, just to make sure. As he ran through the test a third time he continued mumbling, "please be different, please be different." Again, the same results.

He sat motionless unable to fully grasp what he had just calculated. Slowly, his eyes moved to the thimble. He grabbed it like a man dying of thirst would grab a cup of water. With the other hand he pulled the jar of gasoline and the box of matches next to it. His hands were shaking as he twisted off the jar's cap. He breathed in deeply as he positioned the thimble with the open end up. With both hands, he slowly filled it with gasoline and then lit it with a match. "One Mississippi, two Mississippi, three Mississippi...." He continued counting until the fire went out.

With his hands still shaking, he reached for his journal and recorded the number of seconds he had just counted next to the number of seconds from his previous test. His head fell down. After a minute he heard the back door open. Erin stuck her head out.

"You coming in? Your food's getting cold."

Slowly, he raised his head. "Yeah, I'm coming."

"Okay," she said, then disappeared inside.

After a moment he grabbed his journal and headed to the house. The moment he entered he could hear his friends playfully ribbing one another from down the hall. His walk from the kitchen to the conference room seemed to take an eternity. When he finally reached the entrance he stopped for a second, then lifted his head as high as he could and proceeded in.

"There you are!" Erin said joyfully. "You're down at the end where you were earlier."

"Thanks," Jason said as he walked to his seat and sat down.

For the next several minutes, he sat silently looking down at the TV dinner she had prepared for him while his friends bantered about various things they regretted about their childhood.

"I hate that I was so nerdy," said Mike.

"You, nerdy?" Erin said. "No way."

"Oh yeah, I was so nerdy in high school that I didn't ask a girl out until the last month of my senior year."

"Wow," exclaimed Father Tim. "Even I've got you beat on that one."

"What about you, Jason," asked Erin.

He continued staring into his food.

"Yooo hooo. Earth to Jason," she said jokingly.

Slowly he looked up.

"Oh, I'm sorry. I totally zoned out," he replied solemnly.

"Are you okay?" Mike asked.

He tried forcing a smile, but couldn't. He paused a second, then slowly opened his journal.

"Actually, no – I'm not." He looked at each one of them individually. "What I'm about to tell you changes everything."

CHAPTER 21
EYES OF AN ANGEL

Suddenly the room became filled with a heavy angst. Everyone stopped eating and turned their attention to Jason. There had been an increased sense of security and a positive outlook when they were planning for the future, but now Jason was holding information that was threatening to wipe that away.

"I've finished the calculations on the energy efficiency tests I just conducted."

"And?" Mike prodded.

"And it's not good."

No one moved. The tension of Jason's words hung over them like a guillotine. He took a deep breath, as he looked down at his journal, then swallowed hard.

Father Tim placed a reassuring hand on his arm and nodded for him to proceed.

"The energy loss from this last phenomenon was off the charts. The energy we're currently losing has dramatically increased."

"How much?" asked Mike.

"About a quarter of a percent per day."

Mike grabbed a pen and pad and started scribbling. "Oh, my

God! That means we'll be without any form of power in…"

"In about a year," Jason said.

Erin jumped out of her seat. "How can that be?"

"Are you sure?" Father Tim said calmly. "I don't doubt your abilities, but could the test be off some way?"

Jason shook his head. "I tested the food output three separate times."

"What about the gas?"

"I tested it once, but that's all I needed. Proportionately, it lost the same amount which further validated the food loss."

Mike rubbed his forehead and grimaced. "This is going to get bad – like real bad."

Erin put her hands over her mouth, stifling her oncoming sobs.

"Is there any way that this thing could be temporary or reverse itself?" Mike asked, as if pleading.

"There's always the possibility, but it's highly unlikely. It didn't before, so there's nothing that leads me to believe it will now. I'll continue to run tests every day though."

"Is there anything we can do?" Mike asked.

"No, not really." He looked out the window, then turned back to Mike. "Wait, actually there is! Find me Richard Teech?"

"You mean the physicist genius you're always going on about?"

"That's the one. If you can hack into his system or somehow tap into his main lines of communication maybe we can get the latest update on what's going on. If anyone knows what's happening, it'll be him."

Mike pushed his empty plate aside and slid his chair over in front of one of the computer monitors. "The generators are still on, so I'll give it a shot right now."

Jason turned to Father Tim. "Father, we probably need to get going on that additional security system you were talking about while it's still light out. Do you want me to give you a hand?"

"No, I think I'm good. But mind if I steal Erin? She can assist me and keep me company."

It was obvious how upset Erin had become. Perhaps Father Tim was right, and if she were in his presence he could provide some comfort and distraction.

She nodded her approval. He grabbed her by the hand and together they headed out of the room.

Mike was already typing away furiously at his computer. Jason got up from his seat, moved to the computer across from him and began surfing the Internet for anything he could uncover on Teech. For the next hour, they continued searching without any luck.

"Man, this is going nowhere," said Jason. "I can't find anything."

Without looking up Mike replied. "I should have warned you. There's not been much posted lately."

"Why do you think that is?"

Mike continued staring into his monitor while his typing increased at a feverish rate.

"I think the lack of power and people's patience is keeping anyone from posting anything. There's not enough power to keep the Internet up on a continuous basis and people are probably more worried about staying alive than surfing the 'Net. It's just a matter of days anyway before it's entirely shut down."

"What about the government? Have you had any luck with their communications?"

"I'm having a harder time cracking into their stuff, too. They're definitely not posting anything that's public. I'm sure they don't want to alarm those that still have Internet access about the alien encounters."

"The angel encounters you mean," said Jason.

Mike banged his fist down on the table. "I'm so tired of this. I can't find anything. The only thing I've got is that he's in

Washington, D.C. attending some sort of think tank session at the Watergate Hotel."

"You meant to say angel encounters," Jason persisted.

Mike sighed and looked up from his computer. "It's no use. There's nothing."

Jason no longer was concerned with Mike finding Teech. His friend's comment sent up a red flag and he was more concerned now about having him clarify what he meant by alien encounters.

"Mike, listen to me! When you said alien encounters, did you mean to say angel encounters?"

Mike was still frustrated with his lack of success finding any real information about Teech. He had always prided himself on being able to successfully accomplish tasks such as this, and now that he couldn't, his patience was growing thin. He glared at the computer with contempt.

Jason leaned across the table and put his hand on his forearm. "Can you stop a minute, please?"

Mike blinked and looked up at him like he'd just come out of a trance. "What?" he said.

"Just a minute ago you said something about the government not wanting to alarm people about the *alien* encounters. Did you actually mean to say *angel* encounters, instead of *alien* encounters?"

Mike looked back at the monitor and started to withdraw back into the screen.

"Just please let the computer go for a minute!"

"Okay, Okay," he said holding up his hands as he slid his chair back from the table. "I did say alien encounters because…" he hesitated, "that's what I meant."

"So you don't think there's a possibility they were angels? You don't think the girl from the boathouse might have been an angel?"

Mike couldn't look him in the eye. "I'm just not sure any more about all that. There are just too many things going on outside of the whole Tribulation and Rapture theory now."

"You've got to be kidding me! You don't think there's a chance the girl was an angel or that incredible supernatural rain during the second blackouts was angels coming to earth?"

"I'm just skeptical is all," Mike said sheepishly. "If they are angels, wouldn't they have just appeared rather than rained down like that?"

Jason rolled his eyes, not bothering to hide his exasperation. "However God chooses to send his messengers is up to him."

"So what about when the girl was shot? I mean, come on, you can't kill an angel!"

"We don't know that!"

"I know, I know, I'm just playing the devil's advocate."

"You certainly are! What's gotten into you?"

Mike shook his head. "Man, I'm sorry," he said quietly. "I know I brought you in on this and pushed the whole Rapture idea down your throat, but I'm just not seeing it anymore. All that research we did doesn't seem to hold up now. The timing is all off and it's just one contradiction after another. There's no proof. You're the scientist. Can you rationally explain any of this?"

"Do you hear yourself? That's exactly what you first said to me." He paused. "Wait, do you really feel this way or are you still just upset with not being able to get info on Teech?"

Mike's eyes welled up with tears. "I'm sorry, Jason. I'm afraid I do. I can't help it." He turned and started walking toward the door, when Jason grabbed him by the arm.

"You can't lose faith. Not now. We're too close. Father Tim said we'd be tested. That's all this is. It's a test. Don't you see?"

Mike's head dropped. "I don't." he mumbled and walked out of the room and down the hallway to the front door.

A few minutes later the back door opened. "You guys back there?" yelled Erin.

"Yeah, I'm back here," Jason yelled back as he walked toward the kitchen. She and Father Tim met him halfway down the hall. "Did Mike get anywhere with finding your guy?" she asked.

"Unfortunately not."

She walked up beside Father Tim and wrapped her slender arms around his left bicep, then leaned her head up against his massive shoulder. "Father Tim's been talking to me. He's helped show me what I've been missing. I've been so blind, but that's all different now. I believe Jason, I believe! I truly, truly believe!"

"Really?" he said looking at Father Tim.

Father Tim nodded with a big smile on his face.

Jason grabbed her and pulled her to him. As he threw his arms around her, tears came streaming down her cheeks.

"I'm so sorry. Jason, I've been living a lie. I think you've known it, too," she sobbed. "I've been pretending all this time. I pretended I believed in you and Mike. I pretended to believe in the Rapture, the Tribulation, all of it – but I really didn't." She stopped crying and stepped back from him, then took his hands in hers. Her eyes were full of both remorse and joy. "Jason, I confessed to him." She paused a second. "I confessed that I had feelings for you and that was the only reason I pretended to believe like you do. I fooled myself into thinking that you'd care for me if I had the same beliefs." Then she looked over at Father Tim and smiled. "But that's all changed now." She looked upward. "Lord, I do believe." She threw her arms back around his neck. "Whatever happens from this point on, my faith is real! And one day I know you'll be with Kristina and Nikki again. It's going to happen. I know it is!"

Father Tim walked up to them and placed his hands on their backs. "All the angels in heaven are rejoicing this evening."

Jason turned to him. "Unfortunately, I think they may be shedding some tears, as well."

"What do you mean?"

"I had a discussion with Mike while you guys were outside. Looks like he's struggling with his own beliefs."

Father Tim's smile faded, "In what way?"

"He's been trying to rationalize everything and is discounting it by saying everything that's been happening doesn't jive with the *Book of Revelation* anymore. He says all the stuff in the beginning did, but that over time it's gone off track. I told him he sounded like me when we first began. The crazy thing is that he's the one who made me believe. I just can't understand it."

"Do you think he's still open to a discussion?"

"Not from me. I've tried, but my arguments aren't good enough for him."

Father Tim held up a finger. "You might want to put arguments on the back burner. It's faith he needs to find. Logic can sometimes get in the way."

"I'm sorry, Father, I should have known better. That was the physics teacher talking."

"No worries. Do you think he'd talk to me?"

"I'm sure he would."

"Where'd he go?" asked Erin

"He went outside. I think through the front door."

"You guys stay here. I'll be back shortly."

"Please don't be too long, Father," Erin pleaded. "It's already dark out."

"No worries! I'll hog tie him and drag him back if I have to." Then he turned and headed purposefully out the front door.

Erin put her arm through Jason's and gave him a gentle tug. "Wanna help me make dinner?"

He smiled and they walked toward the kitchen. Just as they were about to enter, a loud thump came from the far end of the house.

"Did you hear that?" she said.

Jason jerked back around. "Yeah, it sounded like it was all the way down at Father Tim's room." He squinted his eyes as he looked down the dark hallway. The only light was coming from the conference room, which was directly across from Father Tim's room.

"You stay here," he whispered.

"Are you crazy? I'm coming with you," she whispered back.

He nodded. "Okay, but run to the kitchen first and get me the biggest knife you can."

In a few seconds she was back. "Here," she said as she handed him a large carving knife.

Two louder bangs came from the back. Erin jumped back against the wall and into a small table knocking over a vase and ashtray.

Jason held his finger to his lips. "Shhhhhh." Then he pulled her toward him and whispered, "It's probably just Mike and Father Tim. But we've gotta play it safe."

She nodded hopefully. "Aren't you going to turn on the lights?"

"Not yet. If there's someone back there, we need to sneak up on him."

He motioned with his head for her to follow him.

They slowly moved down the hallway. One foot at a time, they silently tiptoed their way to within an inch of the door. With a vice grip hold, Erin held onto Jason's forearm as he slowly stretched his neck around the corner. The light from the conference room spilled across the hall and into the room. Jason breathed a sigh of relief. The room was vacant.

He flipped the light switch on. "Nobody's here. It must have been the guys doing something outside."

Erin let go of his arm and exhaled. "Oh, thank God. Maybe Father Tim's hog tying him like he said and he's out there bouncing him up against the wall."

She walked over to a window and pulled up the blinds. "I'm going to call them in."

"No, wait! You don't want to disturb them while Tim's talking sense into him."

She stopped. "Yeah, you're right. Thanks!"

As Erin turned back around, something slapped against the window causing her to freeze. For several seconds neither one moved. They stood staring at one another. He tried looking past her to see what it was, but her body was covering the panes. All he could see was Erin, terrified and stiff as a board.

"Don't move." He said holding out his hand. It was too late. In a jerk, she turned on her heels and was now facing the window directly. She clutched her chest, then fell to the floor. Jason leapt across the room. He fell to his knees and threw his arm underneath her head.

"Erin, Erin, are you okay?" he begged.

Just then the sound of fingernails scraping across glass filled the room. His eyes left Erin and moved slowly up the wall. A bolt of electricity shot through his body as he focused in on the ghostly figure of a man on the other side of the window. His hands were pressed against the windowpanes. His skin was beyond pale, and the light from the room made him look almost pure white. His head was turned over his shoulder, as if he were looking for something behind him.

Jason remained cradling Erin in his arms. He was unable to move. He remained fixed on the window, waiting for the next movement to come. Then slowly the man turned his head back to the window. Jason's whole body began to shake as the man turned his gaze upon him. For the second time in two days, he was certain he was looking into the eyes of an angel.

CHAPTER 22
THE SEARCH

The man outside the window had eyes just like the girl from the boathouse. They were the same icy blue, and they shimmered with electricity just as hers had. The same neon circle highlighted the edges. And they were mesmerizing, just as hers had been. Suddenly, Jason stopped shaking. His fear faded and he knew instantly that this wasn't someone or something there to harm them.

Just then, Erin flinched. Jason looked down at her. She rubbed her forehead.

"What happened?" she moaned.

"You passed out," he said softly.

"All I remember was looking out at…" she paused, "a ghost at the window!" She broke out of Jason's arms and pushed herself away from the window. She balled up in the corner trembling. "It was right in front of me." She pointed to the window. "It was right there!"

Jason turned back expecting to see the spectral image on the other side of the glass panes, but he was gone.

She kept pointing. "Did you see it, too? Please tell me you saw it," she begged.

He slid across the floor next to her and put his arm around her shoulders, all the while keeping his eye on the window. "I did see him."

"You're just saying you did. I'm not crazy, Jason. I know you think I am, but I'm not. I'm not, I promise."

"I know that," he said reassuringly. "I really did see it. His skin was white and he had incredibly blue eyes. It was like they were electrified."

"You did see it! Oh, thank goodness! I thought I was losing my mind."

Still looking at the window, he got up and reached down and took her by the hand.

"Come on," he said as he pulled her to her feet, "we've got to go find him."

"What?" Erin said shaking her head. "Why on earth would you want to do that?"

"Trust me," he said, "there's nothing to be afraid of." He took her by the arm and began leading her toward the back of the house.

When they got to the back door she threw her hand up against the frame. "I can't go out there. What makes you so sure he's not going to hurt us?"

Jason turned and looked at her not knowing what to say. She deserved an answer, but he had to keep moving or else he might lose his chance to make contact with him.

"Because…" he paused, "because he's an angel, that's why."

Erin's mouth hung open and her face went expressionless. "An angel?" she said.

He nodded. "I know it sounds crazy."

She looked down as she contemplated the word *angel*. Then she raised her head while slowly dropping her hand away from the door. "I believe you," she said softly.

"Really?"

"I do," she replied.

He tilted his head and smiled. "You know, faith really looks good on you." Then he reached past her and opened the door. "But maybe you actually should stay here. I'll probably come upon them outside, but if Mike and Father Tim come back in, tell them what happened and that I'm circling the house."

"Are you sure?"

"Yeah, I won't be long."

As he headed out the door, she rubbed his arm. "I really do believe you."

He put his hand on hers. "I know." Then he stepped out onto the patio.

The night air had grown cold, but his adrenaline was pumping so hard he was oblivious to it. He desperately wanted to make contact with the man and experience what he had before with the girl. Somehow he knew there was a divine connection with them. This was also his chance to get some answers he'd not been able to get from her.

His first instincts were to call out for his two friends and to conduct his search on the run, but he remembered how timid the girl had been. Anything sudden or threatening could send the man fleeing or cause him to cower in a dark corner where he would be hard to find. Without any sudden movements, Jason slowly turned to his left and began walking to the back corner of the house. His heartbeat quickened with every step. As he approached the window where the man had been standing, all he found were two small shrubs, neither of which was large enough to hide someone.

When he reached the corner he looked back to the patio, then across the backyard. All was calm. No movement in any direction, just a wide open rectangle of grass framed by the shadows of the privacy fence that wrapped around it. He was thankful there was a sliver of moon out that evening illuminating the yard well enough to make out shapes from a distance. Certainly, if something moved he would be able to see it.

As he turned back he placed his hand against the side of the house and slowly inched his head around the corner. If anyone was there he wanted to make sure he saw before they saw him. Fortunately the window blinds to Father Tim's room, as well as the conference room, were wide open allowing their light to pour out onto the side lawn, illuminating it up all the way to the fence. With one glance, he could see no one was there.

Bolstered by the security of the light, he quickly moved on to the front of the house. When he reached the edge, he stopped and took a deep breath. Slowly he peeked around the corner. Because the shades were drawn on the conference room's front windows, there wasn't nearly as much light as on the side of the house. The moon, however, revealed enough for him to see that no one was in the yard, at least up to the edge of where the natural area began.

Mike's front lawn consisted of twenty yards of lush Bermuda grass butting up against an almost impenetrable wall of pine trees, overgrown shrubs, and dense undergrowth that stretched more than fifty yards to the street. Jason knew the only logical way out of Mike's front yard was down the driveway at the far end of the house. If someone was hiding in the natural area, he would never be able to find the intruder. The best he could do would be to hear him rustling around. Taking slow, deliberate steps he stealthily moved across the lawn while listening intently for any other movements. The only sound came from the generators in the garage just around the corner.

As he approached the edge of the house, he heard a twig snap. He stopped and listened – nothing. He took another step and listened – still nothing. On his next step, he stomped his foot hoping to elicit a reaction from anything that was there. In an immediate response, a large object exploded from the natural area onto the driveway. For a second he froze, then in a flash he was sprinting down the pavement in pursuit. Two thirds of the way down the driveway, he realized it was only a deer. He jogged to a stop and bent over to catch his breath. The only thing he could hear over his panting and wheezing was the tickety-tack of the deer's hooves as it ran onto the street.

He couldn't believe he was so winded after such a short chase. It had to be the decrease in their food's energy. All of them had started feeling the effects, but this was his first personal sign that things were getting much worse. After several more deep breaths, he stood up and turned back to the house. The tall pines lining the driveway filtered out the little moonlight there was. And since the only light coming from the house was in the back, it had all but vanished into the night.

Still intent on completing his search he headed toward the garage. As he walked back down the driveway, shapes started to gradually appear. First the edges of the house came into focus. After a few more steps, he could make out the garage and the metal gas tanks adjacent to the back corner. The small light from the kitchen reflected off of the tanks creating a fuzzy dark gray silhouette. He couldn't be sure but it appeared two men, most likely Mike and Father Tim, were standing next to them. He started to call out their names, but hesitated. Just then, there was a loud pop like a firecracker. Then, off in the distance someone shouted, "Shoot now!" followed by POW, POW.

The sudden burst of noise stopped him in his tracks. He blinked his eyes and the figures that were standing beside the gas tanks now appeared to be kneeling. Out of nowhere, a spotlight blazed across the backyard on to the gas tanks revealing the two figures. In an instant he could clearly see the priest kneeling down over another person curled up on the ground. His back was turned against the harsh glare of the light as if shielding them from it.

"Mike! Use your gun!" Father Tim yelled out over his shoulder.

At that moment, a firestorm of shots rattled off, with every other one hitting the gas tank's metal underpinnings. POW, POW – TING – POW – TING, POW, POW.

A tidal wave of adrenaline surged through Jason's body, breaking him out of his paralysis and into a surreal sprint toward his friend. At first it was as if everything was moving in slow motion, each step producing less and less forward thrust. The more he ran, the farther away he seemed to get.

He screamed, "I'm coming!" but nothing came out. Everything was muted – the gunshots, his feet pounding the payment, the hum of the generators, everything was gone. All he could hear was the sound of his beating heart. Then suddenly everything slowed down. In mid-stride he seemed frozen in time as he watched a single spark etch across the side of one of the gas tanks. A split second later came a blast of blinding light, followed by a shockwave that knocked him into the yard.

Unconscious, Jason lay face down in the grass. A minute later he awoke to an ear-piercing ringing running through his brain. His body ached with pain. He grimaced as he rubbed his fingers against his temples. With his head down and facing away from the blast, he slowly stood up. The earth was spinning beneath him. As he regained his balance and his senses came back to him, he realized that night had become day. The entire front yard was lit all the way to the street.

In an instant everything came rushing back. He spun around, then immediately had to throw his hand over his eyes to shield himself from an inferno that lay before him. The entire garage was engulfed in a giant fireball. The ringing in his ears was replaced with the crackling of the fire.

From the other side of the house, he heard Mike shout, "Father! Father, where are you?"

A second later, Erin came running out the front door with her arms stretched out toward him. "Oh, thank God you're all right!" she said throwing her arms around him.

"What happened?"

"I don't know," she cried. "I was in the kitchen waiting for you guys. I heard shouting, so I looked out back and saw Mike run across the patio, then all these firecrackers started going off and then this horrible explosion."

He grabbed her arm. "Come on. We've got to find them."

He started to run straight for the garage and to where he'd seen Father Tim, but the heat was too intense to get close. Plus, the explosion had knocked down the roof to the walkway that connected the garage to the house. He was actually thankful it had, otherwise the fire could spread along it to the house.

"Let's go through the front," he said pulling her with him.

He flung the door open and they ran through the living room, into the kitchen, and out onto the patio. As soon as they stepped outside, he ran into Mike and almost knocked him down. His friend's eyes were wild with desperation and he was breathing heavily.

"I can't find Father Tim!" he yelled.

Jason feared the worst. "I saw him next to the gas tanks seconds before the explosion."

"Me, too," he panted. "I tried going over there, but I can't get within twenty yards of it. The heat is too extreme."

"Maybe he was blown out into the yard."

Mike was shaking his head before he had even finished. "I don't think so. He's nowhere!" He swept his arm from the left side of the yard to the right side. "You can see for yourself."

The fire was raging at full force with the blaze rising over a hundred feet high. The light it was giving off highlighted everything in the backyard from the edge of the house to the large oak tree in the back left corner. Debris from the explosion was scattered everywhere, but Mike was right, there were no bodies anywhere in sight.

He started walking out into the grass. "We need to look for..." He stopped. "We just still need to look."

"I understand," Mike said soberly.

Jason looked back at him. They both knew that whatever they found was going to be more than Erin could handle. Then he looked to her.

"Could you go grab the fire extinguisher and wait on the patio? If the fire starts to spread to the house, you can put it out."

Her eyes began to fill with tears. She knew why they didn't want her to help. "Sure," she muttered turning back.

He looked at Mike. "You take the left side and I'll take the right."

They spread out and slowly began inspecting the yard. There were thousands of pieces of splintered wood interspersed with broken garden tools, lawn equipment, even pieces of their cars. After about ten minutes, Jason heard Mike throwing up next to the oak tree.

"You okay?" he called out.

"No. Can you come here?"

Jason ran across the yard. As he got closer he saw the reason for his friend's reaction. Next to an exposed root coming from off the tree was a hand. It was in shreds just above the wrist. The thumb and forefinger were missing.

"Is it, is it..." he couldn't go on.

"I don't know," Mike replied blankly.

He bent down. "There's a signet ring on the index finger. It's got a cross on it." He looked up at his friend.

Tears were streaming down Mike's face. He slowly nodded. "It's his."

173

CHAPTER 23
LOSING FAITH

Jason bowed his head and silently prayed. Mike stood next to him trying to fight back more tears. But it was no use. The horrible reality overtook him; the man who had helped him through so many troubling times, the man that was like a father figure to him was gone. He fell to his knees next to Jason and buried his head in his hands.

"Why him? He was such a good man."

Jason put his arm around his shoulders. He started to console him, but couldn't find the words. "Come on, buddy. Let's go back inside."

He wiped his eyes. Together they stood up and started the slow walk back to the house. As they approached the fire, Jason was amazed by how quickly it was dying down. A blaze like that, with all that gasoline fueling it, should have burned on through most of the night. It was just another grim piece of evidence validating the severity of the energy they were losing.

When they entered the back door, Erin was sitting at the kitchen table with the fire extinguisher in the chair beside her. She took one look at Mike and put her hand to her mouth.

"Oh, no," she muttered. His tear-stained face told her everything she needed to know.

She pushed her chair back against the wall and ran around the table to him. She threw her arms around him and laid her head against his.

"Mike, I'm so sorry."

Oblivious to her sympathy, he stood there with his arms hanging by his side as she tried consoling him with her hug. After a moment he slowly pulled away. He looked at her with an empty gaze, then without a word turned and walked out of the room and down the hall to his bedroom. She and Jason stood silently in the kitchen until they heard the door shut. As soon as the latch clicked, she turned to him with tears in her eyes.

"You're sure he's gone?"

He nodded.

"What happened?" she pleaded.

"I don't know," he said softly. "Mike was out back with him. I'm sure he knows, but now's not the time to go through it. We'll need to wait until tomorrow."

"You're right."

"Speaking of tomorrow," he said picking up the fire extinguisher, "why don't you go on to bed? It's been a grueling day and you need some rest. I'm going to go outside and spray down the edges of the fire so there's no chance it spreads."

"Do you want me to help?"

"No, that's okay. You go on now."

"But I can…" she continued.

"No, just go on now, okay?"

"Okay," she said softly.

As soon as she had left the room, he put the fire extinguisher down and walked out onto the patio. His fabricated story about dousing the fire had worked. He had already determined that the fire wasn't going to spread, but more importantly, he needed all the light that was left for what he had to do. He stepped out into the grass and looked up into the starless sky.

"Lord, please guide me and give me strength." He lowered his head, took a deep breath and set about the grisly task of collecting the remains of his friend and the man that he had been trying to protect. Without ever raising his head he methodically canvassed the yard, finding remnants of body parts and carrying them back behind the large oak tree. Each new discovery seemed more ghastly than the one before. Every trip was a gut-wrenching experience often resulting in him having to stop and throw up. After nearly two hours, he was exhausted physically and emotionally.

The only other thing he knew he had to do was perform a proper burial or as close to one as he knew how. As much as he wanted to be done, he knew he had to protect the others from the possibility of seeing any of what he had been subjected to. With just enough remaining firelight, he dug a shallow grave next to where they had buried the girl. One by one, he placed the remains into it and covered it up. When he had finished, he wiped his forehead, then dropped to his knees and said a brief prayer. He wanted it to be longer, but he simply couldn't think anymore. He was completely drained.

By the time he got back to the house and into his room he was feeling faint. It was the same feeling he had after running his first half marathon. He walked over and sat in a chair next to the bed. He looked down at his shoes. They were covered with dirt. In fact his whole body was a dirty mess. A minute passed as he waited on the desire to untie them, but it never came. His eyelids fluttered once, then the next thing he knew he was being awakened.

"Jason."

"Hmmm?" he grunted.

"Jason, wake up."

"What…what is it?" he stammered, while rubbing his eye.

Erin jostled his shoulder. "Come on. It's time to get up."

"What time is it?" he said groggily.

"It's almost ten."

He looked down through blurry eyes. His mud-caked shoes were still tied. His pants and shirt were still on. He hadn't moved an inch.

He sat up, then reached around and grabbed his back while rolling his neck in a circle. "I'm so stiff."

"What time did you come in?"

"I don't know," he said scratching his head.

"I made you something to eat."

"Thanks. That reminds me I'm going to have to run another test today. Is Mike up?"

She shook her head. "I don't know. He's still in his room. I knocked on his door earlier, but he didn't answer."

"Do me a favor. Go take him whatever you made me. I'll clean up and be out in a minute."

"Okay." She turned and headed to the door then stopped. "Oh, one other thing, we're running low on a lot of staple items. Do you know where the rest of the supplies are?"

"Yeah, everything's stacked up…" He stopped.

"It's where?" she asked.

He took a deep breath, then slowly turned to her. "Everything was stacked up next to Mike's car in the garage."

"Everything?"

"About ninety percent."

"You've got to be kidding. Really?"

He nodded.

"Jason, what are we going to do now? We've got enough left in the house for about a month and that's it."

"Don't worry. Mike and I will think of something," he said

confidently. He grabbed a towel off the bed. "It'll be alright. Now, go ahead. I'll be out in a second."

He walked into the bathroom and shut the door. He leaned his back against the wall and closed his eyes as the severity of the situation sunk in. He had no idea how they were going to replenish a year's supply of food. Fifteen minutes later, he met Erin coming down the hall with a plate of food.

"He still won't answer the door," she said. "We can't let the food go to waste, so I was bringing it to you."

Jason's concern for his friend showed in his eyes. He looked at her, then down the hall. "You're right. Would you mind taking it back to the kitchen? I'm going to go check on him again."

As he approached his door he couldn't help but visualize what his friend might be thinking. He remembered the depths of his own despair and how he was inches away from taking his life. The loss of his wife and child took him to the abyss and now Mike was suffering his own loss. He had lost both his faith and one of his dearest friends. Jason always seemed to bear the weight of others' grief. Knowing his friend was in distress filled him with sadness. When he knocked on the door, he could almost feel the depression from the other side.

"Mike, can you come to the door?" There was no answer. He knocked again. "Mike, can you please come to the door." Still no answer. A sinking feeling hit him. Just then something crashed within the room. "Mike, are you okay?" he yelled.

Erin came running down hall. "What's going on?"

He banged on the door. "Mike, are you okay?" Still no response.

He stepped to the other side of the hall and prepared himself to break into the room. He took a deep breath, then exhaled slowly. Just as he was about to charge across the hallway, the door suddenly swung open. He waited a few seconds for Mike to ask

178

him to come in, but he never did. Just an open door and an empty room lay in front of him. He began to enter with Erin a step behind. He turned to her and whispered.

"Stay here, okay?"

She nodded.

He stepped through the door and into the room. The bed had been slept in, but no one was there. He scanned the room from left to right, but it was empty.

"Down here." Someone said in a faint, almost childlike voice.

He spun around looking downward. Behind the door Mike lay next to a toppled floor lamp. He tried raising his hand toward Jason but dropped it.

"Help me up."

Jason quickly knelt down beside him. In a few seconds he had him over his shoulder and was carrying him to the bed. He gently laid him down.

"What happened? Are you okay?"

Mike swallowed hard, his eyes half shut. Several times his eyebrows rose as he tried to open them. After a minute he gave up and shut them completely. He began to speak in a raspy slurred whisper.

"I'm okay. Don't worry."

"Maybe he's sick," Erin said from inside the doorway.

Jason put his hand to his forehead. "Are you sick, buddy?"

"Fine, fine."

He turned and looked back at Erin and shrugged his shoulders. "How'd you fall?"

"Juz try'n to get to the door 'ta let you in," he slurred.

"Have you been drinking?" Jason asked, bending down to smell his breath.

"Nah, 'course not. Juz took a sleepy pill." His words trailed off as he fell back into a doze.

Erin ran up to the other side of the bed. "Did he say sleeping pill?"

"Yeah."

"We need to find out how many he took and when," she urged. "He could go into shock, or even a coma."

Jason grabbed him by the shoulders and shook him. "Mike, Mike wake up!"

He didn't respond.

Erin grabbed his wrist and began taking his pulse. "He's only at 35 beats! You've got to wake him up now."

He began shaking him. "Mike, you have to wake up!" he screamed. "He's not waking up." He looked up at Erin, but she was gone.

"Erin! Where are you?" he yelled.

Just then she ran back into the room with a small glass of water, a hammer, and several pieces of charred wood from the fire.

"Keep trying to wake him!" she shouted over her shoulder as she began pounding the wood with the hammer. Thirty seconds later, she had pulverized out a small pile of black powder. She scooped it up and dumped it in the glass of water, then with her finger she swirled it around until the water was a murky black.

"Here, let me get in there," she said as she took Jason's spot beside the bed. With her left hand she slid it under Mike's head and raised him up. "Wake UP!" she screamed into his ear.

One eyelid opened. "Whu?" he muttered.

"Wake the hell UP!" she screamed again.

His head swayed back and forth. "I'm up," he slurred.

"Mike, you have to wake up and drink this NOW!" she demanded.

For the first time his eyes opened fully. "Why do I...?"

Before he could finish, she was pouring the black liquid down his throat, half of it spilling out of the sides of his mouth and down

180

his chin. "Keep drinking," she urged.

He took a willing gulp, then started to gag. "Oh my gah this'z awful!"

"Keep drinking!"

He took another gulp. "Uh-uh, I can't do no more," he said and awkwardly pushed the glass away.

She gently laid his head back on the pillow, then turned to Jason. "Keep him awake. I'll be back in a minute."

He nodded his head as she ran out the door and down to her room. A moment later she returned with a small black pouch. Jason moved back out of the way so she could take his place again. With her thumb and forefinger, she reached into the bag and pulled out a plastic wrapped syringe and a vile of pink liquid. He stood in awe as she deftly peeled off the wrapper, filled the syringe with the mysterious substance, and then injected it into a large vein protruding from Mike's right arm. He didn't flinch. He just shut his eyes and drifted off to sleep.

She stood up and let out a long sigh. "Okay, that should do it."

"Is he going to be okay?" Jason asked.

"He should be fine now," she replied. "He evidently took multiple sleeping pills because his vital signs were so low. Just one sleeping pill wouldn't have had this type of effect."

"What did you give him?"

"The black stuff in the water was charcoal. It'll help absorb the remains of any of the sleeping pills he has in his system. And the pink stuff was an adrenaline and B-12 mixture, which is for boosting energy levels. When I was a nurse we'd use it in emergencies similar to this. Together, they should bring him back to a normal alert state." She took his wrist and started counting silently. "Good, his pulse is already starting to come up."

Jason smiled at her, but didn't say anything.

"What?" she said. "Why are you staring at me like that?"

"You're just amazing."

She smiled back. "Listen, I can stay here and monitor him if you'd like me to."

"Sure, actually I need to run another energy efficiency test this morning. Do you need me to do anything?"

"No, I think we'll be all right."

"Okay then." He turned and headed to the door.

"Jason," she said, catching him just as he stepped out into the hall. "Do you think he was trying to...well, you know... was trying to..."

"I don't know," he replied solemnly. "He's always been such a positive guy, but all of us have our breaking points."

She looked at him, her eyes pleading her thoughts before she even spoke. "Will you please promise me something?"

"What?"

"Promise me you won't ever consider that type of way out."

He smiled. "I've got too much to live for." Then he disappeared around the corner.

CHAPTER 24
FOUR

Jason went to his room and grabbed the cardboard box containing his calculations journal and everything he used to perform his tests. On his way outside he stopped in the kitchen and devoured a full bag of pretzels and a half rotten banana. It was another mental note to himself that his hunger was still on the rise while his own energy was diminishing. When he reached the patio he sat down at the glass top table where he had performed his previous test. He opened his journal and scribbled down the day and time. Next to it he wrote: *Hunger level rising.*

As he set up the apparatus for the food test, the steady and precise movements that had enabled him to quickly assemble it before were now shaky and much slower. After completing the setup he added a second notation in his journal: *Increased physical and mental fatigue.* He then picked up the bag of potato chips and poured out the remaining pieces onto the table. With his thumb and forefinger, he pinched off a small piece of chip and placed it in the testing device.

A few minutes later he was recording his findings in his journal. Before beginning the final calculations he silently prayed, as he had done before, that the results would be favorable. He prayed for a miracle and that somehow the energy loss had reversed itself. With each stroke of his pen, his heart beat faster. He began to perspire and his anxiety grew. By the time he had finished, it was all he could do to scribble out the remaining line of his equation. He dropped his pen and stared down at the last figure of the lengthy computation. *Four.* The number sat there on the page like an ominous symbol depicting the end of everything he had come to know.

Several seconds passed then he angrily grabbed the page, ripped it out of the journal, crumpled it and threw it to the ground. He arched his head back and drew in a long deep breath. As he exhaled, he bent over placing his head face down into the palms of his hands. With his elbows resting on his knees he sat silently breathing in and out trying to erase the results of his test, trying to figure out how to tell his friends, trying to rationalize a solution.

There were limited amounts of food and energy remaining and there was precious little time left before it was completely gone. Was there even an answer, or was it time to let go and let it all end? He was sure of his faith and sure of Erin's, but not Mike's. Over the past weeks he had seen it weakening, then after the loss of Father Tim he had seen it completely destroyed. There were still answers to be found, and for the sake of his friend he simply could not give up.

Suddenly he knew exactly what he had to do. As his idea was taking shape, the kitchen door opened and Erin came walking out.

"Mike's pulse has stabilized and he's resting comfortably now. He's out of the woods, but he'll probably be sleeping the rest of the day. So what did the test reveal?"

"Oh, I – I wasn't able to finish it," said Jason, hoping he sounded convincing.

"Really, what happened?"

"Unfortunately, several things I needed were burned up in the fire."

"Gosh, what does that mean for us now? How can we make plans if we don't know what we're up against?"

He knew he had to come up with a solid response. "It's okay. I actually think I've got enough data to make some good projections that'll help us figure things out."

Just as she was about to ask another question he quickly redirected the conversation. "Erin, last night I buried Father Tim behind the oak tree in the backyard. I wasn't able to really give him a proper service. Would you mind if we took a moment and at least said a prayer over his grave?"

She turned to the direction of the tree. "Sure. I think that would be nice," she said softly.

He took her by the hand and they silently walked to the corner of the yard. Behind the tree was a small mound of dirt next to a larger one. He still had not told her about the girl.

"Why are there two graves?"

He put his hand on his chin and looked down at the two barren patches of ground. He had seen how her courage had grown over the past months and was sure nothing at this point would faze her, with the exception of his test results from that morning. He would continue to withhold that particular piece of information until the time was right. So for the next fifteen minutes he told her about how he had discovered the girl in the boathouse. He told her how mesmerizing, gentle, and childlike she was. He told her how she had been killed. Then he explained how he had seen Father Tim bending over a mysterious man as if he were protecting him. And finally he told her why the graves were different sizes.

She was speechless. She stood looking down with her mouth hung open.

"Do you think the girl was an angel?" Her voice was full of

wonder.

He nodded. "I do. Why else would someone just explode and vaporize into thin air when they had attacked them. And Erin, the sensation I got when I touched the girl was incredible. It was like nothing I've ever experienced before with another human being. That's why I wasn't scared when we saw the man in the window."

"You think he was an angel, too?"

"Yes. His eyes and skin were just like the girl's. I'm almost sure that was who Father Tim was protecting."

"But if they're angels, how can they be killed?"

"Mike said the exact same thing. In my heart, that's just what I feel. If God sends them in this form, that's how He does it, and if they're vulnerable, then there's a reason for it. All I know is that bad things happen to those who harm them."

"Does he think they're angels?"

He slowly shook his head. "No, he thinks they're aliens. At least that's what he led me to believe before last night."

Erin looked back to the graves. "What about all the Tribulation and *Book of Revelation* stuff. Does this fit with that?"

"I'm not sure. During the Rapture or vanishings, everything was a perfect fit. I'll be honest; ever since the second blackouts I can't make heads or tails of anything. And with no TV, radio, or Internet there's no way to find out what's going on. But none of what's happened after the second blackouts is mentioned in the Bible, and I'm not a theologian so I'm not able to interpret it."

She turned back to him and placed her hand on his shoulder. "Maybe we're not supposed to. Maybe we just have to have faith."

He smiled. "Thank you for that. That's exactly what we're supposed to do."

Just then there was a slight rustling from the other side of the tree. Erin looked at him, her eyes growing wide. The sound grew louder. It sounded like something pushing through the leaves along the ground, slowly making its way through the yard toward them.

"Don't worry. It's gotta be Mike," he assured her.

He took her by the hand and they walked out from behind the tree.

Standing twenty yards away from them was a hunched figure in overalls, a flannel shirt, and work boots. Whoever it was had long white hair falling down over the face, making it impossible to tell if the person was male or female. For a moment, no one moved. Without saying a word, the person shuffled a few feet closer to them and then stopped.

Jason glanced at Erin, then back again. "Can we help you?"

Slowly the unknown visitor's head began to rise. Erin inhaled and sunk her nails into Jason's palm. As the hair from the stranger's head fell back, it revealed the face of a kindly old man with the same unearthly blue eyes as the girl from the boathouse and the man from the window. His skin was wrinkled, but of a smooth texture and it was pale but not as much as the girl's or the other man's. Jason suddenly felt a sense of security and excitement. The stranger's eyes were more than enough to convince him that he was again in the presence of another divine being. He let go of Erin's hand and stepped forward.

"Jason, wait!" she begged him.

"Don't worry, it's okay," he said as he approached the man.

"Is there some way we can help you? Are you here for something?" he asked anxiously.

The man shuffled to within five feet of him. Unlike the girl, he seemed unafraid of them. He tilted his head slightly and put his lips together as if about to speak but nothing came out.

"Are you okay?" Jason asked.

The man squinted his eyes and pushed out in a breathless wisp of air, "Wheeerrrree." The word seemed foreign and difficult for him to produce. His brow furrowed in thought, as he appeared to

187

be struggling to construct his sentence. He took a breath, then closed his eyes and made a second attempt. In a soft choppy whisper he said, "Where - am - I?"

Jason stood speechless staring at him, not knowing how to respond.

"You're in the city of Lake Royale," Erin said stepping up beside Jason.

The man opened his eyes. "Lake…"

"Lake Royale," she repeated. "It's in North Carolina."

"Which is in America," Jason added.

The man wet his lips. "I - don't – understand," he said in a slightly stronger voice. He looked down at his hands, turning his palms upward then downward again as if he were examining them. "I'm lost."

Erin looked at Jason for a response.

"Do you have family?" he asked.

The man stopped looking at his hands, then stared up at Erin. "Family?"

"Yes, do you have any family?" he asked again.

The stranger continued staring at Erin for several seconds. Then his eyes grew sad and he dropped his head. "I, I don't know."

Erin turned to Jason and whispered out of the side of her mouth. "This is crazy, but he looks vaguely familiar."

"Really?"

She turned away from the man to prevent him from hearing. "He kinda looks like my Uncle David, but he had brown eyes. And the last time I saw him was over twenty years ago, when I was just a teenager."

Jason looked back at the man. His head was still hung down and he was studying his hands again.

"Hmmm. Why don't we get him back to the house?" he said.

Together they turned back toward the stranger.

"Will you follow us?" Jason said in a slow, deliberate tone.

The man stood motionless not knowing how to answer.

Erin looked at Jason. "I'll lead him back."

"Here, let me help you, sir," she said reaching out to take him by the hand. As her hand drew within a few inches of his a tiny arch of electricity jumped from his forefinger to her index finger, sending a tingling sensation running up her arm. "Ahhhh!" she jerked her hand back.

The sudden reaction startled the stranger, causing him to lose his footing and stumble. Right before he was about to fall, she jumped forward and grabbed him around the chest. As she stood there holding him steady there was a sudden loud pop above them, followed by a crackling noise and a steady hum. Then ZAP! Jason looked up just in time to see the spotlight Mike had installed at the top of the oak tree come on.

He looked at Erin, then back up at the light. "What the...!"

Erin slowly stepped back from the man. "I, I'm sorry!" she said timidly. "I didn't mean to alarm you. I was just..."

The man held up his hand. "It's okay." His words were raspy, but clearer and fuller than before.

For a moment no one spoke. Jason continued to process what he had just seen while Erin composed herself. Finally, the stranger broke the silence.

"I just don't know."

"Don't know what, sir?" he asked.

The man looked to the sky, then back to the ground. He began to slowly turn in a circle, looking in every direction and examining everything in his sight. "Where I am, or who I am," he said.

Jason's hands began to tremble. He couldn't contain himself any longer. He had to ask.

"Are you an angel?"

The man blinked. "An angel?" He touched his chest, then felt the sides of his face. "Am I dead? Is this heaven?"

Jason's heart sank. God could surely send his messengers in whatever form He chose, but how could they not know who they were? His rational mind began taking over. Suddenly, his faith was on the line. "No, this isn't heaven," he said softly.

Erin saw the dejection on Jason's face. She slid her arm around his, then whispered in his ear, "It's okay." With her other hand, she slowly reached out to the stranger. "Will you come with us?"

He looked at her with his shimmering blue eyes, then down at her outstretched hand. There was no trepidation as he reached up and wrapped his fingers gently around hers. The moment their skin touched, the tingling sensation shot up her arm again. She flinched but instead of recoiling she gripped his hand tighter. At the same time the light above them hummed louder. For a few seconds they didn't move. She closed her eyes and took a long deep breath. As she slowly exhaled, a smile crossed her face. Then she opened her eyes.

"Okay, let's go," she said.

Slowly they began walking toward the house. When they reached the patio, Jason turned his head back to the tree and up to the light. Even from so far away, he could still hear the steady hum of electricity flowing through its circuits.

CHAPTER 25
THE CONNECTION

The time it had taken them to walk back to the house was enough to send Jason's thoughts flying in every direction. Angel or not, he had just witnessed a supernatural phenomenon that was the direct result of Erin's contact with the stranger they were now befriending.

As they walked through the kitchen door he asked her, "Would you mind taking our guest to Father Tim's room and settling him in? I'm feeling really light-headed and need to get something to eat."

"Sure," she said. Then she turned to the man. "Are you hungry?"

He shook his head.

"What about you?" Jason asked. "Do you want anything?"

She thought for a moment. "No, I'm good." Her face lit up. "In fact, I feel great."

Jason gave her a puzzled look as she led the man out of the room and down the hall. How could it be that she was so chipper and he felt like he had just run five miles? He opened the door to the pantry and surveyed the half empty shelves. All that remained were canned goods and boxed cereals. If his calculations held up, they would be out of rations and starving within a week. He pulled out a can of beans and franks and in less than ten spoonfuls had finished it off while standing. Still hungry, he grabbed a second can and sat down at the table. As he was about to peel back the top, Erin walked in. Her face was beaming.

"Jason, how awesome is this?"

"You mean our new guest?"

"Of course," she squealed. "What just happened was incredible. You wouldn't believe what I felt when he touched me. It, it was like a river of energy rushing through me. It felt so good. I was worn out this morning, but when I held his hand it was like all these cobwebs were washed away and I felt great. I actually feel better now than I have in weeks! Did you feel the same thing when you touched the girl in the boathouse?"

"I did get a tingling up and down my arm, but that was about it. So how is he doing now?"

"He's just sitting in the chair next to the bed."

"Is he okay?"

"Yeah, he seems to be fine. I didn't ask him a bunch of questions because if he's got amnesia or something it's not wise to force things. At least that's what I remember from nursing school."

"Yeah, I think you're right. We'll wait a little while."

He looked over at the pantry door and thought about the depleted contents on the other side. "Erin, can you sit down a second. There's something I need to tell you."

She looked at him warily as she pulled out a chair and sat down with her back to the hall entrance. "I've heard that tone before. What's wrong?"

He pivoted his chair toward her and then dragged it up to where their knees were touching. "Remember the test I was supposed to do this morning?"

"Yeah."

"Well, I…" he stopped for a second, then reached out and took both of her hands in his. He looked down racking his brain to find the best way to tell her that their world was about to end in less than a week.

"What is it?" she begged.

As he raised his head to answer he was shocked to find the stranger standing in the kitchen doorway directly behind her. His appearance was different than before. His skin was no longer pale, but full of color and his cheeks were even rosy. But the most remarkable change was his eyes. The alluring ice blue had changed to a normal everyday dark brown. He gazed at the transformation in amazement.

"What is it?" she said turning around to see the object of his attention.

"Oh, my God!" She exclaimed pushing her chair back. "You startled me."

For a moment, neither she nor Jason said anything as they sat staring at him, examining the radical changes.

The stranger's face was expressionless, and then ever so slowly the corners of his mouth turned upward into a smile. "Erin?" he said drawing out both syllables in a gentle, southern drawl.

"Yes," she replied.

"Erin - Bannister?"

She sat motionless as she processed the sound of her last name and the fact that he somehow knew it. Suddenly she stood up with her hand to her chest.

Jason looked on, stunned by the revelation that the stranger knew this information, but more so by Erin's reaction.

She inched toward him. "You - You, know me don't you?"

He nodded, his smile becoming more confident.

She took two more steps toward him then stopped. Her eyes

encircled his face as she inspected every curve and wrinkle. He stood patiently, allowing her to absorb the physical signs that would help her remember.

A moment passed. "Oh my!" she gushed. "It's you, Uncle David. It really is you!"

His smile widened as tears began to roll down his cheeks.

She threw her arms around his neck. Simultaneously, the kitchen light exploded above them, the garbage disposal began grinding away, and the blender blasted on with such force it sent the top flying in the air. It was a three-ring circus of noise…beautiful, electrically-generated noise.

Jason spun around, astonished by the effects of the mysterious power surge around him, while Erin and her uncle remained oblivious to the phenomenon their embrace was creating. For the second time that morning he was observing the power these two beings could create. He couldn't help but smile. Suddenly he burst out laughing.

"Erin!" he shouted. "Look around." He put his hand on her shoulder. "Look! Every appliance is running." He reached over and turned on a small table lamp. "Everything in this friggin' room is running!"

She let go of her uncle and turned to him. "WOW! It is!"

"Can you believe it?"

"But how?" she asked.

"I have absolutely no idea," he said while laughing. "But isn't it incredible?"

"We don't have another generator, do we?"

"No. It all happened when you hugged our guest, I mean, your uncle. And it happened earlier when we were out by the tree. Do you know what this means?"

She looked back at the stranger standing in the doorway and smiled. "I know it means I've found a dear uncle I haven't seen in over twenty years."

"Yeah," he nodded as he turned off the blender and garbage disposal, "that's definitely true. But it also means that there's some sort of connection with him that can produce electricity." He turned and looked out the window contemplating all of the possibilities. "In fact, he could even have some sort of reverse effect on the energy loss."

Erin's uncle ambled up next to him. "Not sure what all that meant," he said in a clear, southern drawl.

Jason smiled at him. "Sir, are you starting to remember other things now?"

He averted his eyes downward. "Not really," he said sadly.

"So how did you know Erin was your niece?"

"It just came to me when she touched me out back."

"So you don't know where you're from or how you got here?"

"No." he hesitated. "Only thing I remember is light - lots of light."

"What do you mean 'light'? When did you see it? Where did it come from?"

"I, I don't know. I can't put it in to words." He winced and put his hand to his temple. "I get a headache if I try to think on it too long."

Jason nodded. "That's okay, sir. Don't worry about it."

"Sonny, I wish I could help but I don't even know my last name." He turned to Erin and put his hand over his heart then reached out with his other one and took her hand. "All I know is that I'm David, and this pretty young lady is my niece." His movements were slow and deliberate, just as his speech was rich with southern charm. It was obvious why Erin would have adored him in her youth.

Jason put his hand on his shoulder. "Actually, you can help." He turned to Erin. "Would you mind if I ran some tests with your uncle?"

"I don't know. Why don't you ask him?"

Before he could ask, her uncle chimed in, "I'm okay with it. But will it hurt?"

"No, not at all. I just want to test your sphere of influence."

"My what?"

"Sorry about that. I just want to see if the effect you have with Erin is the same with others." He reached over and turned off the small lamp, then turned it back on again. Nothing happened. "Hmmm."

"What's the *hmmm* for?" Erin asked.

"Will you hug David again?"

"Sure."

She bounced in front of her uncle and wrapped her arms around him. Immediately, the lamp came on.

"Okay, you can let him go now." He turned the lamp off, then back on. "Good," he muttered to himself. He looked out the window toward the spotlight in the oak tree and saw that it had gone out.

"What's going on in that scientific brain of yours?" Erin inquired.

"I expected this to be the case. It appears your uncle's effects are temporary. The reaction is creating enough energy to power things up for a period of time, but then it dies out. It's just natural. There's no continuous energy source like our power plants used to provide."

"So is that it for testing?"

"I've got one more." He reached over and placed the lamp next to her uncle. "Let's see if you can light me up too," he said with a grin.

Jason walked in front of him and stretched out his arms. "All right, here we go!"

Uncle David lifted his chin high and straightened his body into a military grade posture. His arms pinned closely to his side.

Jason chuckled. "At ease soldier, I'm not going to hurt you."

"Sorry," he apologized, dropping his chin and shoulders, "maybe I was in the military or something."

"Holy cow!" Erin shouted. "You *were* in the military. I remember it now. That's why I didn't see you for all those years. When I was a teenager you went into the service and were shipped overseas. No one saw you for years because you stayed abroad after you were discharged. I went off to college and we lost touch after that. Oh, wow! Do you remember any of this?"

His wrinkled face contorted as he struggled for a memory. He shook his head. "I'm sorry. I don't remember any of it."

"Not to worry." Jason said. "I'm sure everything will come back to you over time. In the meanwhile, would you like to take a break?"

"Oh no, I'm fine. We can go on."

"Are you sure?"

"Yep, I'm ready when you are."

"All right," Jason said as he awkwardly put his arms around him and gave him a limp hug. The light flickered on, then off. He stepped back. "Let's try again. This time you hug me instead." With an unexpected enthusiasm, Erin's uncle threw his arms around Jason, burying his entire upper body, including his head, in a hearty bear hug. After about fifteen seconds Jason, tapped him on the shoulder.

"Okay, Okay," he said in a muffled voice. "That's enough."

Uncle David opened his arms and Jason staggered back against the kitchen table.

"Wow! You sure do know how to deliver a hug."

Erin laughed. "That's one thing I also remember about him. He loved a good bear hug."

"So, what happened with the light?" Jason asked.

"It came on just as he wrapped you up, but then went out a few seconds later."

Uncle David turned to Jason. "Is there anything else I can help you with? Whatever you need me to do, I'll do it." His desire to please was apparent and it touched Jason to see how appreciative he was for taking him in.

"I do have one other little thing, but it'll have to wait."

"Just let me know when. In the meantime, do you think I can ask you folks a favor?"

"Absolutely," Erin said.

"Is there any way I could get a cup of coffee?"

"Oh, I'm afraid we can't get the coffee maker working because it needs…" she stopped and looked at him. "No, I think we can arrange that," she said with a big grin. "It's just going to cost you one big hug!"

Jason smiled as he stepped out into the hallway. "Listen, I'm going to check on Mike while you two conjure up your brew. Just make sure not to blow any fuses in the process."

Several minutes later he returned to find Erin and her uncle sitting at the kitchen table chatting over two warm cups of coffee.

"How's he doing?" she asked

"He's still asleep."

"Did you check his pulse?"

"Yep, I checked all his vital signs and everything's normal again."

Just then something banged against the kitchen doorway. "Why, I'm in tip-top shape," Mike said as he staggered around the corner.

"Mike! You shouldn't be up," Erin exclaimed jumping to her feet.

Jason turned around just in time to catch him as he stumbled into the room.

"What the hell are you doing?" he said, helping him into a chair.

His head slumped down onto the kitchen table with his mouth pressed hard against the Formica top. "When you leave a room," he slurred, "you make a ruckus, like a big ole cow."

Erin pushed her cup of coffee in front of him. "Here, you need this more than me."

He lifted his head and stared at it.

She grabbed the paper cup and lifted it to his mouth.

"Okay, okay, I got it," he said, snatching it away from her and guzzling it down. He smashed the cup against his head then let out an obnoxious burp.

"How's that?" he asked.

"Impressive," Jason said blandly. "Listen, don't you think you need to get back to bed?"

Erin walked over to the kitchen sink and ran cold water over a dishtowel. "Actually, it may be best if he stays awake." She walked up behind him and placed it on his neck.

"Whoa!" He reached around, grabbed the towel and threw it back toward the sink. "I'm awake already. I promise." His speech was suddenly much clearer.

She leaned over and looked into his eyes. "Pupils are back to normal."

"I told you," he chided. "Honestly, I'm awake and actually I feel…" He stopped and looked at Erin's uncle as if he had suddenly appeared from thin air. "Hey, who's he?"

"This is my Uncle David," she said.

"Your uncle?"

"Yeah. While you were out, he came to us. We're not sure how he found us or why he's here, but it's a blessing for sure."

Mike looked at the elderly man suspiciously. "What do you mean you don't know how he got here? Didn't you ask him?"

She put her hand on his shoulder. "It's a long story. Trust me for now, he's our friend."

"I really am her uncle," the elderly man said as he reached across the table to shake Mike's hand. "I really want to thank you fine folks for taking me in."

Jason leaned forward as the last request he had mentioned wanting from Erin's uncle was about to happen without him even having to ask. Slowly, Mike stretched out his arm and grabbed his hand.

"Glad to meet you," he said, half-heartedly stifling a yawn.

There were neither sparks nor an electrical surge of any kind, not even enough tingling to cause him to flinch or jerk away.

CHAPTER 26
THE QUEST

Jason looked on, waiting for even the smallest reaction from their handshake – a spark, a flicker of a nearby light, anything. Erin's connection with her uncle resulted in large power surges and his had even created a minor electrical spike. Mike's contact with him did nothing. His assumption that Erin's uncle could induce power through contact with others was false. His notion that he could somehow supply them with enough power to survive was nothing more than wishful thinking. Nevertheless, there was hope, but along with it came more questions, questions he wasn't capable of answering on his own. He was again at a dead end, and so his plan further crystallized.

Over the next twenty minutes, he carefully watched Mike as he grew more coherent. When he was finally convinced his friend could comprehend it, he asked Erin to tell him about their initial encounter with her uncle. He then politely excused himself and headed to his bedroom. As he walked down the hall, numbers and equations began filling his head. Over and over he continued calculating the same figures.

He entered his room and began stuffing a duffle bag with

clothes and other essentials, as he would to ready himself for a weekend getaway. All the while he continued to silently work the numbers and prayed for a different result. Once the bag was filled he threw it over his shoulder and headed outside to some bushes where he had hidden his motorcycle. He pulled it upright and wheeled it next to the gas grill on the backyard patio.

For nearly a half hour he feverishly worked to remove the grill's tank and then attach it to the back fender of his bike. As the transformation progressed, all his number crunching was replaced with thoughts of strategy for his own survival. As he tightened the last screw to secure the tank to the motorcycle, the kitchen door opened.

"You coming back in?" Erin asked.

He tossed the screwdriver onto the table and headed for the door. "Sorry about that, I was just fixing my bike."

"How?"

"I'll tell you in a minute," he said as he passed by her on his way into the house.

She shut the door behind them. Her uncle and Mike were still sitting at the table.

"I really missed a lot when I was out," Mike said looking over his shoulder to him. "Erin told me everything."

"Everything?"

"Yep," she said.

Jason looked him up and down. "You seem to be feeling better."

"I am now. The sleeping pills' effects have pretty much worn off and Erin fixed me something to eat."

"That's good. I need you to be lucid to help me with something. Can you come with me a second?"

"Sure."

They walked out of the kitchen and into the living room.

Jason pointed to the sofa. "You might want to sit down for this."

Mike quietly obliged. "This is going to be serious, isn't it?"

"As serious as it gets," he replied walking across the room and back. He stopped and cleared his throat. "Before I begin, did Erin really tell you everything?"

"I guess. I mean how would I know if she didn't?"

"True. Did she tell you about the first time we met her uncle and how similar his appearance was to the girl in the boathouse and the man she and I saw at the window?"

"Yeah. By the way, the man you guys saw is who Father Tim was protecting when he was blown up."

"So what actually did happen that night?"

Mike looked out the window and sighed. "It all began when Father Tim started talking to me on the back patio about how strong my beliefs were. If I believed in angels and demons, God, the end of times, all those things. Then all of a sudden he saw the man at the window. You know how fast he could run. Well, he bolts over to him and doesn't tackle him, but more or less puts him in one of those wrestling holds of his. I'm still standing on the patio, watching in amazement, when he suddenly lets the man go, puts his arm around him and starts walking him back my way."

"As he's coming toward me I hear two guys jumping the fence in the backyard. Like an idiot, and without thinking, I run toward them. They begin shooting at me. Father Tim was yelling for me to shoot back, but I didn't have a gun." He stopped and hung his head down. "If only I had my gun he'd still be here." He paused for a moment as his eyes filled with tears. "When I looked back, I saw him next to the gas tanks. He was bending down over that man and he had his back toward the guys who were shooting. He was actually protecting him! That's the type of person he was. That's how he treated me all the years I knew him." He wiped his eyes. "Evidently, they began shooting at him too, and one of the bullets hit a gas tank."

"What happened to the guys doing the shooting?"

"When the tanks blew, they jumped back over the fence. I guess it was the gas they were after."

Jason put his hand on his shoulder. "I'm so sorry. I truly am."

Mike looked up at him forcing a smile. "So was that what you wanted to talk to me about?"

He shook his head. "Unfortunately not." He walked to the corner of the room and dragged a chair out in front of the sofa. He sat down with his hands clasped in front of him, then leaned forward. "There's no way to tiptoe around this, plus we don't have much time so I'm going to get right to it. I ran another test this morning to determine our food and fuel efficiencies and the results were bad."

"How bad?"

He took a deep swallow. "We have approximately four days left until all our energy sources are entirely depleted."

"WHAT! Are you sure?"

"I'm positive."

"What if we're able to find more food or fuel?"

"That's not what I'm talking about. What I'm saying is that none of our resources will have any effect. After four days, nothing we eat will have any caloric value. No matter how much we take in, it won't help. The planet is in its death throes."

"Wait a minute!" Mike's eyes lit up. "What about Erin's uncle? They showed me how together they could make energy! Isn't that a type of power source we could tap into?"

"I - I don't know. I'm sure it's a possibility. I just don't have the knowledge to determine if it has any impact on our food supplies. It's simply beyond my abilities."

"How about the way it made her feel? She told me when she

hugs or touches him, she feels invigorated and even her hunger subsides."

"That's true. It does appear to have that effect. I even experienced it. It wasn't as strong as what she felt, but I did feel it when I touched him. I also felt it with the girl in the boathouse. I do believe Erin and her uncle will survive longer because their connection is so powerful. And based upon what I felt, I think there's even a possibility I could probably survive longer.

"What about me?" Mike asked. "Maybe I have a connection with him. Maybe my chances of surviving are longer?"

Jason shook his head. "I'm sorry, Mike, there's not a connection with you."

He stood up. "How do you know that?"

"Because you've already been in contact with him."

"No, I haven't!"

"But you have. Remember when you shook hands at the table?"

"Yeah."

"Did you feel anything, an electrical surge or a tingle of any kind?"

"Well, no, but…"

"I watched the entire interaction hoping there'd be some sign of an electrical spike, but there wasn't any."

Mike plopped back onto the sofa and buried his head in his hands. "I'm screwed. We're all screwed," he muttered under his breath.

Jason pulled his chair directly in front of him. "I don't know what these connections mean or why certain people are affected the way they are. Maybe there's a possibility everyone could benefit from them. All I do know is that I have to try to find out, and I'm going to need help."

Mike raised his head. "But I don't know squat about physics or science. I'm just a tech guy and without Internet I can't even do that." He dropped his head back into his palms. "I'm useless."

"Don't say that." He leaned forward and put his hand on his friend's shoulder. "If it weren't for you, I wouldn't have the leads I need for finding Teech."

Mike dropped his hands to his side and straightened up. "Teech. What're you planning?"

"There's only one man that I know who could possibly have the answers, and it's Richard Teech."

"Why him, and what answers are you talking about?"

"He's been the lead scientist on all these supernatural phenomena since they began. If these blue-eyed beings have any connection to it, he'll know."

"These blue-eyed beings you're talking about are just regular people. Their skin and eyes change back to normal. I know you think they're angels, but they're not. They're just everyday people who've had something different happen to them during these blackouts and after a while it wears off."

"What about the video, the rain, the girl who just appeared from out of the sky?" Jason contended. "None of that was normal."

"Erin's tape had to be bad."

Jason pursed his lips as he suppressed his frustration. "Whether they're angels or not, I believe these individuals are here for a reason or they've been changed for a reason. If there's any chance they can guide or assist in our survival, we need to know how, and Teech is the one who'll be able to tell us."

Mike shook his head. "Man, this is such a long shot. We can't even get in touch with him. Before the Internet went down completely, all I could find out was that he was in D.C."

"Yeah, and he was staying at the Watergate Hotel. That's all I need."

"But he could be long gone by now."

"Maybe not. Remember, we're some of the lucky ones who even have transportation."

Mike laughed. "Transportation? The last time I checked our car was blown to kingdom come by two thugs trying to steal our gas."

"But not the motorcycle."

He rolled his eyes. "D.C. is almost four hours from here. Your motorcycle won't have enough gas to get there and back, even if it does get a lot better gas mileage than a car. And what about the decrease in fuel efficiency?"

"I've been doing calculations and with the reserve tank I just added and figuring in for the rate of efficiency loss, there'll be just enough to make the round trip."

"Just enough to make the trip. Do you know how absurd that sounds?"

He nodded. "I know, but I love you and Erin enough to take the risk."

Mike stood up and stared at him for a moment then smiled. "Well, if you're crazy enough to want to try it, then I'm just insane enough to go along for the ride. When do we leave?"

"Thanks buddy, but this is a trip I'll have to take on my own."

"What?"

"Someone has to stay here with Erin and her uncle. Besides, my calculations only allow for one person's weight on the bike."

"Jason, I can't let you go alone. It's too dangerous."

"It'll still be dangerous here, as well. You have to stay and protect the others."

"Are you sure about this? What if you're lucky enough to find him and he doesn't have any answers? Then what?"

"Then at least I'll have tried." He paused. "You just have to have faith."

Mike groaned. "The little faith I had went up in that damn explosion."

"Don't say that. We've come so far and there's still a chance. You have to believe."

"Nothing I've believed in has worked out, so why should I start now?"

Jason understood his friend's anguish. Although it had been almost seven months since his wife and daughter had vanished, he still felt the pain. The only difference was that his faith had grown stronger while Mike's had died.

He took his friend by the shoulders. "Look at me, Mike. There's not much time left. Yes, it's a long shot, but we have to take it. To make it happen you *have* to believe - now more than ever!"

Mike looked back at the kitchen door. "I'll stay here and do the best I can to protect them, and I'll do my best to believe that you'll make it back. Just don't ask me to believe in anything more. If you want me to truly believe in angels and that Father Tim died for one, or that there is a God, then get your ass back here with some proof."

Jason wanted to shake him and explain that faith wasn't based on proof, but he didn't have any more time for debating. He simply had to make it back.

"I'm going to. I promise." He paused. "Come on now, I need some help."

"What do you need?"

"I've got to go make one more adjustment to the motorcycle. Can you go tell Erin and her uncle what's going on? But whatever you do, please don't tell them about the four days. Erin's toughened up so much, but that type of information could send anybody over the edge."

"I promise." Mike started to say something else but stopped. He felt guilty for venting to his friend and wanted to apologize, but it seemed too late. Nothing mattered anymore. They would all be dead soon and that was the one thing he was sure of. He just nodded, then turned and walked into the kitchen.

For the next fifteen minutes he masked his emotions with false hope, as he told Erin and her uncle of how Jason was going to find Teech. He described how Jason had it all planned and asked them not to worry. It would only take a few days and when he returned he'd have the answers they needed to survive in the hell that their world had become.

CHAPTER 27
A LONELY ROAD

Jason threw his leg over the seat of his motorcycle and started the engine. At the same time, Erin came flying out the back crying. She ran up to him and wrapped her arms around him, almost knocking him over.

"You big idiot! You don't have to do this!"

He cut the engine. "Now, listen to me Erin." His voice was resolute, yet comforting. "This is something I have to do."

"But why? If Kristina were here, she'd want you to stay. Please do it for her."

"I *am* doing it for her. I'm doing it for her and Nikki. I'm doing it for all of us. "

"Then, can't we all go?"

"It's actually safer if I do this alone." His stomach churned as the deception of the statement weighed down on him. "It'll also be much faster. I'll be back in a day or two. I promise."

Mike and her uncle had come up behind her and were now standing next to them.

"You weren't going to leave before saying goodbye were you?" Mike said.

"No, of course not. I was just cranking the engine to make sure it started okay."

"Have you got everything you need?"

He leaned down and picked up his duffle bag. "I've got some clothes, a bag full of protein bars, and canned food. It's enough to last me there and back."

"How about this?" Mike said reaching into his pocket and pulling out his handgun. "I hope you don't need it, but better safe than sorry."

"I'll be right back," Erin said as she turned and ran into the house.

Jason took the gun and stared at it for a moment. "Yeah, I hope I don't need it either, considering I don't even know how to shoot one."

A moment later she returned with a small black pouch.

"Is that the bag of adrenaline B-12 shots you used on Mike?"

"Yep," she said stuffing it into his duffle bag. "There are two vials left. They'll give you an energy boost in case you need it."

He looked down at the gun in his hand and smiled. "I thought that's what this was for." Then he placed it in his bag and started to zip it up.

"Wait, don't forget this," Erin said handing him one of the pagers Mike had given them during their strategy meeting.

He raised his eyebrows. "Anything else? Alarm clock, kitchen sink, maybe a fruitcake, or some other nice parting gift?"

Erin wiped a tear from her cheek. "Listen, smarty pants, just get your butt back."

He smiled. "Don't worry. I will."

She hugged him, then stepped back as her uncle leaned forward and patted him on the shoulder. "Come home safe, son. We'll be praying for you."

All the while Mike stood looking at him as he tried to

comprehend the magnitude of his friend's decision to risk his life for them.

"Are you absolutely sure this is the right thing to do?"

"I'm positive," he said with a nod.

Mike stepped closer to him. "You know, this is going to be like finding a needle in a haystack, don't you?"

"No need to worry," he smiled. "I'll be stopping for directions along the way."

Mike glanced at the others then leaned down and whispered into his ear. "Damn it. I'm serious."

"I am, too. I'm stopping at Silas McCain's house. It's just off highway 95 this side of Richmond – it's more or less halfway to D.C."

"Who's Silas McCain?"

"Remember, he's the teaching buddy I used to work with that knows Teech? He might have some info about him I can use. It will probably be getting dark by the time I get there, so it's the perfect stopping point."

"I don't care how you plan to get there, but I am counting on you to get back. With or without answers, you get back here okay?" Mike quickly wiped his eyes before the tears touched his cheeks.

Jason stood up. Straddling the seat, he reached out and wrapped his arms around his friend. "Don't worry, my brother. I'm coming home." He leaned back, threw his duffle bag over his shoulder and with a quick kick, his motorcycle rumbled to life. "Just remember," he shouted over the pounding pistons, "HAVE FAITH!" He smiled and put on his helmet. With a quick wave, off he went speeding down the driveway.

As he pulled onto the street, a mix of emotions washed over him. He felt sorry about leaving his friends, but knew that what he was doing was for the greater good. He was excited about the possibilities of what he might learn and how important his task was, but at the same time he was fearful of the danger his endeavor promised. Despite this, a sense of freedom and peace was enveloping him, since he knew he was approaching a point of resolution. He was putting everything in God's hands. Whatever dangers he may encounter or whatever the final outcome, he knew he would be reunited with his beloved Kristina and Nikki.

Back at the house the three remaining friends started to head back inside. As they walked up to the door, a breeze swept through the yard sending leaves and debris swirling around them. Several leaves, along with a crumpled piece of paper, floated onto the doormat in front of them. Erin bent down to pick up the paper, intending to throw it in the trash, when she noticed Jason's handwriting on it. She unfolded it quickly and scanned the mishmash of numbers and computations. She stopped, unable to process the final figure of the page.

Scratched out in bold labored strokes was the number *4*. Next to it were the words *days left*. Her chest contracted, as all the air rushed from her lungs. It was as if she had just read her own obituary. The paper fell from her fingertips and drifted to the ground. She turned and gazed down the driveway as the sound of the lone motorcycle faded in the distance.

The roads and highways were barren and wide open spaces free of chaos. There were no long lines or traffic jams, just abandoned cars and trucks everywhere. Jason had started his journey with a wary eye. Every second he was flashing from one side of the road to the other waiting for the ambush he was sure would come. Except for the occasional stray dog or cat, the landscape was devoid of life.

After a while his confidence began to rise. His fear of being attacked was disappearing, but now the inevitable foe he knew was going to strike was stirring from within. He was already starting to feel tired and weak. The energy loss he had so accurately computed was starting to take its toll. Up until now he'd been able to eat and replenish his energy as needed, but after an hour and a half on the road he hadn't dared to stop once. By the time he reached Silas McCain's house, it was dusk and his stomach was in knots.

McCain's home was on a small hill at the top of the highway off-ramp next to an old abandoned gas station. Quite fitting, Jason thought, considering how rundown it was. Most homes now had their share of neglect, but this was an exception. It was a shabby split level with tattered aluminum siding. Streaks of rust ran down the sides giving the appearance it was bleeding. Two-foot high weeds had choked out every blade of grass, and with the exception of a narrow gravel path running up to the front door, there was no access to it. Like so many homes, all the windows were boarded up. But something was different. His had been built with a cross shaped opening in the middle. A rather odd symbol, considering he remembered McCain to be a staunch atheist.

As he pulled up to the front of the house he panned the yard for signs of life. There was no movement anywhere. The amber hue from the day's final light cast a hopeless feeling about the property and a sense of dread came over him. What if McCain had abandoned the house? It certainly looked as if he had. Or what if he had been killed? What if someone else was waiting inside to do the same to him?

He stared at the small stoop leading to front door. It was guarded by two overgrown cypress trees, engulfing it like the shadowy entrance to a cave. As much as he wanted to turn around and get back on the road, he knew he had to stick with his plan. He had come this far and he was tired and needed shelter. Most importantly, he needed any information he could get about Teech.

Stepping off his motorcycle, he reached into his duffle bag and pulled out the gun Mike had given him. He stuffed it into his pocket and took several apprehensive steps toward the house. This was the first time in months he had ventured into anyone else's domain. The common act of knocking on someone else's door was now surreal and full of foreboding. His heartbeat quickened as he inched his way onto the stoop.

"Stop right there!" barked a deep male voice from the other side of the door.

He froze. A bead of sweat rolled down his temple. He started to reach for his gun, but realized he was being watched. Any threatening move could cost him his life.

"Who are you?" demanded the voice.

"My name is Jason. Jason Sto..."

"What do you want?" the voice clipped him off with a growl.

He looked around searching for a peephole or crack through a window where he could identify himself to the person on the other side.

"I'm looking for Silas McCain. My name's Jason Stover, and I used to work with him."

Several seconds passed.

"Why do you want him?" This time the reply was more even-toned.

"I need some information about a friend of his."

"Go the hell away!"

"Wait, wait," he stammered searching for the right response, "that's true, I'm looking for information but I have some for him too – information that could help save his life.

Again, there was silence. He took a deep breath as he waited for a reply. His head was starting to ache from lack of food. Suddenly it gave him an idea. He blurted out. "Tell him I also have food."

Immediately the door jarred against its frame, coupled with the sound of metal scraping against metal. Following in quick succession were the sounds of deadbolts and chains being unlatched. The handle jiggled once then stopped. Slowly the door creaked open.

He inhaled while inconspicuously sliding his hand into his pocket and around his gun. Inch by inch the door swung open revealing nothing more than when it was shut. It was as if the very air behind it had been painted black.

Sweat fell down his face, burning his eyes as he struggled to find a silhouette or even a shadow of something on the other side. From out of the darkness, a pale hand reached across the threshold then withdrew back inside.

Jason stared motionless into the pitch-black opening.

"Come in," the voice requested.

He remained fixed, gripping his handgun. Just as he was about to pull it from his pocket a tiny fireball crackled to life from inside the doorway. He watched as a matchstick hovered through the air and onto the end of a cigarette hanging loosely from the outline of a man's lips.

"You don't have to be afraid," the man said sending the red-hot edges of the tobacco bouncing up and down.

"Silas? Is that you?"

The cigarette burned brighter as the man pulled the nicotine into his lungs. Then with a long exhale he filled the entrance with a cloud of smoke. "Yes, it's me," he replied flatly.

Jason sighed as his anxiety subsided. "Man oh man, am I glad it's you. I've got something to tell you and I was hoping to get…"

"You said you had food."

"Uh, yeah, I - I do. Let me go get my backpack."

He leapt off the stoop and ran out to grab his bag. When he returned there was no one there. He stood at the door's edge and leaned into the darkness.

"Where'd you go?" He hesitated a moment then stepped inside.

PHWAM! The door flew shut behind him followed by the manic sounds of deadbolts and door latches locking shut.

He dropped his bag and spun around waving his arms blindly. "What the hell! Who was that? Silas, is that you!"

"Yes, yes, calm down damn it!" he barked.

"Why'd you shut the door?"

There was no answer, only the sound of feet shuffling about the room. He tried backing himself toward the door, but kept running into furniture. He reached into his pocket and pulled out his gun.

"Tell me what's going on or I..."

Another match lit.

"Or what?" Silas said placing the flame to a candle's wick.

Instantly the room filled with flickering light, revealing to Jason the haggard features of the man he had once worked with and called a friend. The last time they had seen each other Silas was a strapping, clean-shaven, health buff with tightly cropped jet-black hair. Jason was aghast at the depth of his transformation. His once robust two hundred pound frame was at least forty pounds lighter, and his head was a scraggly mess of long hair and an unkempt beard. Both were knotted with streaks of gray and his ruddy complexion was now ashen and weathered. He wore a dirty beige bathrobe held closed by a large leather belt, and a machete was affixed to its side.

Jason eyed him cautiously, wondering why his former colleague had yet to acknowledge their friendship. He watched him take a drag on his cigarette and then nervously blow it toward him. His movements were quick and jerky, each one Jason interpreted as a stronger warning to keep his distance. Unconsciously, Jason's eyes fixated on the machete as he waited for any form of cordial response.

"So, where is it?" Silas asked gruffly.

"Where's what?" he replied, still staring at the weapon.

"The food you said you had. Can't you see I'm starving here?"

"Oh, oh yeah. I'm sorry, I forgot." He grabbed his duffle bag and held it out as his offering.

Silas leaned over and looked inside, then smiled.

"I'll take it all."

"Really? But I'm going to need…"

Silas burst into a cackling laughter, then stopped abruptly.

"Relax, I'm just kidding."

"Oh, thank you," he sighed.

"I will take half though. It's been a couple of days since I've been able to bag a decent meal." He glanced over to a heap of fur piled in a corner. Jason's stomach turned, realizing they were the remains of some dead creature.

Silas took another hit from his cigarette. Then he reached in, helping himself to protein bars and cans of food, and shoving them into his pockets.

Jason watched helplessly as his supply was promptly cut in half.

When his pockets were full, Silas pulled out one last bar. He stood marveling at it, the way one would gaze upon a precious jewel. Then with a snarl he ripped into it with his teeth. In seconds he devoured the entire bar along with a third of its wrapper. When the feeding frenzy was over, he wiped his mouth with his sleeve. Then he stared up at Jason like a wolf that had just tasted its first drop of blood.

Jason took a wobbly step back as Silas slowly moved his hand onto his machete. As he wrapped his fingers around the blade's handle, his eyes widened displaying their glassy yellow tint. Slowly, he pulled the machete from its sheath. Fiery tongues of candlelight flickered against the blade.

"It's time," he whispered.

CHAPTER 28
THE TALLY MAN COMETH

Jason pulled his gun and pointed it directly at Silas's face. His hand was trembling uncontrollably. He had never shot a gun, let alone aimed one at somebody.

"Don't come a step closer!"

Silas stared down the shaky barrel for a second, then began moving toward him.

"I said don't come any closer!"

Silas slowly raised his hand. Jason's body stiffened. He suddenly had no control over his own reflexes. He could neither fire nor retract the weapon.

"Get that thing out of my face," he said defiantly as he brushed by him on his way to the other side of the room.

Jason watched him place his machete onto a small table, then reach around and pull out a rifle. He clicked the lever, sending a bullet into the firing chamber, then turned and glared into his eyes with a contempt born from months of living in desperation. Jason's heart pounded. His knees grew weak and the sweat on his palms caused him to almost lose grip of his weapon.

Silas tilted his head and snarled, "If you're going to use that thing you might want to put your finger on the trigger."

He made a quick glance at his gun hand, validating his own error. He didn't know whether to be angry or embarrassed at Silas's observation. All he knew was his own humanity was in jeopardy. He'd gone his whole life without ever losing control or even coming close to hurting another person. And now he was on the verge of killing a man he had once considered a friend.

But this wasn't the same Silas McCain. Physically, he was a fraction of the man he once knew. Mentally, he was even less. The aftermath of the vanishings, the tumultuous living conditions and hardships of day-to-day survival had caused him to slip into a dark existence. Even though life had been difficult, Jason knew, by comparison, he had fared better than most. He had planned well and had his friends to lean on, but most importantly he had his faith. Silas McCain had none of these.

Slowly, he lowered his gun – an uncomfortable act considering the man in front of him was holding a rifle and probably on the edge of insanity. But he couldn't maintain his aggression. He had to stay strong and not succumb to the ugliness of what the world around him had become. If he were to kill him, it would cost him his soul. He would just have to use his wits to coax Silas into giving up details on Teech's whereabouts. Once he had that information he would sneak out into the night and be back on his way.

Jason opened his hand letting the gun fall to the floor with a thud. Surely, this gesture would win him over.

"I'm sorry, Silas. I didn't mean to be so defensive. I was just scared. I promise I don't want to hurt you."

Silas rocked his head from side to side with a puzzled look that quickly turned sour. "Don't be a fool. Pick that back up. You're going to need it."

Why would he need it? He had just disarmed himself, Jason thought. Why would Silas want to give him back this power? Was he challenging him?

"But I really don't need it. I told you I'm not here to harm you. Honestly, I'm your friend. Don't you remember me?" he pleaded. "We worked together at the school."

Nothing was registering with him. In an instant, Silas's angry glare melted into a blank stare. Then suddenly his eyes darted to the far side of the room, then to the door, then from corner to corner.

"Listen!" he shouted. He quickly stepped one way then another. Like a squirrel caught in the middle of the road, he couldn't commit to a direction.

"What is it?" Jason urged.

Silas backed up against the front door. "Shhhh! He's outside."

"Who's outside?" Jason whispered.

In a burst of erratic energy Silas spun around and thrust the barrel of his rifle through a window's cross-shaped opening and fired a shot into the darkness.

"Where are you, you bastard?" he screamed while jerking the barrel up and down, then from side to side. The percussion of the shot in the tiny room caved in on Jason from every corner, causing him to wince in pain. He clasped his hands over his ears as he watched Silas rush fanatically from window to window blasting random shots into the night.

"What are you shooting at?" he yelled above the ringing in his ears.

Silas paid no attention to him as he ran back and forth across the room. All at once he came to an abrupt stop, falling to one knee. He leaned his head to the side and cupped his hand around his ear.

"Hear that?" he said in a childlike whisper.

Jason looked around the room. Other than the residual ringing from the gunfire, he didn't hear a thing.

"The Tallyman cometh." He paused and looked up at him. Then he grinned and winked. "He cometh for you." He crouched down and with his arms spread wide began to dance around him like a tribal warrior preparing for the hunt. In a low guttural voice he began chanting, *"the Tallyman cometh, time to fear, the Tallyman cometh, bringing his cheer, the Tallyman ..."*

Jason stood in the middle of the room watching the flickering candlelight drape his former colleague and friend in a blanket of madness. Whatever information he could get out of him wasn't worth the risk staying to find out. Imaginary or not, he didn't care who or what was on the other side of the front door. All he knew was that he had to get out of there. But how? The front door was sealed shut and all the windows were boarded up. He had only been in this one room. Most likely, the rest of the house was a virtual vault as well.

He looked down and saw the candlelight reflecting off his gun's silver-plated barrel and for a moment contemplated using it to negotiate his exit. But he quickly rationalized that Silas had reached the tipping point and would probably not hesitate to shoot him if he reached for it. Besides he had already failed to use it before. But more importantly, he had made the decision not to use violence.

He decided he would try again to win his confidence, then somehow lure him out of the room so he could escape through the front door.

"I hear it!" Jason exclaimed with as much dramatic effect as he could muster. "Silas! I hear it!"

The chanting and dancing continued.

"I hear the Tallyman!" he yelled louder.

Silas stopped and peered up at him with suspicious eyes "You hear the Tallyman?"

Jason nodded.

"How do you know it's *him*?" he said raising his rifle toward him.

"Because, because I - I've heard him before."

"When?" he demanded, while poking him in the rib cage with the end of the barrel.

Sweat poured down Jason's face as he racked his brain for a narrative worthy of Silas's approval. Suddenly, he remembered Erin's description of the hooded figure she claimed to have seen floating outside the kitchen window. Maybe that would satisfy him. He slowly began telling her story, spinning it as if it were his own.

"It was several months ago. It was on a night very much like this one. I was standing in my kitchen looking out the back window into a big tree when I started to see the image of something appear within its branches."

"It was a man?"

"Yes, a man."

"Did he have a black hood?" Silas asked like a child egging his father on for the next detail of a ghost story.

"Why, yes. He did."

"And did he have really pale skin?"

Jason looked at him quizzically as Silas lead him through his description with an uncanny way of predicting everything he was about to say.

"Yes, his skin was very pale. It was almost white."

He nodded eagerly. "Yeah, yeah…what about his chin? Freaky looking chin, huh?"

Jason swallowed, then nodded. "It was big and pointed and it had…"

"A huge scar!" Silas blurted. "Kinda like a chin from one of those masks you buy at Halloween."

Jason stepped back with his mouth open. It didn't seem possible for Silas to know detail by detail the exact image Erin had described to him. He turned to the door envisioning the sinister presence of the hooded man lurking somewhere on the other side. Could two people imagine the same exact thing? Could it be this ghoulish phantom was more than imaginary? Then he remembered Father Tim telling them how they would be tested during these times and how Satan would manifest himself to those without faith. He had appeared to Erin before she began to truly believe. And Silas was a hardcore atheist. Of course he would be susceptible.

Jason turned and looked into the crazed eyes of his friend. But now when he looked at him he saw something different. He saw a man in need, a sick man who had lost his soul. Instead of running away from him he wanted to wrap his arms around him and make him well again. He wanted to explain that his salvation was in reach and that all he had to do was believe. It wasn't his mission to escape from Silas, but to help Silas escape from himself.

He closed his eyes for a moment and silently prayed for God to grant him wisdom and guidance to help him. When he opened them Silas was standing against a window on the right side of the door. His face was pressed into the cross-shaped opening.

"Peek-a-boo, Mr. Tallyman." His words were muffled between the window's boards. "I see you. Do you see me?"

Jason walked up to the window on the other side of the door and leaned toward its opening. He closed one eye and looked through as if it were a telescope. The light of the moon illuminated the jungle of weeds that stretched across the front lawn, transforming it into a field of shimmering reeds swaying gently in the night air. With the exception of two small maple trees, the only other object he could clearly see was his motorcycle standing at the edge of the front steps.

"Tee hee hee," Silas tittered.

Jason scanned the yard looking for the source of his amusement. "What's so funny?" he finally asked.

"He's messing with your ride."

"What?" Jason panned back to his motorcycle. "I don't see anything."

Silas continued giggling like a second grader sneaking a peek through a girl's bathroom peephole.

"I still don't see anything."

Silas pulled back from the window and glared at him. "You moron, he's standing right next to your motorcycle." The sudden agitation in his voice made it clear to him that it was time he played along.

"Oh, wait!" Jason shouted. "Yeah, yeah, there I see him now."

"What do you think he's doing to your bike?"

He'd have to be keen with his responses, or else Silas would see how he was trying to placate him. "I'm not sure. What do you think?" Jason replied.

"I think he's trying to booby trap it."

For the next few minutes, Jason pretended to follow the hooded figure's movements as Silas continued to describe what he was seeing. With one eye on his motorcycle and the other on Silas, he watched as his friend's emotions irrationally turned from fascination to anger.

"That's it. I've had enough of this shit."

He slowly lifted his rifle to the window and eased it through the opening. In contrast to his frantic shooting spree from earlier, this time he was calm and controlled. Gently, he eased his cheek against the wooden gun stock. He closed one eye as the other peered down the barrel in the direction of the motorcycle and the specter of the demon that was tormenting his soul. Just as he was about to squeeze the trigger, Jason found himself rushing over and grabbing him by the arm.

"Wait!"

Silas jumped back, his rifle clanking against the sides of the cross-shaped opening.

"What the hell? Don't you ever touch me!" he roared.

"I - I'm sorry. I didn't mean to frighten you."

Jason stepped back trying to understand his own actions. He didn't know why he had prevented him from firing. All it had accomplished was to shorten the fuse of an already ticking time bomb. He had to think fast.

"I don't think you want to kill him."

Silas turned from the window and focused his anger squarely on him.

"Why not?" he yelled. "He's been trying to kill me!"

With military drill precision he spun his rifle around and jammed the butt into his gut. Jason doubled over as the air rushed from his lungs. Silas bent down beside him gnashing his teeth inches from his face.

"I remember you, Mr. Jason Stover," he snarled. "I remember your goody-goody ways, your church going, your community group kumbaya crap, and all that holy roller religious shit of yours." Then with both hands he shoved his writhing body to the floor. "You make me sick!"

Jason lay on the ground clutching his stomach and gasping for air; each breath an effort in futility. After a few moments the pain started to subside and the muscles in his diaphragm began to relax. As oxygen started filling his body, he slowly regained awareness of his surroundings and the vicious situation he was in. Standing over him was Silas's dark silhouette, the candle's backlight creating a towering black figure of neurosis.

For fear of inciting any more rage he frantically pushed himself into a corner only to have Silas follow him. With no possibility of escape, he cowered in the dead end he had created.

"Please, don't hurt me," he begged.

"Tsk, tsk, tsk," came Silas's reply. "Oh, how your God hath

forsaken you yet again."

Jason lay motionless, staring up at the lurid image of the man who was now in control of his fate. How had it all come to this? How had he been so stupid, he thought, as to go on such a quest so naively? He bowed his head and began praying aloud.

"Yea, though I walk through the valley of the shadow of death, I will fear no evil: for thou art with me; thy rod and thy staff they comfort me…"

As the last word of his prayer left his lips, a scolding white light exploded before him along with a blunted pain that swept him from the flickering glow of the room's lone candle into a void of blackness.

CHAPTER 29
JEKYLL AND HYDE

While Jason was out there were no dreams, no thoughts, and no pain, only sweet relief from a situation gone horribly wrong. Ever so slowly, out of the nothingness, remnants of thoughts began to form within his brain, a fragment of a thought, then a blur of an image, until finally a complete thought. As he gained control of his reflexes he slowly pulled himself up on his knees and willed his eyes to open. The full force of the light blinded him, causing him to block it out with his hand. As his eyes adjusted, he peeked through his fingers. It was a scene aglow with warmth and a vague familiarity. His heart fluttered.

Stretched out in front of him was the luminous shape of a cross, emblazoned against a field of mahogany. For a second he could not breathe. Thoughts of salvation were at his fingertips. Slowly, he reached out toward it. As he approached its edges his fingers began to glow, then his whole hand was awash in its light. He turned his palm upward and stared enchanted at the halo around the crucifix and the warmth of its energy. When he rotated his hand back, his gaze moved past his fingers and onto the shadowy image of another hand several feet below. Every time he moved his, the other followed. He made a fist, it made a fist. He spread his fingers and its fingers spread.

Turning his head he followed a beam of light away from his hand and up to the cross-shaped opening in the window on the far side of the room. The rays of sun flowing through the opening had deceived him and he dropped his head as his surroundings and the memories of the previous evening rushed in on him. A dull ache suddenly emanated from the back of his head and down his shoulders. He reached around and noted a goose egg-sized bump just behind his left ear. There was no blood – only a throbbing that was matched with a painful hollowness in his stomach.

He looked around the room. The light from the openings in the windows revealed a less oppressive atmosphere than from the night before. It was just one very messy living room, typical of any bachelor. Even the remains of the animal carcasses he thought he had seen in the corner turned out to be nothing more than a dog's play toy. The best revelation, though, was that his nemesis was nowhere in sight. Now was the time to make his move.

As he began to stand, he fell back to his knees. After several attempts he was finally able to pull himself upright. He took a deep breath and began walking to the door. On his second step his left leg jarred to a stop while the rest of his body lurched forward. His ankle was securely bound by a makeshift zip-tie shackle and chain that ran from his leg to underneath the sofa.

"What the…" he muttered under his breath.

He bent down and peered into the underpinnings of the furniture, only to find the other end securely wrapped around a thick metal support rod. As he stood back up he became light-headed, and his knees wobbled. He fell back into the sofa with a long exhale. It was day two of his odyssey and he had already missed a full day of meals. By his calculations he wouldn't be able to accomplish his task, let alone survive, without forcing himself to eat every two hours. And being bludgeoned certainly didn't help matters.

For several minutes he sat still trying to collect enough of his thoughts to devise an escape plan. With only three feet of chain, his ability to survey the house from his tiny corner of the room was null. The only exits he could see, other than the two windows beside the front door, were an opening to a hallway and one to a kitchen thirty feet away. Suddenly he heard movement from somewhere in the house. A bed mattress squeaked, then moments later he heard snoring. He'd have to move soon before Silas woke.

Slowly, he stood up. His only option was to try to drag the sofa toward the kitchen, where hopefully he could reach a knife or scissors to cut the plastic ties. The wooden floors should have made pulling the small sofa easy, but after five or six minutes he had only managed to budge it a couple of feet. Dejected and exhausted, he fell back onto the cushions.

He couldn't believe how rapidly the energy loss was affecting him now. Unless he suddenly regained his strength he would never make it to the kitchen before Silas woke up. He needed food and water to give him enough energy to accomplish the task. But even if he had both, it would still take time for them to produce any strengthening effect. He looked down at his hands. They were starting to shake from fatigue and his thoughts were growing fuzzier. Then suddenly he remembered the vials of B-12 shots Erin had placed in his duffle bag.

He rapidly turned his head back and forth scanning the room. Hopefully Silas had not taken it with him. His heart jumped when he saw the strap peeking out from around the edge of the end table on the other side of the sofa. Even though it was only fifteen feet away it seemed like miles. To conserve his energy he quietly rolled onto the floor. He took a deep breath and stretched out his body, only to fall two feet short. He paused a moment, then slowly climbed to his feet. He bent over and grabbed the armrest. Then with everything he could muster he leaned back and began pulling the sofa diagonally away from the wall, when suddenly he lost his grip and crashed to the floor knocking over a lamp.

He lay on the cold mahogany surface holding his breath waiting for Silas to come rushing in. When he finally heard the sound of snoring again, he drew in several sharp breaths then rolled onto his side, stretched his body along the sofa's edge and reached out past the table toward the bag. When his fingertips came to within a fraction of an inch from the strap, they stopped. No matter how hard he strained he couldn't grasp it. Exhausted, he rolled onto his back. As soon as he did the knobby texture of the canvas pressed gently onto his fingertips. Blindly, he arched his hand backward until he was able to firmly wrap his fingers around the elusive handle and pull it over onto his chest.

"Thank you, dear Lord," he whispered breathlessly.

With the bag still on his chest, he reached inside and pulled out the little black sack containing the B-12 shots. His hands were shaking so much he could hardly hold the vials steady enough to insert the needle. After several attempts he was able to successfully fill one of the syringes and inject the precious serum into his vein. Almost immediately, his head stopped hurting and the haze began to lift.

As his fatigue began to dissipate he raised himself onto the sofa and devoured a couple protein bars for safe measure. Although he was not nearly as strong as the day before he felt ready enough to continue his escape plan. He tossed his duffle bag onto the cushions and began pushing the sofa slowly toward the kitchen. A minute later he had slid it into the kitchen doorway well enough to reach in and grab a carving knife from the counter.

As he began cutting through the plastic straps he heard something on the other side of the front door. There was a

231

shuffling sound followed by the scraping of feet against a doormat. Then came three loud knocks. At the same moment, two of the six zip-ties snapped apart. BAM, BAM, BAM came another three knocks. He feverishly continued his cutting. POP, POP, another two zip-ties snapped. Down the hall, the snoring stopped. POP, POP. The last two pieces of plastic flew apart. Grabbing his duffle bag he ran to the front door and began flipping deadbolts. No matter who was outside, this was his ticket to freedom.

"Hey, you!" a voice boomed from behind him.

He froze and then slowly turned his head to find Silas standing in the middle of the room with his rifle pointed directly at him. Sweat beaded up on his forehead and his palms became moist. He was so close to escape. He had to chance it and yell for help. Just as he opened his mouth, a female's voice shouted out from the other side of the door.

"Silas, are you going to let me in?"

"Yeah. I'm coming," he yelled back. With his gun he motioned Jason toward a small wooden stool in the corner. "You, sit down," he commanded.

Jason obligingly sat down. Meanwhile, Silas kept his rifle aimed at him as he circled to the door. After unlocking the last deadbolt he flung it open. The light instantly flooded the room washing away the sun-etched cross that had stretched over the floor.

Standing in the threshold was a thin, fair skinned girl in a man's red flannel shirt. It was tied up in a knot at the waist, exposing the toned, smooth skin of a teenager. She wore flip-flops and jeans that were faded well past fashion acceptability and the jagged edges of her short straight auburn hair denoted a do-it-yourself attitude. She was cute with soft puppy dog brown eyes that said she was a kind and gentle person. But it was her posture that spoke more about her. It was the silhouette of the downtrodden. She leaned slightly forward and kept her hands tightly folded against her chest. Her shoulders were slumped over reflecting her downward gaze.

"What's going on?" she said in a soft voice. She looked at Jason. "Is everything okay?"

Silas closed the door and locked it. "Everything's fine except for the fact that this guy broke into my house and…" He stopped abruptly. His mouth fell open as his expression turned to one of amazement.

"Oh my word – Stover, is that you?"

Jason was taken aback with his apparent lack of memory from the previous night. "Yes, it's me," he said cautiously.

"What on earth are you doing here and how the heck did you get in?" His tone was full of pleasant surprise.

"I, uh…well." He hesitated not wanting to get into the sordid details from the previous evening for fear of triggering a potential relapse.

"I came by late last night. You let me in, then we sat up for a while talking, then you went to bed and I slept out on the sofa." It was as vague an answer as he had ever given, but anything more would have prompted too many questions.

"Really?" Silas scratched his head. "Man, I don't remember any of that." He looked across the room. "How come the sofa's in the kitchen door?"

"I'm sorry, I didn't mean to rearrange your living room. It's just that there was a bit of a draft where it was so I moved it over there."

"Oh, no problem," he said still scratching his head. "Man, I'm still clueless on yesterday though." He slapped Jason on the shoulder. "But whatever, I'm just glad to see you." He turned to the young girl. "Zoey, this is a good friend of mine, Jason Stover. He and I worked together as teachers. We taught all those young bozos the exciting world of physics."

The girl extended her hand. "How do you do, Mr. Stover?"

"Pleasure to meet you. Please call me Jason."

"So, tell me buddy, what brings you to my dumpster on the hill during these apocalyptic days of ours? It must be pretty important."

Jason couldn't believe the hundred and eighty degree turnaround in his friend's persona. He was so pleasant, even jovial. Whatever had caused it, he was just glad his old friend seemed back to normal. But he was even more excited that he could tell him why he had come and hopefully he could get more information on Teech's whereabouts. Just as he was about to speak, Silas looked down and realized he was still holding his rifle and wearing his bathrobe.

"I'm so sorry," he apologized, placing the gun in the corner. "I can't believe I didn't recognize you right off the bat. It's just that I've had intruders before and things got nasty, so I've had to arm myself. I'm sure you've experienced some stuff too."

"You wouldn't believe it," he replied.

"And I'm sorry for the mess I'm in right now. I'm excited to hear why you're here, but would you mind if I go wash my face and change clothes real quick?"

"Sure."

"Good, I'll be back in just a minute. Meanwhile, you and Zoey can get acquainted."

After Silas left the room, Zoey averted her eyes from him and cleared her throat nervously.

"So how do you know Silas?" she asked breaking the awkward silence.

She leaned toward him, still looking away and whispered. "Were you really here last night?"

"Yeah. Of course."

She looked around the room as if trying to detect eavesdroppers. "You're pretty lucky, mister."

"What do you mean?" he asked with piqued interest.

"Silas is a great guy, but he's got some problems." She shifted her weight from one side to the other. "We all got problems. I'm not sure why he's got 'em, but seems like his are a little bigger than most."

"What kind of problems are you talking about?"

She leaned back and looked at him suspiciously. "How do you know Silas again?"

"We were both teachers near Lake Royale. What kind of problems are you talking about?" he asked anxiously.

Suddenly her tone became defensive. "You're not here to take him away are you?"

"No, no, of course not. Why would I take him away? I'm here to *help* him."

"How are you going to help him?"

"I've got some information that could save him. It could save you, too. I just need to talk to him and get some information from him that will…"

"What kind of information?" she interrupted.

Just then, Silas walked back in wearing a clean pair of khakis and a denim shirt. Although his beard was still unruly, his hair was pulled back into a ponytail giving him a much cleaner appearance.

"What kind of information were you referring to?" he said as he tossed a stick of beef jerky to him. "I gotta eat this mess or else I'll keep losing weight."

Jason began salivating as he examined the sliver of meat. "I've encountered something of a phenomenon," he said excitedly. "It's something that could have a major impact on us. It's something that could potentially save us. But I think it's going to take someone who understands the whole energy loss crisis. Someone like…"

"Like Richard Teech." Silas said, finishing his sentence.

Jason smiled wide. "Exactly like Richard Teech."

CHAPTER 30
AN UNEASY TRAVELER

As Jason described his encounter with the girl in the boathouse and the man in the window, Silas began slowly pacing the room. By the time he had finished describing the energy surge by Erin and her uncle, his pace had doubled. He walked back and forth across the room, lost in thought as he assimilated every syllable of every detail.

"This is pretty incredible. Do you think it can be replicated?"

"I don't know. I tried it with her uncle and had some success. What's odd is that I had another friend try and he didn't have any results."

"Hmmm. That is odd. Maybe it's connected with their DNA."

"I don't think so. They weren't blood-related, and of course, I wasn't either."

"What about kinetic energy?"

"Excuse me," Zoey squeaked from the corner of the room.

"Yes, honey, what is it?" Silas said.

"Maybe it's something else."

"Like what?"

"Well…" she hesitated. "How about love?"

"What do you mean?"

"I'm no scientist like you guys, but maybe their love is what caused the blender and the lights and all that other stuff to go on like that. Couldn't they love each other enough to make that kind of energy?"

Silas walked up to her and gently placed the palm of his hand against her cheek. "Ah, sweet youth. Maybe that could happen in the movies, but not in real life. I wish it could, but as a man of science I know that's impossible."

"I don't know about that," Jason chimed in. "The Lord works in mysterious ways and I've seen my share of strange things since the vanishings." He wanted to mention Silas's own Jekyll and Hyde transition, but opted to stay silent.

Silas turned. With a sigh and a smile he said, "My good dear friend, you don't seriously want to debate me on all this God stuff, do you?"

"There's actually nothing I'd like more, but unfortunately we don't have enough time."

"Not enough time? Do you know something I don't?"

Jason looked at him in disbelief. "You're a physics professor. Certainly you've been tracking our energy efficiency levels?"

"Not for several weeks now. Why?"

"Oh man! I can't believe you don't know this."

"I'm sorry," he said motioning with his eyes toward Zoey, "but I've been dealing with other issues in my life."

Jason gave a slight nod, then breathed in deeply. "I've been testing regularly. Two days ago, I performed one that revealed devastating results." He paused. "The test revealed that we had four days left until all our energy sources would be depleted."

Silas turned to Zoey. Her face was expressionless. He turned back to Jason. "So we've got two days remaining now? That's what you're telling me – just two days?"

Jason nodded.

"And you're sure?"

He nodded again.

"And you think Teech might be able to figure a way to take what your friend Erin and her uncle did, and translate that into a global energy reversal solution?"

"It's a possibility," he said.

Silas threw his hands in the air. "Well, hot dang buddy, we're on the road to salvation!" Suddenly shades of the previous evening's madness crossed his face. "Are you out of your God-forsaken mind?" he bellowed.

Jason stepped back into the corner as Silas began vigorously rubbing his temples.

Then as quickly as he had flown off the handle, his demeanor changed course. He dropped his hands to his side and exhaled.

"Jason, I'm so sorry. I didn't mean to blow like that. But man, that's some heavy shit you just dumped on us. And how do you think all this can happen in less than two days? Even though I'm pretty sure I know where Teech is staying, it's a crap shoot that he's still there."

"So you do know where he is!"

"At least I did while email was working."

"Is he still in D.C.?"

"No, he's moved to Fredericksburg, Virginia to be with his sister."

"Fredericksburg - that's great! That's only a couple of hours from here. Do you have the address?"

"Actually, I do. He gave it to me in case I wanted to visit him." He took a long, deep breath. "Well, I guess I do. "

"What do you mean?" Jason asked.

"I guess now might be as good a time as any for a visit." He chuckled sarcastically.

"Wait!" Zoey said grabbing him by the arm. "What do you mean visit? You can't go anywhere. You know you can't."

"If we leave now we can be back by nightfall," he reassured her.

Jason held up his hands. "Hold up, guys. I don't think you understand. This is a one-man trip. I only have the motorcycle and it can't handle two people." He turned to Silas. "I've only got enough fuel to get there and back. The weight of another person will use too much fuel, plus I'm sure the amount of energy we lost yesterday will sap it even more."

"Ha! You can't go anyway," Zoey said.

The edges of Silas's mouth slowly turned up. "Come with me, my friend." He turned and walked past the sofa Jason had slid across the floor and led him through the kitchen to the back door. After flipping several deadbolts he pulled it open. "Check this out!" he said pointing proudly to a beat up 1966 red Mustang parked a few feet from the back steps.

"Don't worry, the inside has a brand new interior, dashboard, gauges, everything."

"Uh, okay. I'm impressed, I guess," Jason said.

"I've been meaning to finish off the body for years but never got around to it."

"That's great but you know it's not going to run because..."

"Hold that thought." Silas cut him off with a smile. "Follow me." He opened the door and they walked outside. "I know the body looks like crap, but trust me it's the inside that makes this baby so beautiful." He rubbed his hands across the hood as if stroking a cat. "So what makes you think it won't run?" he said, reaching under the hood.

"It would have to be rigged with additional batteries and would have to..."

Just then the hood popped up revealing a shiny new V-8 engine with a row of five new batteries tightly grouped together on one side. A bird's nest of tangled wiring connected them to each other.

"Did you seriously think you were the only physicist who knew how to rig a car and perform fuel efficiency workarounds?"

"So, it actually runs?"

"Of course."

Jason grinned. "This is fantastic, but I had to add an extra tank to my motorcycle to make the trip and it uses a whole lot less gas than any car."

Without a word Silas motioned him to the trunk. With his fist he pounded twice on the rusty metallic horse emblem next to the keyhole, causing it to spring open a half inch. He reached under and pulled it up.

"Ta da!" he exclaimed.

Jason gazed down onto a large metal drum that filled the entire back end of the car. He looked up at Silas with a smile.

"Is it full?"

"To the brim! Compliments of my next door neighbor," he said looking across his yard to the abandoned gas station. "And check out the back seat."

Jason peered through the rear window at another large shiny metal drum. "Don't tell me… another fuel tank?"

"You know it. You might say it's my reserve's reserve."

"Okay, it's official," Jason said, nodding his head. "I truly am amazed."

"So let's get going then!" Silas urged.

Jason couldn't hide how impressed he was at what his friend had accomplished, but the ordeal from the previous night was still fresh in his memory. The last thing he could afford was to be on the road and have Silas's mental circuitry go haywire, though having him on board could have its advantages. He could precisely navigate them to Teech, and if they ran into trouble he would have a second person to help out. Plus, riding in a car instead of on a motorcycle would certainly be less taxing on him physically.

"Before we do anything, there's something I have to know."

"Shoot!"

Jason looked at Zoey. "You mentioned Silas shouldn't go. Actually you mentioned he couldn't go." He turned to Silas. "And Silas you said something about getting back by night. What exactly are you guys talking about?"

Silas cleared his throat. "I knew you'd bring that up, and you're totally right in doing so. The bottom line is I have some sort of nocturnal condition. Mind you it's just *some* time." Silas looked at Zoey, "but it's not *all* the time."

Jason didn't want to let him know he had already been witness to his condition. He would let him elaborate in case there were any other issues he needed to be aware of.

"Honestly, I'm always fine during the day, but sometimes I'll black out and don't remember anything from the previous night."

Jason turned to Zoey. "I assume you've seen some of this."

She nodded quickly. "It's like he's got this split personality. He's always so sweet and nice during the day, but it's like someone flips a switch after dark. He starts seeing things and acts really weird."

He looked at Silas. "What kind of things do you see?"

"I really don't know," he shrugged. "I'm honestly oblivious to everything."

"It's usually a man," Zoey said. "He says he's after him."

"How do you know?"

"I told you. I've seen him when he's gotten this way. He'll start rantin' about this imaginary man and that's when he starts acting all crazy. That's why I don't come around here after dusk."

No one spoke for a moment as Jason weighed his options. He looked at Silas. "My friend, I'm so sorry for whatever you're going through…"

"But you don't think it's wise for me to come," Silas

interrupted.

"No. I was just going to say that I wish I could help you. I most definitely want you to come."

Silas smiled. "Well, what are we waiting for? I'll grab some supplies and meet you back out here in just a minute."

As he entered the house, Jason turned to Zoey and asked. "Do you think everything's going to be okay? I mean with Silas and his condition."

Her lower lip began to quiver. "I don't know," she said as tears began running down her face. "You just have to promise to take care of him. Please, Mr. Stover, he's all I've got." She stopped and looked into his eyes. Without saying a word, he knew what she wanted to say.

"You love him, don't you?" he asked.

She nodded slowly, then turned and ran into the house.

A moment later Silas came back out carrying a small cardboard box of food under one arm, and his rifle and machete tucked under the other.

"Oh, that reminds me," Jason said as he headed back inside, "I brought along some food and supplies too. I'll be back in a second." When he entered the living room he found Zoey kneeling on the floor reaching into his duffle bag.

"Can I help you?" he said.

She turned around startled. "Oh, I'm sorry, Mr. Stover." She stood up quickly and handed him the bag.

"Are you looking for anything in particular?"

"Oh – oh, no," she said nervously wiping tears from her face. "I just thought you might need something for the trip."

"Like what?"

She reached into the bag and pulled out a handful of plastic zip-ties.

"These. In case – well, you know - in case you need to keep

safe."

Jason gave her a warm smile and nodded. "I understand."

"I also found this beside your bag." She held up the silver heart Erin had given him. "Is it yours?"

"Yes – it is," he said softly.

She handed it to him. "It's beautiful."

Suddenly he was back in his office looking out over his backyard. He could feel the breeze coming off the lake and the warmth of the sun beaming across his desk. The smell of the jasmine was sweet. His heart soared as the gentle laughter of his wife and daughter slowly filled his mind. From a distance, he watched as the wavy brown locks of his little girl's hair floated and bounced in slow motion over the back of her neck, revealing her small heart-shaped birthmark.

"Jason, are you ready?"

In an instant, the roar of an engine drowned out the sound of his family's laughter.

"I've got the car running," Silas yelled from the back door. "Let's go!"

Jason looked at Zoey as he stuffed the silver medallion into his pants pocket. "Thank you." Then taking her by the hand, he led her out to the car just as Silas was sliding into the driver's side seat.

"Wait a second!" she said, catching the door as he was about to shut it. She threw her arms around his neck. "Please be careful."

"I will, I promise," he said revving the engine. With a quick peck he pulled the door closed. As Jason jumped in beside him he gunned the engines again.

"Now that's a beautiful sound!" he shouted over the thundering pistons.

Then he threw it into second gear and popped the clutch, propelling Jason's head against the back of the seat. Dirt and gravel went shooting out from the rear tires. Jason looked back over his

244

shoulder. Through the cloud of dust he saw Zoey's image fading away.

Silas turned to him with a big grin. "Man, this is going to be awesome!" he shouted as the car plowed through the weed-infested yard.

Jason wondered to himself how this could be awesome. They had just two days to accomplish a task that, by all rational means, was an almost sure failure, especially considering a self-professed schizophrenic was driving them. As they drove onto the highway, the car bounced hard over a curb sending their supplies flying everywhere, including Silas's machete, which landed in Jason's lap.

"Son of a bitch!" yelled Silas. "That was a helluva a curb."

Jason looked down at the weapon that he had so recently been held captive by. Just as he was about to pick it up, Silas snatched it away and tucked it under his seat. Suddenly, Jason wished he had opted to make the trip alone.

CHAPTER 31
A FAILED EVANGELIST

With the exception of a wispy row of thin clouds on the horizon, the sky was a solid canvas of pastel blue. The temperature was mild and there was just a hint of a breeze. The only thing that kept it from being a perfect day was the ever-increasing fatigue and the knowledge that billions of people throughout the world were starving to death.

With no other vehicles around or the threat of being pulled by police, Silas kept the car at a steady eighty miles per hour.

"At this speed, we'll be in Fredericksburg in forty-five minutes."

"How's the fuel?" Jason asked.

Silas pressed a button next to the gas gauge. "Wow! You really were right. We're burning fuel like crazy. We're only getting four miles per gallon."

Jason exploded. "Four miles! Are you serious? We'll never make it!"

"Don't worry. Between the regular tank and two reserves, I've got almost forty-eight gallons. That'll get us there and back with a full tank to spare."

Jason breathed a long sigh of relief. "We still gotta hurry

because every second our fuel efficiency is decreasing. By tomorrow, it won't matter how much gas we have – it'll all be useless." He began rubbing his forehead "Man, I don't know about you, but I'm starting to feel dizzy."

Silas grabbed a couple protein bars and handed him one. "Here, keep eating. We've gotta keep up our strength." Then he punched the accelerator, sending the speedometer up to ninety miles an hour. "Don't worry, I'll have us there in thirty minutes. We'll be back by lunch and you'll be home before the sun goes down."

"You must be lovin' this." Jason said, as he ripped open the bar's wrapper.

"If you mean this open highway, you're right. You won't believe it, but this is the first time I've actually driven this car since I rigged it up last week. I just realized I really didn't have anywhere I needed to go. I wonder if we'll see anybody else out."

"If we do, it won't be many. Most people are too weak at this point to be very active. Plus, most people don't know how to reconfigure a car's battery system like us."

Silas chuckled, "That's right. I forgot we're the only geniuses left in the world." Just then, a convertible with its top down came flying onto the highway from the off-ramp just ahead of them. A young man was driving while a lady was standing up waving her arms from side to side.

"What's that on the side of the car?" Silas asked.

Jason craned his neck back as the vehicle zoomed by. "It looked like they spray painted the words 'The Apocalypse Is Here' and they spelled it A – P – O – C – A – L – I – P – S."

Silas laughed. "So, now we know there are at least two more geniuses out and about."

"Just no grammarians," Jason joked. In an instant, their laughter became a unifying blessing and Jason's earlier fears that his friend would relapse into his madness started to disappear.

As they continued down the highway he started looking for opportunities to discuss Silas's religious beliefs. He wasn't skilled in theology, and with the exception of his brief attempt at rebuilding Mike's faith, he had never evangelized or even attempted to persuade a hard and fast atheist, like Silas, to believe in God. But he knew he had to try.

"So, how do you know Zoey?" he asked.

"Poor thing – she's had it pretty tough. She's lived next door since she was seven. When she was a teenager she got into a ton of trouble rebelling against her folks. I can't understand it because they were such nice people. Anyway, after they disappeared during the vanishings she was left on her own and in order to survive she started having sex with men for food and shelter. When I found out, I kinda took her under my wing. I gave her food and a place to stay. That is, until we discovered I had this condition."

"What happened then?"

"I boarded up her house and put a security system in place so she'd be safe at night. During the day, she's been staying at my house."

Jason smiled. "That's pretty awesome of you." He paused. "You know she loves you, right?"

"Oh sure – I love her, too."

"No, I mean she's *in* love with you."

Silas turned toward him with a jerk. "Man, that's just perverted. I'm almost twice that girl's age."

"I'm sorry, I wasn't suggesting that you…"

"Besides," he continued, "I'm still in love with my wife."

Suddenly, he saw the chance he had been waiting for.

"You think you'll see her again?"

"Jason, she's gone," he replied sternly. "She disappeared during the vanishings. How will I ever see her again?"

"Well, Kristina and Nikki were taken too, but I'm sure I'll see them again."

"How's that?"

"I'll see them in heaven, of course."

"Oh, so you really do want a debate on the existence of God? If you do, I have to warn you that I'll debunk every miracle or prophecy the Bible has to offer."

He fidgeted in his seat as he contemplated his response. Silas was extremely intelligent and like many atheists had the ability to rationalize away any religious doctrine. He'd have to use another tactic.

"It's not that I want a debate. It's more that I want to help someone I care about find what they've lost, and along the way, find the one true love."

Silas shot him a skeptical glance. "I'm not sure what *type* of love you're talking about, but I did have true love. Her name was Debbie McCain, and she was taken from me through some freaking weird force of nature."

"As were Kristina and Nikki and all of the other people like them."

"How can you logically lump the third of the world's population that vanished into one group? There are just too many variables. Think of the myriad of different factors – all the different demographics, psychographics, and ages. There are classes and religions. There are just too many to say that these people vanished because they were alike. It simply had to be a random factor to the equation."

"You know who you sound like?"

"Who?"

"Me. That's exactly the same way I felt after it happened." A lump came up in his throat and his eyes filled with tears. "But something changed in my life and saved me – I began to truly believe."

"Believe in what?"

"In God. In Jesus. For years, I was faking it. I was just acting out the part of the good Christian. But after the Rapture occurred, or the vanishings as everybody's been calling it, I had a good friend of mine help show me the light." He stopped for a moment, then wiped his eyes. "Answer this one question for me."

"Okay."

"Of all the people you know who were taken, were any of them non-believers?

"Of course!" he said confidently.

"How do you know?"

"Well," he hesitated a second as his confidence dipped, "to be honest, no one can say for sure because most people don't go around spouting off about their beliefs, but there are people like Paul Evans and Wendy Zimmerman who vanished and I'm sure they didn't believe."

"How do you know that?"

"Well for one, Paul cussed like a sailor and cheated on his wife. And Wendy did drugs, had an abortion several years ago, and from what I knew of her she never set foot in a church."

Jason nodded. "You're right. You never can tell exactly what someone's like or what their demons are. Only God can. But absolutely no one is perfect. We're all sinners. He'll always forgive us because He loves us that much. That's the love I was speaking about. That's the truest love there is. All we have to do is believe in Jesus Christ as our savior, then He'll redeem us. Wendy and Paul may have had their faults, but if they truly believed then they were forgiven and worthy of being taken. That's why you and I are still here. It's why my other friends are still here. None of us truly believed."

A moment passed as Silas waited for him to continue.

"So that's it," he scoffed. "That's all you got? Believe and we'll be taken to the Promised Land?" He shook his head. "I'm sorry, but I don't buy it. I'm a scientist, and until I see empirical evidence that the existence of a God, your God, is even halfway plausible, I'm opting out."

Jason's heart sank. He hadn't come close to swaying him. "I just wish you would open up to the possibility and for once go on faith. If you'd just give him a chance, the rewards are everlasting. But you have to have faith."

Silas raised his hand as if he'd heard more than he wanted, then pointed his finger toward him and said, "Let me ask you a question now. If you have so much faith, why aren't you okay with just lying down and dying? I don't mean to be crass, but isn't that your golden ticket to heaven anyway?"

"The fact of the matter is that I'm okay with dying. It doesn't scare me because I know where I'm going. I also know that God has a plan for all of us, but none of those plans include just rolling over and dying. He gave us our lives for a purpose. Giving up isn't a purpose."

"So, what's God's plan for you then?"

Jason shook his head. "I'm not sure. But what I do know is that you're here for a reason and that I love my friends and the world enough to make this journey. Jesus loved mankind enough to give His life for us, so why shouldn't I be prepared to do the same."

"Crap!"

Jason raised his eyebrows. "Why would you think that's crap?"

"No. I missed the turn - hold on!" Silas slammed his foot down on the clutch and jammed the brakes. With a quick turn of the wheel the car spun a hundred and eighty degrees, throwing Jason against the door. Smoke from the burning tires shrouded them like a blanket of fog. In an instant they were speeding back in the opposite direction.

"Man, that was fun!" Silas shouted as they veered onto the off-ramp. Their previous conversation faded away as quickly as he had whipped the car around. The only things occupying his mind now were road signs and landmarks that would lead them to Richard Teech.

"We have to pay attention now," he said as he grabbed a dog-eared map off the dashboard.

For the next ten minutes they wound their way through the forsaken neighborhoods of Fredericksburg. Just like Lake Royale and every other city and town on earth, the streets and yards were deserted as the inhabitants lay wasting away inside their homes. With the exception of an occasional homeless person curled up waiting to die, the landscape was desolate, rendering this once bustling historic city into a virtual ghost town.

After several more minutes of searching they slowly pulled into the driveway of a modest one-story colonial style home.

"Here we are." Silas announced. "118 Callenwood."

"This looks promising," Jason said, jumping out of the car. "The house seems to be in pretty good shape. I bet they're still here."

Silas stepped out of the car and stretched. Other than the average amount of weeds, Jason was right. The house was indeed in pristine condition.

"I sure hope you're right," he said.

For a moment all of Jason's fears and worries vanished. He was about to meet a legend in the world of physics, a man he had admired and followed since he began teaching. As Silas calmly walked up to the house, Jason dug through his duffle bag gathering protein bars.

"I'm sure they'll enjoy one of these," he said walking up the steps behind him.

Silas snickered. "Not a bad welcoming gift for a hungry Nobel Prize winner."

After several knocks with no answer Silas turned the doorknob. "It's open," he said.

Jason peered through the side windows. "I don't see anybody. Maybe they're here but can't get to the door."

Silas push the door halfway open. "Hellooo, anyone home?"

No answer.

"Richard, are you here? It's me, Silas McCain."

Jason leaned around him into the sun-drenched foyer. "Come on," he said pushing past him. "If they're here, they won't mind us coming in."

The interior of the house reflected the Victorian taste of a true English dame. Lace doilies and cross-stitching seemed to cover every inch of the foyer. Turn-of-the-century oil paintings of the English countryside, replete with lords and ladies, adorned the hallways. Peppered throughout were pictures of Teech accompanied by family and friends.

"We're definitely in the right place," he said in a soft voice.

"Why are you whispering?" Silas said. "Richard, are you here!" he yelled.

The two stood motionless, waiting hopefully for a response. Silas slapped his hand against his thigh, "Crap, I don't think anyone's here." Then in a burst he began running from room to room, while Jason remained in the hall admiring a picture of Teech shaking hands with former British Prime Minister Margaret Thatcher.

After several minutes of Silas's stomping about, everything suddenly went silent. Then from the far end of the house he yelled out, "Jason, come here. I'm in the back study."

A moment later, Jason came running through the door. "What's wrong?"

"Nothing's wrong, except that nobody's here."

Jason looked around the room. "And you've looked

everywhere?"

"Yeah. Everywhere."

"For the love of God," Jason said shaking his head with dejection. "Any sign of where they might have gone?"

"Nope. But it couldn't have been long ago. Check out the coffee on the desk."

Jason's eyes lit up when he touched the cup. "It's still warm! They'll probably be back then."

"Can we afford to just sit here? What if they don't come back and we wait for nothing? Like you said, every second means less fuel efficiency and more starvation."

"I think we should wait a bit."

Silas shook his head and laughed. "You amaze me. You actually have some sort of chance of surviving by going back to your friends, but you want to hang out here with my doomed ass."

"Like I said, I'm not sure of the Lord's plan, but there's a reason we're here together."

Silas smiled at him then looked down at the cup of coffee.

"Mind if I have this? I'm about to drop."

"Be my guest."

With a shaking hand, he grabbed the cup and guzzled it down.

Jason watched as Silas wiped excess coffee from his mouth. His hand was nothing more than a thin wrapping of skin over bones and his already gaunt frame appeared ten pounds lighter.

He hadn't looked in the mirror, but he could tell he had also lost a lot of weight. Over the past two days he had tightened his belt a notch each day. Even though he had arrived in better shape than Silas, the effects of the accelerated energy loss had rapidly taken their toll on him. His body was breaking down. Any fat he had was gone and now his system was starting to burn away muscle. Suddenly, his knees became weak and everything went black.

CHAPTER 32
THE HOLY GRAIL

"WAKE UP, DAMN IT!" Silas shouted.

Jason's eyes rolled back from behind his head, and his body began twitching him into consciousness. "What, what happened?" he muttered looking up at Silas's face.

"You fainted. I caught you right before you hit the ground." Silas was kneeling down beside him.

"How long have I been out?"

"Just a few seconds."

With two deep breaths he shook his head clearing the cobwebs from his mind. "I think I'm okay now. Can you help me up?"

Silas pulled him to his feet. The sudden rush of blood to his brain started his head spinning, causing him to bend over.

"You gonna be okay?"

After several more labored breaths, he stood straight. "Okay, I think I'm good now."

Silas put his hand on his shoulder. "Man, you went down like a sack of potatoes. I almost wasn't able to catch you."

"Speaking of potatoes, I think we need to eat something fast or else I'm going to fall out again."

"I agree," Silas said. "Knowing Teech, I'm sure he had his sister stockpile extra food. Why don't you sit down and save your energy and I'll go check the kitchen?"

Jason nodded as an aftershock of dizziness rushed over him. "Yeah, that's probably a good idea."

While Silas ran to the kitchen, Jason shuffled his way to Teech's writing desk in the corner of the room and plopped down into a small tufted leather chair. Looking around the room, he was amazed at its tidiness. It was obvious that his sister was letting him use it during his stay. There were physics books stacked neatly in every corner, but oddly there were no computers — only dozens of books and two leather-bound journals lying next to the leg of the desk.

A moment passed as he sat staring down in disbelief. "Can this be?" he thought. "Could Richard Teech's journals actually be at my feet?" For a lowly physics teacher it was the equivalent of staring at the entrance to King Tut's treasure chamber. A sudden burst of adrenaline pulsed through his veins as he scooped them off the floor. Both were identical with the initials *RT* embossed in the lower right corner.

Holding his breath, he slowly opened the cover of the first one only to find the rich parchment void of any content. He flipped the page and again nothing. He turned another page and again nothing. Picking up the book, he fanned his way to the back. The entire thing was empty. He tossed it to the floor. Surely the second one would have something.

He placed his right hand on the desk with his forefinger just under the edge of the cover. "Come on, Teech, tell me something," he whispered. Then with a flip of his finger the first page appeared before him full of notes, equations, and doodles. His heart skipped a beat. He began running his fingers along the lines at an ever-increasing speed.

Silas walked back in carrying a tray heaped with food. "You're not going to believe what I found!"

Jason glanced up at him. "And *you're* not going to believe what I found. Check this out. It's Teech's journal," he said with a huge grin.

Silas placed the tray on the edge of the desk. "Have you found anything?" he said excitedly.

"Not yet. But man, is this guy brilliant or what? Some of his theories and calculations are out of this world. He's honestly like Einstein smart. I mean this stuff is..." He stopped mid-sentence and began sniffing the air. "What is that tantalizing smell?"

Silas pointed to the tray. There were two glasses of water beside two piping hot plates of food.

"That's my finding!"

Jason gave him a puzzled look. "You found two hot meals?"

"Nope. I found one working microwave and then made two hot meals."

Jason's eyes grew large. "With no generator attached?"

"With no generator," he replied, smiling from ear to ear.

Jason looked out the window processing his friend's remarkable find. "So, Teech must have learned how to create energy AND how to store it." He turned back to Silas with a look of amazement. "And I'll bet he even learned how to increase or transfer energy to food. Do you know what this means?" He jumped up out of his chair and grabbed his friend by the shoulders. "Silas, do you know what this means?"

Silas nodded as tears began streaming down his face. "Yes, he said softly...we're saved, we're saved!" The words grew to a crescendo. "We're SAVED!"

Jason fell back into his chair and let out a sigh of relief. For a moment, neither man said a word, content in the knowledge that their trip had not been in vain.

"Oh, and check this out," he said stepping over and flipping one of two switches next to the door. Instantly, the ceiling fan began to turn. He flipped the second one and the light came on.

"I can't wait to give that man a hug," Jason said.

Silas picked up his plate and began shoveling food into his mouth. It was the first hot food he had had in months. "Hell," he mumbled through a cheek full of mashed potatoes. "I'm going to give'em one helluva sloppy kiss."

A minute later, both plates were wiped cleaned. Jason neatly placed the tray next to the door then sat back down with Teech's journal and began pouring through its pages. Meanwhile Silas combed the room for any more documentation that may have been left behind.

"You may want to look at this journal, too," Jason said with a sigh. "So far I haven't come across anything that seems current. And to be honest, most of it is so beyond me I don't know if I'd recognize his energy solution or not."

Silas poked out his head from a nearby closet. "I thought we were just going to wait for him to return. Now that we know he's got all the answers, we have to wait."

The options began spinning through Jason's mind. Silas was right. If Teech showed up they were saved, but if he didn't they were doomed. If they waited too long, their gas wouldn't be strong enough to get home and they would starve to death. Jason at least had a chance of survival back with his friends. But more importantly, he would have one more opportunity to try and restore Mike's faith.

"Silas, do you honestly think he'll be back?"

"I do. I really do."

"What if he doesn't?"

"Man, I don't have anything else I *can* do. If I go home, I'm dead. I have to take my chances here."

258

"What about Zoey?"

Silas stepped out of the closet and walked over to him. "I know you can't wait here much longer. I know the ramifications." He paused. "If Teech doesn't show within the next two hours, then I want you to take the car back to my house and get Zoey. You can refuel there and take her with you to your friend's house. At least you'll all have a better chance there."

"But I'm not sure Zoey will even have a positive connection with Erin's uncle."

"At least it's a chance." A lump filled his throat. "And if she doesn't, then at least she'll…" He turned toward the window so Jason wouldn't see his tears. "…at least she'll be with people who care about her."

"You know there's also a chance you could have a connection with Erin's uncle. Who knows? It could be the most powerful one of all."

"Hmphh," Silas said, shaking his head. "I doubt it. If yours was just moderate, then I'm pretty sure mine wouldn't even register." He wiped away his tears with his sleeve then turned around with a big grin. "Besides, as soon as Teech does show up, he and I are gonna make our own road trip to beautiful Lake Royale."

The hum of the fan accented the silence that followed Silas's declaration to stay. Jason wanted to try to persuade him, but he knew it was a well thought-out decision. All he could do now was to wait and pray for Teech to return.

For the next forty-five minutes the two men examined the renowned physicist's journal trying to uncover the answers they so desperately needed. Sweat dripped from their faces as the effects of starvation and desperation kicked in. Their minds grew fuzzier with each passing minute, and the harder they tried to decipher his entries, the more frustrated they became. Halfway through the last page, Silas picked up the journal.

"Damn it!" he yelled, as he threw it against the wall. The single burst of anger left him gasping for air.

"You have to remain calm," Jason pleaded.

"I know," he panted. "I just can't believe that stupid book has Nobel Prize winning shit for everything except how to save the world!"

Jason put his hand on his shoulder. "Listen, we need to eat and drink again. We're showing major signs of starvation now. Irritability, dehydration, skin rashes..."

"Skin rashes?"

Jason pointed to two large red spots on Silas's arms.

"Aww shit," Silas said miserably.

"Let's go grab something," he urged.

"I'm not hungry. We've been eating and eating. I can't put another thing in this skinny body of mine."

He stood up. "Apathy's another sign of starvation. You're giving up."

"No, sir. I'm not giving up. I know apathy is on its way, but it's not here yet. I simply can't put anything else in my belly. I've got to digest what's in it first. Besides, whatever we eat now isn't going to amount to a hill of beans for energy anyway – BAH HA HA!" Silas blurted out in hysterical laughter. "A hill of beans – get it?"

"Come on man, keep it together. If your plan is to wait it out here, you've got to force yourself to eat."

"I can't!" Silas countered. "You go eat. I'm going to look around this stupid house to see if I can find another journal or anything that might help us."

Jason watched as his friend staggered out of the room and down the hallway. His gait was uneven. At any moment it looked as if he would drop from the sudden fatigue. Just then, it came to him. In a minute he was in the kitchen digging through the duffle bag he had brought.

"Silas, get in here!" he yelled.

A moment later Silas came bumbling through the door leading to the garage. "Looks like Sir Richard knew how to rig a carrr too," he slurred while motioning out toward the empty parking space. "Wherever they went, it wasn't on foot."

"Never mind that – get over here."

Silas wobbled to him. His eyes were half shut and his head leaned to the side as if too heavy to lift.

"Stick out your arm," Jason said.

"What?"

"Just do it."

Silas slowly stretched his arm out. In one motion, Jason pushed his sleeve up to his bicep and wrapped his arm around his. With his other hand he grabbed a syringe from the countertop and injected it into his friend's arm. Without flinching, Silas allowed the serum to enter into his system.

Jason guided him to the kitchen table and sat him in a chair.

"That'll kick in any minute and you'll be good to go for a while." Then he turned and opened the refrigerator door. "Holy mackerel! We hit the mother lode."

"What kind of mother lode?" Silas said in a more lucid tone.

Jason moved to the side showcasing for him a dozen stacks of protein shakes.

"I never thought to look in the refrigerator," Silas said in clear crisp sentence. "Wow! This is pretty good stuff," he said opening his eyes wide.

"I know," Jason said. "We can down a lot more of these than we can hard food. We'll get more energy, plus it'll hydrate us."

"You're right about that, but what I really meant was that the shot you gave me was pretty good. What was it?"

"A B-12 and adrenaline concoction my friend Erin gave me before we left. Unfortunately, it'll probably wear off in a couple of hours."

"How many more do you have?"

"That was it." He said as he popped the top of one of the shakes and started guzzling it down.

Silas sat with his mouth hung open. "You gave me your last one?"

He licked his lips of the excess liquid from his protein shake. "Yep. You got a problem with that?" He started to raise his drink again, but Silas grabbed his arm.

"Why would you do that?"

"Why not? You'd do the same for me. You know, do unto others as you'd have them do unto you."

"I know, but..."

"No, my friend. You needed it more than I did, and besides, now I can down a couple more of these and I'll be okay for a little longer. He pulled two more cans from the refrigerator then pushed the door shut.

"What just fell behind you?" Silas said.

He turned and looked down. "It's just a calendar that must've been on the other side of the fridge."

After several failed attempts to re-stick it to the front door, he tossed it onto the kitchen table.

"Wait just a second." Silas reached over and picked it up.

His eyes narrowed as they jumped from one day-block to the next. Slowly, his expression turned from curious to concern.

"What are you looking for?" Jason asked.

He leaned his head back and closed his eyes. With a heavy sigh he looked back down onto the spiral-bound pages hoping what he had seen wasn't true. He handed Jason the calendar.

"Look at today's date."

Jason focused in on the meticulously written entry. Every letter matched perfectly with those from Teech's journal. Aloud he read:

Depart for Annabel's. Noon.

Next to it was a heart with the number "two" next to it.

He looked at Silas. "Who's Annabel?"

"Doesn't matter," he responded, his voice full of dejection. "We just missed him."

Jason panned to the margin where someone had sketched in two stick figures holding a heart between them. Just above the heart to the right was another small number "two" written like an equation or like something to the second power. He calmly placed the calendar back on to the kitchen table.

"Do you think Annabel's another sister?"

Silas shrugged his shoulders. "It could be. I don't know. It could be an aunt, a coworker, or a girlfriend. Hell, it could be his mother as far as I know." He shook his head. "But with no way of telling who it is, we don't know where he went."

"Stay here a second," Jason shouted on his way out of the room. A minute later, he returned with a circular Rolodex.

"I remembered seeing this in his study." He ripped out half of the cards and gave them to Silas. "Start looking for any Annabels. Most of these have the entire address, so maybe we'll get lucky and she'll be nearby."

"What if we find more than one, or if we find some Annas? Anna can be short for Annabel right?"

He turned to him with his head tilted. "Just look please."

"Yeah, yeah! Sorry."

"I got one!" Jason exclaimed. "Shoot. She's in Australia."

"Pretty sure he didn't fly there."

"Wait, here's another one," he said holding the card to the light. "This one's an Anna. Anna Kennsington, address is Chicago." He tossed it to the floor.

After filtering through the remaining cards with no luck, Silas walked to the back door and peered up into the sky deep in thought.

"By the sun it looks like it's between two and three. If we leave now, we should make it back with no trouble."

Jason nodded.

All hope of finding Teech and the life-saving answers he possessed was gone. The only option now lay back in the direction they had come.

CHAPTER 33
GOING HOME

Jason grabbed his duffle bag and stuffed it with protein shakes, while Silas packed the remaining cans into a cardboard box. Minutes later, they were back on the highway leaving the potential of Teech's secrets in the rearview mirror. Neither man spoke as they silently reflected on the past few hours and how their best chance of survival had slipped past them. All they could do now was contemplate their futures and what their new journey would bring.

After fifteen minutes, Silas's head bobbed downward then snapped straight up.

"You okay?" Jason asked.

"Yeah, but that juice you pumped into me is starting to wear off pretty quick."

"You want me to drive?"

"No, I'm good." He blinked away the first wave of fatigue. "This might be the last time I get to enjoy a ride like this."

Jason gave him a quick glance. "If you'll just have faith, it doesn't have to be."

Silas looked at him with a crooked smile. "You never give up, do you?"

"I can't."

Silas punched the accelerator. "Do you really think God would forgive me for all I've done in the past? I mean my being an atheist and everything."

His heart jumped. "Of course He would."

"Even now?"

"Absolutely!"

Just then, the car started sputtering and began to slow down.

"Oh no. Don't tell me we're out of gas," Jason said.

"The second tank is." He flipped a switch on the dash and the engine revved back up. "Okay," he sighed, "we're good again."

"Phewww!" Jason said wiping the sweat from his forehead. "By the way, how's our fuel efficiency?"

He shook his head. "You don't want to know."

"Is it enough to get us back to your house?"

He hesitated while he calculated the outcome in his head. "It's going to be close. The problem is I don't know how rapidly we're losing energy now. Plus this last tank isn't connected to the fuel gauge, so I don't know how much we're using."

Jason reached into his pocket and pulled out the silver heart-shaped medallion Erin had given him.

"What's that?" Silas said yawning.

"Just something a friend gave me. Listen, are you sure you're okay to drive? You look like you're going to pass out."

"I promise I'm okay. Anyway, at ninety miles an hour we'll be back at my place in less than twenty minutes."

"Okay, but when we get there I'm taking over, okay? You are planning to come with me aren't you? And Zoey too, of course."

"You can bet on it, my friend."

Jason looked backed down at the heart. Curling his fingers around it he closed his eyes and whispered a prayer asking God to help them make it home safely. As he prayed he envisioned them pulling up to Mike's house and his friends running out to meet them. He could feel the warmth of their embrace. He could hear their laughter. He could see their tears of joy. Slowly, his thoughts faded away as the melodic hum of rubber against road lulled him to sleep. The blissful void from consciousness was a welcome relief from the second-by-second angst brought on by the constant fear of running out of fuel. As he passed into a deeper slumber, his head rolled to the side causing the rest of his body to follow.

For the next several minutes he lay comfortably against the door until suddenly his head was jerked to the left. His body swung upright. Tires screeched as he was tossed violently against Silas, then back against the door. For a split second his eyes fixated past the dashboard onto the spinning landscape outside. Trees blurred into a swirling stream of green and brown. His head slammed into the roof then down onto the dash. A jagged collage of flashing trees, road, and sky spun him back into the unconsciousness from which he had come. The last thing he remembered was the sound of glass crashing in on him.

As the smoke and dust of the wreckage settled around the mangled car, Silas crawled through the shattered front windshield and onto the hood where he lay gasping for air. His heart was pounding. With every beat a fresh flow of blood streamed down his forehead and across his eyes. The world about him was a smoldering blur.

"Jason!" he yelled blindly. "Where are you?" The only response was the clicking of the engine as it slowly died.

Frantically, he pulled off his denim shirt, then ripped the T-shirt he was wearing underneath into several large pieces. He wiped the blood from his eyes and wrapped one of the strips around his forehead. Slowly, the horrific scene came into focus. Sitting sideways in the middle of the road was one half of the car with the other half nowhere in sight. Pieces of the mutilated Mustang lay scattered over forty yards in every direction.

Climbing to his knees he yelled again. "Jason, where are you?"

But still there was no reply. He turned one way and then the other. He looked up and down the road and out into the fields of thick weeds bordering the asphalt.

"Oh God, please help me find him," he pleaded aloud.

"I heard that," came a weak, raspy voice from below the car.

He twisted his head in every direction. "Jason, is that you?"

"Who else would it be?" he groaned. "I'm down here."

"Down where?"

For a second there was no response. "I think I'm beside..." his voice trailed off.

Silas grabbed the top of the passenger door that had flung open during the crash and leaned over the edge of the car. Lying unconscious next to the front tire was Jason. A large bruise spanned from the right side of his forehead to his temple. His left pants leg was shredded into pieces revealing the white of bone protruding through his skin just above the ankle.

As he jumped to the ground a sharp pain ripped through his abdomen causing him to fall face down beside his friend.

"Ohhhh," he moaned clutching his stomach.

Every breath he took was like a searing hot dagger to the gut. The deeper the breath, the more intense the stabbing. After several minutes the pain subsided enough for him to bring himself to a kneeling position. He laid his hand on Jason's forehead and felt the large mass of blood-filled flesh on his palm. He looked down at the shattered bone in his leg. Then he sighed and dropped his head to his chest as the bleakness of the situation set in. How had he let himself fall asleep at the wheel? Why had he not let Jason drive? His selfishness and arrogance had sealed their fate. And his own lifetime of denial had now led him to the edge of eternal damnation.

Placing his hands together he raised his head and gazed into the sky. As tears began to fill his eyes he whispered, "God, please forgive me. Forgive me for turning my back on you. Forgive me for renouncing you, for not believing in your son." He covered his face with his hands and began to sob. Tears rolled past his palms onto Jason's chest. "Forgive me, God. Please forgive me."

With all his strength he grabbed the door and began pulling himself to his feet. As he stood, the pain in his stomach leveled off, only to be replaced with a dull ache running from the top of his head down his spine. He paused a moment to catch his breath and to steady himself. Then holding onto the remains of the car he slowly worked his way around the wreckage, searching for anything that might help him attend to Jason's leg. Each step was a singular ordeal of torture.

By the time he had made it to the driver's side he was sweating profusely and his head had started to bleed again, creating a constant stream of blood down his face. He wiped his eyes and stuck his head through a large gaping hole the crash had ripped in the door. Grimacing in pain he reached his arm through it. Blood gushed from his forehead, burning his eyes and blinding him again.

A few seconds later he pulled himself back from the car holding the machete he had placed under his seat. After wiping the blood away from his eyes, he surveyed the debris field that lay in front of the car. Beyond the seemingly infinite pieces of glass and shards of metal, he spotted Jason's duffle bag along with dozens of protein drinks scattered nearby. The twenty yards he walked to retrieve it were excruciating. Whatever was wrong with him internally was growing worse with every step. By the time he got back to his friend he was doubled over in pain. He dropped the bag and passed out at his feet.

For the next two hours, the earth stood still as the two men lay unconscious. No birds or butterflies fluttered about, no clouds drifted by, no cars zoomed past, only the shift of the day's light as the sun progressed toward twilight.

Beep – Beep – Beep. Silas's eyes fluttered as the chirpy little tone teased him awake. Gingerly, he raised his head from the asphalt. Beep – Beep – Beep came the tones a second time. He identified the duffle bag as the source of the annoying sounds and turned it over spilling out its contents. For a moment he lay staring at a T-shirt, a bottle of water, some protein bars, and a roll of plastic zip-ties.

Beep – Beep – Beep came the sounds again. Stretching out his hand he grabbed the T-shirt and flung it back revealing the pager Erin had given Jason. Only two words appeared on the digital screen, "Coming for." He tossed the device to the side of the road, then slowly lifted himself off the pavement and into a kneeling position at his friend's feet.

He had to work fast while Jason was still unconscious. And with the sun low in the sky he knew he didn't have much time to complete the task as himself. In surgical fashion he neatly laid out the items for his procedure. Then grabbing the machete he positioned himself for the difficult next step.

Thirty minutes later, Silas sat motionless against the side of his once-prized Mustang. His shirt was drenched with sweat and blood. Stretching out before him was the long and lonesome river of asphalt that had been carrying them home. He closed his eyes hoping to maintain the little energy he had left.

With his right hand he reached over and placed it onto Jason's chest to make sure he was still breathing. He smiled as it slowly moved up and down. Just as he was about to remove it, something no heavier than a butterfly's wing tapped against his finger. Then another tap, followed by another. He opened his eyes to find Jason reaching up to him.

"Silas," he whispered in a feeble voice. "Are you okay?"

Silas managed a chuckle. "You're amazing. You're almost dead and you're worried about me."

"What happened? I feel like crap." He grabbed Silas's hand and squeezed it, sinking his nails into his palm. "AHHH! My leg! What happened to my leg?" he screamed.

"We crashed. It was my fault. I fell asleep and lost control."

Jason pulled himself up on his elbows and looked down at the T-shirt covering the bottom half of his leg.

"It feels like it's been…" He stopped. "NO, please tell me you…"

Silas reached down and quickly pulled the T-shirt away. "I had to set the bones while you were out. I used the machete as a splint and the zip-ties to secure it."

He winced as he stared at the makeshift apparatus, then fell back to the ground laughing.

"For a minute I thought you'd done something drastic."

"I'm sorry, Jason. It was all my fault."

"It wasn't anybody's fault," he said patting him on the knee. He started to raise himself up then fell back. "Do me a favor and prop me up. This huge bump on my head is throbbing. If I'm upright, I think it'll feel better."

Silas slowly stood up biting his lip while masking the sudden onset of pain. As gently as he could, he pulled Jason up against the car next to him. When he sat back down he wrapped his arms around his abdomen and began coughing up blood.

"You sound horrible. How do you feel?"

"Could be better, I suppose," he said forcing a grin. "I tore up something inside, that's for sure. It's tough breathing, so it might be a punctured lung."

"You wanna know something funny?"

"What's that?"

"Those zip-ties you used on my leg were actually meant for you."

Silas nodded. "I should've known." He hesitated a moment to catch his breath and to deal with the increasing pain. "I don't think I'll be much of a threat tonight." Then he turned and looked down the road and out over the horizon. Only a fraction of the sun remained above the tree line, just enough to produce the most glorious shades of lavender, gold, deep purples, and soft violets. "Man," he wheezed, "I'm really going to miss sunsets."

Jason turned to him and smiled softly. "Yeah, me too."

For the next few minutes they sat in silence as they coped with their injuries and the increased fatigue of the relentless energy loss. Quietly, they reconciled with themselves that the end was upon them.

As the remaining splendor of the day's light faded into darkness, Silas reached over and took Jason's hand. With a long painful breath he said, "Will you say a prayer for me?"

"Of course I will." He hesitated a second. "But I need to ask you something important first."

He raised his head. "Sure," he said in a small voice.

"Have you accepted Jesus as your savior?"

As he eagerly awaited his response, Silas began to breathe heavily. His hand pulled away from his.

"What's wrong?" Jason asked.

"Do you see it?"

"See what?"

"The light," he said pointing down the road.

He squinted. "I don't see anything."

"There," he said in a breathy plea. "It's right there."

Jason straightened up as a tiny speck of light dotted the center of the highway. Slowly, it began to get bigger. Then off in the distance, ever so faint, a hum. As the light continued to grow, the

272

hum gradually morphed into a rumbling. Jason and Silas sat in anticipation when suddenly the light accelerated toward them. At two hundred yards, the rumbling became more defined as the firing of pistons filled the air. At a hundred yards, they could feel the percussion of sound against their chest.

In an instant the light was directly on them, blinding and pinning them against the car. Too weak to stand, all they could do was shield their eyes. Suddenly the engine stopped. A second later the beam of light swung to the right illuminating the car and destruction surrounding it. As their eyes adjusted, they watched as the dark outline of a man stepped off a motorcycle and walked toward them.

CHAPTER 34
ARMAGEDDON

The stranger stopped fifteen feet from them and knelt down. "Jason, is that you?"

"Mike?"

Slowly, the image of his friend appeared before him.

"Mike, is that really you?"

"Yeah, it's me. What the hell happened, buddy?"

"Oh man, am I glad to see you," he said excitedly. "We crashed. We were trying to make it back and we crashed. Mike, we almost found Teech. We were so close. We were in his house and he's got the answers. Mike, he found out how to generate energy and maybe store it and maybe even transfer it to food and..."

"Hold on! Slow down. You need to conserve your energy."

Jason held up his hand. "Right," he said breathlessly. He gulped, then slowly inhaled. "What are you doing here?" he said, gritting his teeth in pain.

"I came after you, of course."

"Whose motorcycle?"

"Yours. I got to your friend Silas's house and the car I rigged died. So I took yours. Zoey told me about Teech's move, so all I had to do was follow your trail. Sooner or later, I knew I'd either catch up with you or meet you coming back."

Jason turned to Silas. "Did you hear that? He's going to get us out of here!"

Silas was curled up shivering with his head tucked into the car's wheel well.

He turned back to Mike. "You can see we're pretty banged up. I'm afraid if we don't get him out of here quickly he'll go into shock."

Mike took a step closer. He bent down and tilted his head in Silas's direction. His eyebrows furrowed with a disregarding glance.

"He'ssss a goner." The callousness of his words seemed to hiss from his lips.

Jason was momentarily taken aback by what he thought he had just seen and heard. His condition was shaky at best, and given how fuzzy his mind was becoming, he couldn't be sure of anything. What he did know though was that Mike was one of the most compassionate people he knew. Surely, he had misheard him.

"I'm sorry. What did you say?"

"I said I think you're right. Silas is hurt pretty badly."

"He's a lot worse than me. Why don't you take him back and I'll stay here? There are enough protein cans lying around to keep me going for a while."

"NOOOO!" Silas screeched. He grabbed Jason by the arm. "NOOOO! NOOOO!" Then he buried his head back into his safe haven between metal and tire and began mumbling. "No, no! Not going! No, not going!"

Jason looked at Mike. He wanted to explain his friend's nocturnal condition, but didn't know how. He turned back to Silas and placed his hand on his shoulder as he watched the madness take control.

"Don't worry my friend. Everything's going to be okay. Mike's here to help."

Silas began gnawing at his fingers and shaking his head. "Not here to help. Not here to help."

"But he is," Jason said reassuringly. "Trust me. He's going to take you home. Everything's going to be okay."

"NOOOO!" he screamed.

Jason glanced at Mike. "If you can just get him on the bike, I think he'll be okay."

Silas threw his arm around Jason's neck, buried his head into his ear and whispered. "No, no, please, don't let him take me. Pleeeeease!"

Jason pulled back and looked into his eyes. Tears were streaming down his cheeks. He took him by the shoulders. "It's the only way. You'll die if you stay here. You have to go with him."

Instantly Silas's face became pale with an intense fear. He leaned forward and slowly whispered in his ear. "Mike not here to help." He squeezed his arm, digging his fingers into his bicep. He pulled him closer. "Tallyman here to steal soul."

Jason looked at him, heartbroken at how quickly the neurosis had hit him. When he turned back to Mike, he found him bent down next to Silas. He was staring intensely at him as if he were looking below the surface of his skin. The light from the motorcycle cut sharp angular shadows into his face stealing away the kind and gentle features that had always made him so approachable. He rolled his head to the left and then the right.

Out of the corner of his eye, he stole a menacing glance in Jason's direction. A sudden wave of pain shot up his leg and his head began to throb. His mind became a blurry haze as he began to drift into a semi-conscious state. As the scene unfolded, it became hard to separate reality from dream.

"Silasssssss," he whispered. "It's time to come with me."

Jason watched his friend recoil against the car. As if in slow

276

motion, he saw Mike reach out his hand and curl his fingers back into his palm, motioning Silas to come with him. His nails appeared long and sharp. His skin was a grayish pale.

"Silassssss. It'sssss time," he hissed.

Jason's head bobbed down then jerked up as he fought from passing out. Silas had wrapped his arms around his and was lodged between him and the car. He could feel his body trembling.

"No, please don't take me! Please, don't take me!" He buried his head behind Jason's shoulder. "Jason, please help me," he begged.

Fatigue and pain were seconds away from overtaking him when suddenly Jason willed himself into a moment of clarity.

He grabbed Silas by the hand. "Pray with me!" With a deep breath he began...

"*Yea, though I walk through the valley of the shadow of death...*"

Silas followed along repeating after him, his voice shaky but firm.

"*...I will fear no evil: for thou art with me; thy rod and thy staff they comfort me...*"

As they spoke, Mike's eyes narrowed and his face became contorted with anger. Slowly, he began to back away from them. His body appeared to hover above the ground.

"*...Thou preparest a table before me in the presence of mine enemies: thou anointest my head with oil; my cup runneth over...*"

As he continued speaking, Jason's mind became clearer and the pain and fatigue began to lessen. He watched in horror as Mike's body suddenly rose into the air and morphed into a black hooded figure. His skin was deathly pale. His eyes and top of his face receded under the dark folds of the hood as a large pointed chin appeared from nowhere. He paused as he stared at the hideous scar that ran across it. It was exactly like the one Erin had witnessed in her unholy encounter.

The specter then arched backward and spread his arms letting out a beastly moan. Rising higher, he grew to twice his size. A clash of thunder sounded and suddenly his arms transformed into giant scaled wings. A serpent's tail emerged from behind and whipped around him just over their heads. The car began to rattle and the ground began to shake.

Silas averted his eyes while Jason remained defiantly fixed upon the demonic figure. Jason squeezed Silas's hand to continue "

"*...Surely goodness and mercy shall follow me all the days of my life...*"

With another clap of thunder, a blast of air hit them then swirled around them as a bolt of lightning struck the road in front of them.

Raising their voices above the wind's fury, they screamed the prayer's last line,

"*...AND I WILL DWELL IN THE HOUSE OF THE LORD FOREVER!*"

Everything went black. The air stilled and all was quiet. Darkness surrounded them. Suspended above them was a large black mass, deeper in pitch and more void of light than the rest of the night sky. Slowly it disappeared. Both men sat motionless, not having the words or breath to express their thoughts. After several minutes, Silas turned to Jason. The edges of his mouth slowly curved upward and he began to laugh. Jason looked at him guardedly as he anticipated another level of neurosis to appear.

"What's so funny?"

Silas patted him on the knee. "How often do you have the chance to send the devil packing?" His words were clear and lucid.

Jason leaned his head back and chuckled. He let out a sigh of relief. The black cloud of his friend's condition had miraculously been lifted.

"How do you feel?"

He looked about his body. "I feel different." He hesitated a second then looked up into the sky as he chose his words. Then he looked at Jason and smiled. "I feel – reborn."

Jason's heart soared. "That's because you *are*."

A tear rolled down Silas's cheek as he grabbed his hand. "Thank you. Thank you for not abandoning me. Thank you for helping me see the light and showing me how to believe."

For the next several minutes the two men reflected on the extraordinary experience they had just been through. Then fighting through their pain and fatigue they sat and talked through the night as they savored their last precious moments on earth. They talked about their past, their regrets in life, their triumphs and disappointments. They shared the love of their family and friends. But most of all, they talked about the power of faith.

Shortly before sunrise, the fatigue and stress of his injuries overcame Silas, and he slowly passed away. Jason lowered his head and silently said a prayer asking God to receive his friend. The sadness of losing him was suddenly replaced with a sense of joy as he thought back on the miraculous spiritual transformation he had made and how he had received his salvation. Jason smiled, fulfilled in knowing that he would see him again soon.

It was now just a matter of time before he too would fade away. He was at peace in knowing that he had finished strong. He had learned how to believe and to lead by faith. Most importantly, he had sacrificed for his love of others. He had finally become the man he had always wanted to be.

As the first ray of sunlight reached into the sky, it tinted the horizon with cool tones of purple and blue. Reluctantly, the night was giving way to morning. With the sky growing brighter his breath grew shallower and his heart slowed. He gazed down the road that had been leading him home. He was now ready for the final journey, content with where he had been.

His chest rose then fell one final time. Gently the breath of life left his body. On the last beat of his heart, his eyes closed and the morning's light faded back into night. There were no shadows, silhouettes, or shades of gray, just a solid space of darkness now. Time stood still. There was no beginning or ending, just a frozen moment void of sensation, emotion, or thought. He was without presence – he was no more.

From out of the unknown, ever so slowly, a pinhole of light appeared. Slowly, the genesis of awareness ignited and he began to feel his own being. As he watched the light expand toward him, cognitive thought emerged from within and each of his senses returned. But somehow the anguish of his final hours had vanished. He was without a body, but he felt whole. He felt alive and vibrant, but without the trappings of his physical self. There were no worries, stress, sadness, pain, or fatigue, just a blissful feeling of joy and happiness.

As the light continued to approach, its warmth intensified. But there was no fear of heat, as fear did not exist anymore. In an instant the light was before him. Like an endless wall it stretched infinitely in every direction. It was a light that he had never seen before. It was beyond white with a purity that did not exist on earth. For a moment he remained suspended in space, gazing into its magnificence. Then suddenly it began to move forward. The top, bottom and sides began to bend and wrap around him. Like a blanket, the light enveloped him.

Awash in its all-embracing warmth, a presence reached out to him. There was no form or shape to it, just the essence of spirit and light, and the undeniable knowledge that he was about to encounter the divine. As it approached he began to feel an overwhelming sense of love; a love so great and powerful that it was beyond mortal comprehension.

Without a spoken word, it communicated to him that he was loved unconditionally, his soul was redeemed, and that his purpose in life was yet to be completed. At that moment, off in the distance, he heard a hum. Like a tender lullaby it began pulling him from the light and into a dreamlike state. Slowly the brilliance of his surroundings began to fade and he slipped back into darkness. Time and space were again suspended.

Somewhere within the recesses of his soul, he began to feel a tingling. Then the darkness about him began to vibrate and an invisible force grabbed him, pulling him backward through space. Faster and faster he flew, out of the abyss and into the light of day. In an instant he lay lifeless amidst the wreckage of the car, next to the body of his dear friend.

He tried opening his eyes, but could not. He tried moving his arms and legs, and again could not. The only sensation he felt was an icy coldness that ran through his body. It was the only thing letting him know he existed. Ever so slowly he began to feel warmth around him. As the feeling grew stronger, another feeling emerged – love. He felt it as he had before. It was unconditional and without description. It entered from every part of his body and coursed through his veins. With a gasp he took a breath, then another and another.

When he opened his eyes, the glare of the morning sun blinded him causing him to quickly close them again. Suddenly, he felt a pressure from his torso down to his waist. He cracked his eyelids just enough to see the wavy brown hair of a woman below his chin. Her head was buried in his chest and her arms were wrapped tightly around him.

"What – Who – Who are you?" he stammered. His voice was groggy and hoarse.

Her head immediately popped up, blocking the sun while concealing her face within a dark silhouette.

"Oh my," she gasped. "You're alive! You're ALIVE!" She turned to the side and screamed. "It worked! HE'S ALIVE!"

At that moment a little girl jumped up from behind her. Leaping onto his chest she wrapped her arms around his neck and cried. "DADDY! You're back!"

Jason's heart began pounding.

She sat up on his chest. "I missed you daddy!"

"Oh, dear Lord," he said breathlessly. He stared at her for a second. "Nikki, is that really you?"

"Of course it's me," she giggled. She turned her head around revealing the tiny heart-shaped birthmark on the back of her neck. "Mommy, Daddy wanted to know if it was me."

She turned back and hugged him. As she did, the face of his beloved Kristina appeared just over his little girl's shoulder. Tears were streaming down her face.

"Kristina?" he whispered.

She smiled.

His heart skipped a beat. "Is this real? I'm not dreaming, am I? Please tell me I'm not dreaming."

She fell to her knees and kissed him. She hugged and kissed him again and again. "Yes. Yes!" she said through her sobbing. "Yes! You're alive!"

He lifted his arms and pulled them both into him. A tidal wave of emotions rushed over him. He wanted to speak, but he couldn't catch his breath – all he could do was cry. His joy and love held him captive in a way that he didn't want to be freed of. His two most precious gifts were in his embrace. All the pain and suffering he had been through was suddenly gone and the world about him was warm and full of love again. He buried his head between his wife and daughter and continued to weep.

"Maybe the next time you take a trip you'll let me tag along."

Jason recognized the voice. He lifted his head. Still unable to form a complete sentence, he held out his hand and muttered, "My friends – my dear friends."

Standing next to a school bus, with a huge grin, was Mike. Beside him were Erin and her Uncle David.

In a joyous rush they ran to his side and joined his wife and daughter in wrapping their arms around him. For the next half hour they remained gathered over him hugging, laughing, crying, and praising God for the miracle of his return. All the while, he held Nikki and Kristina in his arms afraid to let them go.

After wiping the tears from his face, he placed his hand gently against Kristina's cheek and gazed into her eyes. "What happened?" he asked softly. "How did you get back?"

Before she could answer, Mike put his hand on his shoulder. "Maybe you should relax right now. There's plenty of time for explanations. Why don't we get you home?"

He smiled and nodded.

With Mike directing, they all circled him and carefully picked him up and carried him to the bus. A few minutes later, Jason was sitting with his broken leg stretched across the front seat with Nikki on his lap and Kristina curled up next to him. Erin and Mike sat in the seat behind them.

As Erin's uncle pulled the door shut, Jason turned to Mike and asked, "Are you sure this is going to get us home?"

Mike looked at the others then turned back with a big grin. "Jason, as long as we stay together, we can go as far as you want."

CHAPTER 35
LOVE STORIES

Uncle David turned the ignition and the engine roared to life. As they pulled away from the wreckage, Mike looked out the rear window.

"It's a miracle you didn't die instantly in that crash."

Nikki laid her head on Jason's shoulder. "Mommy said the angels brought you back."

He looked around at his friends. They were all smiling in anticipation of his fatherly response.

"They sure did, honey," he said softly. In an instant all of his attention was focused back on his daughter. He tilted his head and smiled warmly at her.

Mike leaned over the seat. "You were right," he said. "They really do exist."

"What do you mean?" he said, while stealing a kiss first from Nikki and then Kristina.

"Angels. They exist."

"I know," Jason smiled, "I think I'm in a busload of them right now."

Erin laughed as she leaned forward next to Mike. "He's being serious. You remember how Uncle David came to us?"

He kissed Nikki on the forehead and began stroking her hair. "Yeah, I remember."

"And you recall how you thought he was an angel and how you thought the girl in the boathouse and the guy at the window was, too?"

"I remember."

She paused and looked at Mike. "We believe they were all sent by God."

"Even Kristina and Nikki," Mike added.

Jason stopped running his hand through Nikki's hair and turned to them with a puzzled look. "You think my wife and daughter are angels? I love it, but I'm not sure I follow."

"Well maybe not angels exactly," Mike began, "but we believe they were taken and then sent back for a reason."

Kristina leaned down and whispered in his ear "I love you."

Mike smiled, looking on as his best friend and his family displayed their undeniable love for one another. "I apologize," he said. "Maybe we should wait until we get home to tell you all this."

Kristina quickly sat back up. "Oh no, I'm sorry, Mike. Please go on."

Jason looked at his wife. His heart warmed as he remembered how caring and sensitive she was for others.

"Are you sure?" Mike said.

"Absolutely," she replied enthusiastically, "he's all yours. Besides, I don't think I'll ever get tired of hearing this."

Mike nodded. "Well, if you insist." He paused, then slowly began. "The day you left, Erin and I sat in the living room talking all afternoon. Not to get all sappy, but through her testimony she helped reaffirm my faith. When we finished, I asked the Lord to forgive me for losing my faith and not believing."

Touched by the impact of his words, Jason put his hand to his heart. "Is that what made you decide to come after me?"

"Partially, but it's what happened immediately afterward that really did it."

Uncle David looked over his shoulder. "It's when I put the mojo to him."

Mike chuckled. "Thanks, Uncle Dave!"

Erin put her hand on Jason's knee. "What happened was another miracle. Uncle David had overheard our conversation and was so moved by Mike's prayer he couldn't help but come in and give him a hug."

Nikki wrapped her arms around Jason's shoulders and squeezed him as tight as she could. "Just like this," she said with a grunt.

Everyone laughed.

"That's exactly it," Mike said. "And that's when the fireworks began. Every light in the room went on, the ceiling fan took off, and the security alarm began blaring."

Jason turned to Erin. His eyes grew larger. "It was just like what happened between you and your uncle!"

She started laughing. "You should have seen him jump. He looked like he'd been hit with a cattle prod."

Mike was almost standing in his seat. He smiled at Erin. "It was the best shock I've ever been given. In an instant, I felt energized. All the fatigue and stress I'd been feeling were gone. It was like I'd been hooked up to a human battery pack." He turned back to Jason. "That's when it hit me!"

"What did?"

"That maybe we could take the results of this energy generation on the road."

Erin smiled. "And that's when he told me and Uncle David that we were going to your house to try and find your friend Silas's address so we could go after you. I even paged you we were coming."

Mike's smile continued to grow. "So the next morning we all set off on foot to your place, with the intention of testing my hypothesis out on the first vehicle we came across."

"Don't tell me…" Jason said.

"That's right. Good ol' Oakwood Elementary bus number three was the lucky winner."

"It sputtered the entire way, but it got us there," Erin chuckled.

"This is amazing!" Jason said, almost bouncing in his seat. "So, our initial thoughts about the connections being beneficial were actually correct."

"Yep." Mike replied back with a big smile.

"Keep going – how do Kristina and Nikki fit in?"

"Oh, let me tell this part," Erin begged.

"Sure," Mike smiled.

"When we got to your house we immediately started digging through your files for Silas's address. After about fifteen minutes we found an old Rolodex with it, so we headed back to the bus. Just as we were about to get in, I heard someone giggling in a bush." She turned to Nikki with a big grin. "When I walked over to it, guess who I found?"

"Me, me!" Nikki squealed as she bounced up and down on her daddy's lap.

"That's right," Erin said playfully. "I found our littlest angel hiding in the bushes."

Jason looked lovingly at his little girl and smiled, then turned to Kristina. "And what about my other beautiful angel?" he asked.

"At the same moment, she walked around the corner. Both her and Nikki's eyes had a bluish tint to them and their skin was pretty pale."

"They were rather confused, too." Mike said.

"But not as much as Uncle David," she added. "The effects of whatever had happened to them were wearing off just as they did with him."

Jason turned to Kristina. "Do you remember anything or where you went for so long?"

"I don't have a clue. It only seemed like we were gone for a couple minutes. One moment we were playing tag around the clothesline, then the next we were wandering the backyard in a daze. It was like coming out of a deep sleep. Initially, I couldn't remember who or where I was, then slowly everything started coming back to me. I didn't even realize our appearance was different until Erin and Mike told us later." She paused, then turned to Nikki and smiled. "But there is one thing we do remember."

"THE LIGHT," they exclaimed in unison.

Jason's heartbeat quickened.

She looked out the window for a second then turned back to him. Tears filled her eyes and her smile turned to joyous laughter. "Jason, darling...you wouldn't believe it. It was the most magnificent thing I've ever experienced. It was..." she hesitated, searching for the correct words. "It was..."

"It was love, Daddy!" Nikki exclaimed. "The light loved us!"

Jason smiled as a tear rolled down his cheek. "I know," he nodded. "I know."

"Well, I'll tell you one thing," Mike chimed in.

"What's that?" Jason said as he wiped his eyes.

"This bus sure loved them. The moment we brought them on board the engine roared and the sputtering stopped. Even the gas efficiency's gotten better."

Uncle David looked at him through the rearview mirror. "That's right. I'd say we're using between ten and fifteen miles per gallon. Pretty dang good, considering these elephants probably average on the low end of ten per gallon."

"Seems to be affecting what we eat, too," Mike said. "All the way around, it appears energy's being regenerated when we're in the midst of these three. Look what it did for you."

Jason tilted his head. "What do you mean?"

Mike's eyes welled with tears. "When we pulled up, you weren't breathing. You didn't have a pulse and your skin was blue – Jason, you were dead. I'm not sure for how long but your body was ice cold," his voice cracked. "I tried administering CPR, but nothing."

"That's when it happened," Erin continued. "That's when Kristina and Nikki ran to you. Kristina wrapped her arms around your chest and Nikki around your waist."

Mike wiped his eyes with his sleeve. "A few seconds later, you gasped. Your eyelids fluttered and you began breathing."

Nikki snuggled up to his cheek and gently kissed him. "But you're all better now."

Erin looked down at his makeshift splint. "So, how do you actually feel right now?"

He stared at her for a second as his thoughts flew back to those exact words he had asked Silas before he passed away. He flinched as he recalled the terrible crash and their horrifying encounter with evil. Then he smiled as he remembered the warmth of the light and the promise of unconditional love and redemption. He looked down at his leg, then back to Erin. "How do I feel?" He gave Nikki a hug, then gazed up into his wife's eyes. "I feel blessed. That's how I feel – utterly and completely blessed."

CHAPTER 36
FIREFLIES

A month later, Jason was sitting on his back porch in his shorts and T-shirt watching Nikki chasing fireflies across the yard. By all logical reasoning it should be freezing out with no fireflies in sight for at least three months. Not caring to stress himself for any more answers, he just smiled and enjoyed the moment.

"Daddy, I got another one!" she exclaimed clamping the lid onto the jar. "That makes twelve."

As night slowly fell, his daughter's features began to fade into the night. He smiled as he tracked her by following the illuminated jar bouncing about between the trees and shrubs.

"I think twelve's about enough, don't you?" he shouted.

"Yeaahhh – I guess," she answered reluctantly.

Just then, Kristina stuck her head out of the kitchen window. "Honey, the news summit is on in two minutes. You'd better hurry."

Nikki came running up onto the porch. "Look how much my bugs are glowing," she said proudly. "They sure must have a lot of energy."

"Come on sweetie. We need to get inside. There's a man on the

TV who's going to tell us just how those little fellas got all that energy back so soon."

"Oh wow! Let's go! Let's go!" she said jumping up and down.

Jason put his crutches under his arms and they headed inside.

As he hobbled his way through the kitchen, Nikki ran past him into the living room.

"Wow! That's a lot of fireflies," Kristina said as Nikki presented the jar to her.

"Daddy says there's a man who's going to tell us how they got their energy back."

Jason plopped down on the sofa next to Kristina. "And that's the man right there," he said pointing to the image of two men on the screen.

"Who?" Nikki asked. "The man with the tie?"

"No, that's the anchor man. It's the older gentleman. His name is Richard Teech."

"He looks like that famous smart man we learned about in school – Alvin Einstein."

Kristina put her finger to her lips. "Shhhhhh. He's about to start talking."

"Thank you, Sir Richard, for joining us," the news anchor began.

"My pleasure," Teech replied with his customary polite nod of the head.

"Sir Richard, it's been a month since the energy loss phenomenon reversed itself. Since then, there seem to be thousands of theories as to what happened and how the earth, for lack of a better term, righted itself. Your theory has been the most anticipated of all. Can you explain for us this evening your thoughts on the matter and what your theory is?"

"Yes, sir," Teech said. "I'd be happy to." He cleared his throat, then smiled into the camera. "Before I begin, I always like to offer disclaimers and to apologize in advance if my views offend anyone. So to begin, I'd just like to say that I'm sure my thoughts are not going to be received well by some, but I anticipate those numbers will be extremely low."

He paused and took a deep breath. "A month ago, our world was on the brink of disaster. It was dying rapidly due to what was being referred to as the global energy drop phenomenon. Many thought it involved black matter. And of course there were the vanishings. The most common theories revolved around black holes, or that they were associated with the Rapture. Regardless, none of these have been able to be explained. But I do believe we can explain how the earth righted itself, as you put it."

"For a theory, you sound pretty confident, Sir Richard."

"I understand. Most of my theories have been just that — theories. This one, however, involves personal experience along with millions of testimonials. I'm not sure if your viewers know this, but my entire life I've been an atheist. I'm a scientist. Scientists live and breathe empirical data, hard and fast certainties and facts. It's how we do our jobs. It's also the reason I wasn't taken in the vanishings."

"Would you mind expanding on that?"

"Certainly. Just this week our global reporting system indicated that almost all missing persons from the vanishings have returned. We can't say for sure how all of them reappeared, but there have been thousands of testimonials and some actual video evidence that leads us to believe they did so during the supernatural rain storm we experienced."

The anchorman nodded. "That's also when the second energy loss phenomenon began."

"Correct - that's when the energy loss escalated. During the days that followed, these individuals slowly began showing up at their homes or places where family or loved ones were.

Unfortunately, many people perceived them to be aliens or a threat because their appearance was temporarily altered. Slowly, their normal physical features returned but they had no memory of how they came back or where they'd been. It was at this stage that the energy loss began to reverse itself."

Nikki bounced up and down on the sofa. "Is this where he tells us about the glow bugs?"

"I think so, honey," Jason replied.

"This is when millions of people's lives changed." Teech closed his eyes for a second. When he opened them, he looked off-camera as if addressing someone specifically in the audience. "It's when mine certainly did."

"What exactly happened?" asked the news anchor.

Teech looked back into the camera. "During this time, a third of our world's population that wasn't taken in the vanishings starved to death. Those of us who didn't are here, because we were able to make a supernatural connection with someone who had returned – especially a loved one. Those connections created life-sustaining energy and started a chain reaction throughout the world that brought it back to life."

The anchorman nodded. "Do you have a theory that explains those connections?"

Teech cupped his hands together and took a slow breath. "I don't actually have a theory. I have something more important – I have a belief. It's without empirical data, there's no quantifiable evidence, but I know it to be true. I know this because without it, I wouldn't be standing before you today.

The newsman smiled. "Please continue," he said warmly.

"As a lifelong atheist I never believed in anything other than what was based on logic. From the vanishings up until they returned, I continued to try and explain everything through scientific means. I racked my brain to find the answers. When I couldn't, I did something I've never done before…I reached for the Bible." His eyes filled with tears. He looked off-screen again and then back to the camera. "Through it, and with the help of someone very special, I found what I'd been looking for."

"Which was?" the anchorman asked.

A tear rolled down his cheek. "Faith," Teech said in a tender voice.

"What kind of faith?"

"Faith in God – faith in my savior Jesus Christ – and faith in loving my fellow man."

A moment passed as the anchor sat smiling. The kindly professor reached over and touched his arm. "I suspect you're here for the same reasons."

The newsman nodded.

"Those without such faith or belief couldn't make the connection," Teech said. "Those with it were able to."

"One last question, Sir Richard. I, for one, believe that what's happened is associated with the *Book of Revelation* and that the vanishings were indeed part of The Rapture. Could you tell us your thoughts on this?"

Teech glanced upward, as if listening for something. Slowly, he looked back down into the camera.

"I've read the *Book of Revelation* and I understand that a lot of what has occurred has matched with it. But as a scientist, I've also observed that a lot of things don't line up. What I will tell you is that I choose to view it as a man of faith. Whether it is or isn't part of *Revelation* doesn't concern me as much as knowing I must continue my journey.

"And what is your journey?"

"That I continue to believe in God and in Jesus Christ as my savior. I have to continue to believe that He has a plan for all of us." He paused a moment. "I'm sorry I don't have the answers

294

everyone is looking for. I'll never have them. And no one else will either. We won't have them until we get to heaven. And you know – I'm okay with waiting."

As the news anchor signed off, Nikki picked up her jar of fireflies from the coffee table. She studied it for a moment, turning it slowly from side to side. With a tilt of her head, she turned to Jason.

"Daddy, is it okay if I go back outside for just a minute?

"Why, honey?"

"I want to set my glow bugs free." She held the jar in front of her and smiled, then gently kissed the lid. "I think it's time for them to share their light again."

ABOUT THE AUTHOR

Chris Pennington is a marketing and Internet entrepreneur by day and a closet creative in the evenings. He graduated from East Carolina University in Greenville, North Carolina with a degree in Graphic Design and Journalism. Upon graduation, he moved to New York City where he began his career as a marketing manager at *Omni Magazine*. Chris conceived and is a founding partner in the website, *CodeOfKindness.com*, which is based on helping better the world by promoting random acts of kindness. Feel free to contact Chris at chris@codeofkindness.com.

Made in the USA
Lexington, KY
01 October 2013